Liar

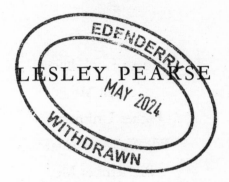

LESLEY PEARSE

MICHAEL JOSEPH
an imprint of
PENGUIN BOOKS

MICHAEL JOSEPH

UK | USA | Canada | Ireland | Australia
India | New Zealand | South Africa

Michael Joseph is part of the Penguin Random House group of companies
whose addresses can be found at global.penguinrandomhouse.com

Penguin
Random House
UK

First published 2020
003

Copyright © Lesley Pearse, 2020

The moral right of the author has been asserted

Set in 13.5/16 pt Garamond MT Std
Typeset by Jouve (UK), Milton Keynes
Printed and bound in Great Britain by Clays Ltd, Elcograf S.p.A.

A CIP catalogue record for this book is available from the British Library

HARDBACK ISBN: 978–0–241–42660–9
TRADE PAPERBACK ISBN: 978–0–241–42661–6

www.greenpenguin.co.uk

MIX
Paper from
responsible sources
FSC® C018179

Penguin Random House is committed to a
sustainable future for our business, our readers
and our planet. This book is made from Forest
Stewardship Council® certified paper.

I am dedicating this book to all the frontline workers – doctors, nurses, carers, teachers, police – and all those many other people who have so valiantly given their expertise during this frightening coronavirus, without concerning themselves overly about their own safety. Then there are all those checkout angels in the super-markets, who haven't snapped back at the idiotic people who blame them for shortages, risking their health when we breathe on them. I salute you all for your kind-ness, compassion, good humour and for working above and beyond the call of duty.

I wish to mix up a huge dollop of sympathy too for all the self-employed, who, at the time of writing this, have no idea if any financial help is coming to them. You deserve better.

People have told me that my books have helped them fill the long hours of self-isolation. Thank you for that. And may I thank all the other writers who have enter-tained me in this bleak period.

We will get through it, I'm sure. I wonder if next year there will be countless books on sale about pandemics? Not from me though. Living through it is enough.

God Bless you all.

Lesley

I

Shepherd's Bush, 1970

The stink from the bags of rubbish piled against a wall in Scotts Road made Amelia involuntarily gag and cover her nose. The local dustbin men had gone on strike, and the council appeared disinclined to make any alternative arrangement. People had resorted to piling their refuse on side roads like this one – anywhere just as long as it wasn't outside their own home.

Amelia lived just around the corner in Godolphin Road. It was a street of Victorian three-storey houses with basements. They had been built as family homes with rooms for servants, but now practically all were in multiple occupation. The luckier tenants had a self-contained flat, but mostly the houses were divided up into bedsitters, with as many as ten rooms sharing one bathroom.

Amelia thought herself lucky. Her room on the first floor of number twenty-two was large and light, and there were two bathrooms in the house, along with a separate lavatory. But, then, her landlord was a decent sort – he lived in the basement flat and kept an eye on his tenants and his property.

Pleasant he might be, yet his house was still shabby. Cracked lino in the hall, a threadbare stair carpet and, despite all the tenants getting on quite well, no one was in favour of a cleaning rota. Mostly it was Amelia who cleaned the common parts. She daydreamed of having a real flat, with a proper kitchen instead of a cupboard, and her own bathroom, where she could arrange fluffy towels and pretty bottles of bubble bath. But on twelve pounds a week from her job at the *West London Weekly*, she couldn't afford anything better.

'In The Summertime' by Mungo Jerry had been in the top twenty for most of the summer. It wafted out of shops, houses, and from car radios all the time. But while that song created a lovely image of sunshine and flowers, stinking piles of rubbish were growing all over London. Now in late August, this one in Scotts Road had become a small mountain. Mike, who lived in the bedsit next to Amelia's, claimed he'd seen rats running around on it the previous night. He thought the army should be called in to take it away.

Amelia usually averted her eyes from it and hurried past as fast as she could, but she saw something white out of the corner of her eye and turned her head to look.

There on the rubbish was a pair of the gorgeous white boots she'd been aching to own. She'd seen an advertisement on the tube for them, a black girl with an Afro hairstyle sitting naked on a rock wearing only the boots. A girl in the office called them Durex boots because the legs were tight, stretchy and quite difficult to get on.

Amelia couldn't believe that anyone had just dumped them there – the soles looked hardly worn. Glancing around first to check no one was watching, she went closer, braving the smell. She couldn't see a size, but they looked like a five, her size. Checking around her once more, she climbed over a couple of bags and grabbed one of the boots.

It didn't move, so she pulled it sharply. The rubbish bags shifted and, to her horror, she saw the boot was attached to a human leg.

She screamed and almost toppled over backwards as she let go of it. On reaching the pavement she saw the pile had collapsed further with her weight and now a tanned thigh was exposed.

2

Seeing a man who lived two doors away from her house coming towards her, Amelia ran to him, stammering out what she'd seen and pointing back to it. He caught hold of her shoulders to calm her. 'Okay, love, horrible, but you'll be all right,' he said soothingly, glancing at the exposed leg. 'I'll go to the phone box and ring the police. You'd better stay here. They'll need to speak to you.'

Within a minute he was back, and put his arm round her as she was shaking from the shock. 'They're coming. Now, let's cross over so the smell isn't so bad. I'm Max, by the way. You aren't going to pass out on me, are you?'

'I don't think so,' she said, and gratefully let him lead her away.

She'd seen Max dozens of times, but mostly only from her window. He was perhaps thirty, slim and tall with dark hair, always smartly dressed in a navy blue suit with well-polished shoes. Close up, he was much nicer-looking than she'd expected, green eyes, a tanned face and even white teeth.

'Do you think she's been murdered?'

'I can't think of any other reason for her being on

a pile of rubbish,' he said. 'Let's hope the whole girl is there, not just a body part.'

Amelia shuddered. 'I saw the boots and thought someone had dumped them,' she admitted. 'I never expected they'd be attached to legs.'

They stood together in silence. Amelia was normally something of a chatterbox, but shock had made her mute.

The police arrived soon after. They cordoned off the area, preventing anyone coming into the street, and removed some of the rubbish from around the body to take photographs.

A policeman came across to speak to them. He looked close to retirement age and his face was deeply lined. 'You'll be the young lady who found the body,' he said. 'And is this the gentleman who telephoned us?'

Amelia nodded. 'I'm Amelia White, and I live at twenty-two Godolphin Road. I just saw a leg and I ran to Max here as he came around the corner.' She couldn't bring herself to admit she'd wanted the boots. In the light of the girl being dead it sounded so ghoulish.

'Would you both come inside the cordon to see if you recognize her?' the policeman asked.

They nodded agreement and followed him, ducking under the rope of the cordon.

They were now close enough to see she was a young,

very pretty girl, with long blonde hair. She was wearing red hot-pants, the kind with straps and a bib, and a blood-stained white T-shirt or blouse beneath the straps. Somehow the outfit made it even more distressing as it was the kind Amelia yearned to wear, but she felt she was too plump. 'I've never seen her before,' she said, biting back tears. 'I don't think she lives around here.'

Max said the same and the police officer thanked them, took down their names and addresses, then said they would be called on for a written statement.

'How was she killed?' Max asked.

'The pathologist is examining her now. We'll establish her identity and contact her next of kin. But you can both go now.'

'Well, that's it, dismissed,' Max said, in an obvious attempt to lighten the mood as he led her away. 'You're as white as a sheet, Amelia. Shall I come in with you and get you tea or something? I don't want to leave you alone after such a shock.'

'That would be so kind,' she agreed, glad he'd offered because she felt she'd fall apart if she was left on her own. 'But only if you've got nothing more pressing to do.'

'Even if I had, I'd postpone it,' he said, with a weak smile. 'Besides, I'm as shaken as you and I need a cup of tea too.'

As he followed her up the stairs to her room, Max

spoke up. 'How funny is this? I've been seeing you most days for ages, but we've never spoken before. Well, it's not funny – in fact it's sad that something bad had to happen to make us speak.'

Amelia had spotted him moving in about two years ago. She thought he was too straight for her taste, with his neatly cut hair and smart suit. Even when he wore jeans and a T-shirt he still managed to look as if he'd stepped out of Burton's window. 'That's London for you,' she said, as she unlocked her door, glad that she'd tidied up before going to work. 'It takes an accident or a drama of some sort to make people speak to one another. The hippie scene made it more friendly for a while, but that's drifting away now.'

'You were a flower child when I first saw you,' he said. His smile was an engagingly wide one that made his eyes crinkle. 'You were wearing one of those loose cheesecloth dresses and a beaded band round your forehead. I think you had bare feet too.'

'Did I really?' She giggled. 'The thought of bare feet among the rubbish and dogs' doings turns my stomach now.'

Max stood for a moment, looking around her room. Amelia had painted it all white, including the table, chairs and an old wartime sideboard. She had a big jug of red gladioli on the table, a patchwork quilt covering an old armchair, and dozens of brightly coloured paintings on the walls. Even her bed in the corner was covered with a red blanket and cushions in primary colours. With the late-afternoon sun coming through the large sash windows, it looked beautiful.

'Are the pictures by you?' Max asked. 'It's obvious you're extremely artistic.'

Amelia smiled. 'Extremely nothing! I couldn't draw to save my life, but I appreciate art. I picked up most of these from the artists who hang their work on the railings outside Kensington Gardens. I do sew, though – the patchwork quilt is my work – and I paint furniture.'

'It's a lovely room,' he said. 'Mine's pretty squalid.'

'Do sit down.' Amelia waved her hand to a small sofa covered with a vivid turquoise Moroccan mirrored throw, then pulled back a curtain in an alcove that held a sink and a tiny Baby Belling cooker atop a fridge. She filled and switched on an electric kettle, then took two mugs down from a shelf. 'This place was hideous when I moved in, but it was cheap and it had potential. I've grown quite fond of it now.'

'So what happened to the hippie chick?' he asked.

Amelia glanced at herself in her long mirror. She liked to think of her present style as Girl About Town: a black and white mini dress, her brown hair cut in a sleek bob. Back when Max had first seen her in 1968, she had modelled herself on the Pre-Raphaelites with a curly perm, and used henna to dye it a deep red. She'd worn flowing dresses, jingling bracelets and no bra.

'She grew up.' Amelia sighed. 'It was a fun time, but

not, as it turned out, the Nirvana we'd imagined. Brian Jones dying, then Jim Morrison, not to mention the Vietnam War still going on and so many American soldiers being killed – all good reasons to take life a bit more seriously. Then the Conservatives got in early this year, and that just put the lid on it. But what about you? Did the sixties change you?'

'It did internally,' he said, taking the tea she offered him. 'I liked the way it opened people up, me included! The music, the freedom to express yourself . . . But I'm an accountant and for that you have to look quite straight. Maybe I just reverted to type.'

Amelia sat down opposite him. She thought Max was rather scrumptious, and he was articulate. He wasn't the type she normally went for, but she'd had her fill of weak men who relied on a spliff to face the day and wanted a woman to keep them. While it was true some of the hippie men she'd known were great in bed, they'd perfected their technique by staying there all day and taking mind-altering drugs.

'So, what do you do, Amelia?' he asked, breaking her reverie.

'I work for the local paper,' she said. 'I say I'm a junior reporter, but the truth of the matter is I sell advertising space, make the tea and act as the office gofer.'

'So do you write? I mean for yourself.'

No one had ever asked her that before. Maybe people thought her too shallow, too much of a party girl to do so.

'Yes,' she admitted sheepishly. 'I'm writing a book, but I've never told anyone that until now.' She hoped he wouldn't ask what it was about because a book about a girl growing up in the sixties sounded so trite. Free love, drugs, and the inducements to abandon all morality changed her heroine and, doubtless, readers would think it was autobiography. In fact, it was based on observations she'd made about people she'd been close to. She hadn't lost her own moral compass and she didn't need drugs, but she certainly understood those it had happened to.

'I'm not going to ask what it's about,' he said, surprising her. 'My grandmother wrote short stories and she hated us asking about them. She'd say, "Wait until it's in a magazine. You spoil it for me by asking. It makes me question too hard what I'm writing about."'

'Gosh, that's so true,' Amelia said. 'When I try to write a synopsis it sounds pathetic.'

'So have you got secret aspirations to write a killer column in one of the broadsheets?'

Amelia spluttered with laughter, almost spilling her tea. 'No! I'm learning the craft of writing with a view to getting my book published, not to be a real journalist – they're all so cynical and jaundiced. I bet when I go in tomorrow and tell them about the girl in the rubbish, they'll all want to be my best friend for the day.'

'Speaking of which, wouldn't you like to know who the girl is, who killed her, why he dumped her there?

Her background and everything else about her? I know I would.'

Amelia liked that he had that kind of curiosity. She found men generally didn't care about people's back story the way she did. 'Yes, I would. Ideally I'd like to be asked to write a feature on her as a person. What she did, her place in her family. But I think my paper will only be interested in sensationalizing her death, the lurid stuff. We might be a local paper but even they take their lead from the *News of the World*.'

Max smiled. 'Maybe this is serendipity. If you were to find out about her, get the real lowdown, you could use that to make your book really great.'

They had more tea, then Amelia made them cheese on toast and they talked as if they'd always been friends. She learned that until six months ago Max had had a steady girlfriend called Gloria. 'I was fond of her, but not in love, whatever that is,' he said. 'She kept hinting we should get married but I thought if I'm going to marry someone it's got to be because I can't bear to be without her. I suppose I think that's what real love is all about.

'I felt bad that I backed out. Gloria was very hurt,' he went on. 'She actually said she hoped I'd be miserable without her. Well, that didn't happen, but I think she jinxed me. Some of the girls I've seen since seemed promising at the beginning, but they soon wore thin. I guess that makes me very shallow,' he said.

Amelia liked him even more for saying that. 'Not

shallow, just honest. I don't think I've ever experienced real love either,' she admitted. 'I've found the bullies, the vain ones, the pathetic ones, the mean ones. Not to mention the ones not too keen on personal hygiene. Once or twice I've felt hurt when I was dumped, but in a day or two I felt relieved I'd escaped. So now I can't really be bothered to date anyone. I'd rather sit here at night and write.'

Max smiled. 'Last winter I often saw your light on late at night. I got the idea you had a wild romance going on. I never imagined you writing a book.'

'All my wild romances are fictional ones,' she admitted, and laughed. 'I'm so glad you came along when you did today. You've managed to cheer me up.'

At midnight, Amelia was still awake. Max had finally left at about ten o'clock. She was quite staggered by how much she liked him. He wasn't what she called a Normal Norman at all, and she felt a bit ashamed that until today that was how she'd seen him, without knowing a thing about him.

He was so easy to be with. He didn't talk about his work, or the people he worked with: he said that was deadly dull. Instead she'd found out that he played cricket and belonged to an amateur dramatic society, so far playing small parts. He also liked singing and rock-climbing.

'I like the idea of a singing rock-climber. Are the hills alive with the sound of music?' She giggled.

He had laughed at that but, then, he laughed read-ily. He said being the youngest of four boys he'd had to learn to laugh at their cruel jokes or be labelled a cry-baby. He had grown up on a moorland farm in Devon, but his parents had sold it the previous year to retire to Sidmouth. They had hoped one of their sons would want to take it on, but two of his brothers had joined the RAF, while the third had just finished his training as a vet and moved to Edinburgh. Max had never wanted to be a farmer, even though he said his childhood spent on the farm had been idyllic. He had started rock-climbing at seven on wild patches of Dart-moor. Now he liked to go to Scotland or North Wales to climb.

They kept coming back to the murdered girl, though – he was as interested as Amelia in who she was and why she'd been killed. He pointed out that narrow Scotts Road, which ran from Goldhawk Road to Uxbridge Road, existed to give access to all the wider roads it crossed and had been chosen to dump her body as garden walls on either side obscured any view. The upper storeys of the houses offered little more because of the tall plane trees that grew along the road.

'Still, a strange place to dump a body,' Max remarked. 'She wasn't there this morning – I would've seen those boots – so she must have been put there during the day. Possibly not long before you passed by. The killer must've driven her there, so why didn't he go further out of London? Unless the rubbish was the attraction. Maybe he saw her as rubbish.'

Now as Amelia lay in bed, turning things round and round in her head, she realized not only was she burning to know about the dead girl, but she also wanted to see Max again.

3

After almost two hours in an airless interview room with a chain-smoking, dour, middle-aged copper, who appeared not to believe her story, Amelia had had enough.

'I've told you absolutely everything that happened,' she said, glaring at him, 'and now I want to go to work!'

At eight that morning two officers had arrived at her home and insisted she accompany them immediately to the police station to give her statement.

She was worried she'd be late for work, but they'd waved aside her protests. As she had told them everything on the previous day and had nothing else to add, she couldn't imagine it taking more than twenty minutes at absolute tops. But she was mistaken.

'I told you I don't know her. I've never even seen her before,' she said wearily when, once again, he produced a photograph of the victim. The girl looked very pretty, although the photograph had been taken after her death. 'Look! I didn't see anyone put her there. I didn't see anyone hanging around looking suspicious, either.' She paused, her irritation rising and threatening to spill over into anger. 'How many times do you need me to tell you the same thing? I just saw the boots and

I wanted them. I didn't expect them to be on the legs of a dead girl. I thought they'd been thrown away.'

'You didn't tell the officer at the scene yesterday that you'd tried to take the boots. Why was that?'

Amelia rolled her eyes in despair. 'I got a huge shock when I realized they were attached to someone. It frightened the life out of me. I didn't want to admit the truth, which was that I've wanted boots like that for ages and I was just going to look at what size they were.'

'So you were going to take them?'

Amelia stared hard at him, astounded that he was making such a thing of it. 'Well, yes, if they'd just been thrown out and were my size.' She knew she was shrieking but she couldn't help it. 'But the moment I realized there was someone under that rubbish I backed away in shock. That was when my neighbour Max came along and he ran to phone 999. Now please may I go to work? I can't tell you anything else.'

'Fair enough,' he agreed. 'But we'll need your fingerprints before you leave so we can eliminate those from any others we find on the boots.'

'Have you found out who the girl is yet?' Amelia asked, as they left the room. 'She looks so young and lovely. Her family must be wondering where she is.'

'That's our job, not yours,' he said curtly. 'Now come with me and I'll take your prints.'

It was nearly eleven when Amelia finally arrived at her office on Shepherd's Bush Road. She was furious at what she'd been put through and she went straight into the editor's room to explain why she was late. To her surprise, he greeted her pleasantly, getting her a cup of tea and inviting her to sit down and tell him the whole story. He agreed that it was wrong for the police to be so aggressive to someone who was guilty of nothing more than reporting a crime.

Jack Myles was not known for being kind. His bad temper, savage character assassinations, and humourless personality were legendary. Amelia described him to friends as a bulldog, with heavy, sagging jowls, brown teeth and a bad case of BO. He ran the newspaper like a military campaign and was hard on anyone who didn't jump to his commands. So even as Amelia basked in his sympathy, she knew that a wily old fox like him probably sensed the murder as a huge story, and as Amelia had found the body, he could make it a scoop.

'When the police release the girl's name and how she was killed, it would be a kind thing for you to call on her family,' he said, once he'd exhausted his feigned sympathy.

Amelia's mouth dropped open. She hadn't expected something as obvious as that. 'I couldn't,' she said in alarm. 'They'll be beside themselves with grief.'

'That's when people most need to talk,' he snapped. 'You found the girl, her mother will feel a bond with you, and she'll spill it all out.'

Amelia gulped down any further argument. She

was horrified by Jack's lack of sensitivity . . . but maybe he was right. The girl's mother would feel something for the person who had found her, just as Amelia felt something for the dead girl. Truth to tell, she wanted to know her background, to put a character and personality to the person who had worn the white boots.

Jack asked her still more questions about the crime scene.

As he listened, he propped his elbow on his desk and supported his head with his right hand. With the left, he rubbed his chin thoughtfully. Amelia had seen him sitting like that a hundred times and it was usually followed by his version of the story he'd just been told.

'The murderer saw her as trash,' he said, when Amelia had finished. 'No one waits by a pile of rubbish hoping to kill someone, then tosses them onto it. But he knew that heap was there. He killed the girl elsewhere and drove her there to dump her body. I wouldn't mind betting he'd been following her for some time too, perhaps some ugly bastard who knew he couldn't have a girl like her for himself.'

'She could've had a fight with her boyfriend, and he killed and dumped her,' Amelia suggested. 'There's piles of rubbish all over London since they stopped collecting it.'

'A man who loves a girl doesn't dump her on rubbish. He'd have buried her in woods or some beauty spot.'

Amelia nodded. That sounded logical. 'But if the

killer was a stranger, how on earth will the police find him?'

'Because he'll do it again,' Jack said. 'He'll have got a kick out of killing this one, and he'll want to repeat it.'

'He took a huge risk dumping her where he did,' Amelia said. 'The houses at either end of the road might not have any view from their back windows because of the trees, but a great many people walk through that way at any time of day or night.'

'I expect that added to the excitement,' Jack said, getting to his feet, clearly dismissing her. 'I'm going out now to have a chat with a contact at the nick. On your desk there are some leads for firms who might advertise with us. Follow them up.'

Amelia felt hurt that he had terminated their talk so abruptly. Until that moment she'd felt he was engaging with her and understood what a shock she'd had. But remembering that other staff had said he was selfish to the core, she got on with her work and tried hard to stop dwelling on it.

Jack didn't return until nearly four in the afternoon, stinking of cigarettes and whisky. 'My office!' he said, as he lurched past Amelia's desk.

There was nothing unusual about Jack being drunk: he often was after he'd been meeting a contact. Sometimes he fell asleep on the couch in his office. There was a story, often repeated, that he peed in his waste-paper bin when he was sozzled.

'Did you find out anything useful?' Amelia asked.

Jack had collapsed onto his couch and she averted her eyes as his flies were open. She just hoped he wasn't going to do the peeing thing in front of her.

'Course I did. I'm a ball of fire when I want information,' he said, slurring his words. He fished in his jacket pocket and pulled out a piece of paper. 'Her address! She was a stripper. Name of Lucy Whelan, age twenty-five. Her killer will be a punter from the strip club – they're raiding the place tonight. Get around to her folks and butter them up for some background. They've been informed their daughter is dead, but there hasn't been enough info leaked about this yet to get all the newshounds round there. Advise the family not to speak to anyone else.'

Amelia wanted to say he could show some consideration for a bereaved family, but she didn't dare. She shot off hurriedly, not because she was keen to go to the address in Chiswick but to get away from Jack's stench.

The combination of cigarettes and whisky was an unwanted reminder of her father, Bill White, or Chalky, as he was known to his pals. Those same pals thought him brave, wise, generous and tough, but the reality was that he was cruel to his wife, Gillian, and their children, kept them short of money, treated them like they were nothing, and they were terrified of him.

He'd joined the army at eighteen in 1929, and very quickly rose to corporal. Within ten years, at the outbreak of war, he was made a sergeant. Bill was possibly the only person in England who was delighted to go to war – he couldn't wait to get stuck into some real fighting. Amelia had no doubt that her mother was equally delighted to see him go, but as she wasn't born until 1945, she couldn't be certain of that. The three children Gillian had had then were evacuated to Norfolk, and she got a job as a clippie on the buses. From the odd things she'd said about that time, it seemed she'd enjoyed it, at least until she'd got pregnant with Peter.

If he was to be believed, Bill was a war hero, though Amelia wasn't convinced that all his stories were true. He had been decorated for rescuing a severely wounded officer in the withdrawal to Dunkirk, that much was true – he was always showing off the medal – but he certainly couldn't have been in all the dangerous and faraway places he claimed, not as he had come home on leave and impregnated Gillian, first with Peter and then with Amelia.

Amelia was happy to think he might have been in an Asian PoW camp, as he claimed, for that would mean he couldn't be her father, and maybe the real one was a kind, decent man.

As the youngest of five, with a sister and three brothers, she hadn't been knocked about quite as much as the others. But she'd learned at an early age to listen to Bill's wartime stories with apparent eagerness and excitement, especially when he was drunk.

It was her oldest brother Michael and their mother who took the brunt of his bad temper. Bill blamed

Gillian for everything he didn't like: being invalided out of the army on medical grounds, having five children, being forced to drive a truck to earn a crust, and for living in a council house in White City. By all accounts he had never liked Michael because he was quiet, timid and gentle, characteristics he certainly hadn't inherited from his father.

When he had been evacuated, Michael was chosen by a childless doctor and his wife in Norfolk. At their comfortable home, he discovered books, learned to play chess and listened to classical music. The doctor and his wife became very fond of him and gave him a first-class education. Christine and James were in the same village, but billeted with a farmer and his wife.

Back in 1960, when Amelia was fifteen, Michael confided in her that he had considered killing himself when the war ended and he'd had to return home. He was just twelve then, and the thought of being forced to live in squalid conditions under the same roof as a violent bully, and to be jeered at for his bookish ways, was too much to bear.

As it turned out Michael's return home was even worse than he'd expected. He didn't know four-year-old Peter, his youngest brother, and Amelia was just a baby. The council house in White City was small, damp and cold, with only an outside lavatory. He had to share a bed with his three brothers, there was an acute shortage of food and coal for the fire, and Bill never stopped belittling him. He thought all boys should be out playing football or roaming the streets in gangs as he'd done as a child. Each time he caught Michael with a book he hit him.

Finally Bill was so drunk one night that he beat Michael to within an inch of his life, resulting in a broken arm, cracked ribs and his whole body bruised and battered. Christine ran to the corner shop and begged them to call the police and an ambulance before Bill killed her brother.

Although the police arrested Bill, Gillian knew they wouldn't be able to hold him for long, so in desperation she rang the doctor and his wife and asked if they would consider taking Michael when he came out of hospital.

They were only too happy to agree – in fact, they came to London immediately and arranged for Michael to be brought to Norfolk in an ambulance. It was said they spoke to Bill while he was still being held in custody, and told him they would have him prosecuted for cruelty to children if he ever came near Michael again. Whether that was true or not, Amelia didn't know but, thanks to the doctor and his wife, Michael went on to university and eventually became a doctor too. Something that had made their father seethe.

Amelia met up with Michael occasionally. They tried hard to bond, if only because they were both family outcasts, but he'd been almost grown-up when she was born, and they'd spent only a few weeks under the same roof. Now married with two children, Michael was in a practice in Bury St Edmunds and he didn't get to London often. When Amelia did see him, no matter how hard Michael tried to be a real brother, she sensed he would have preferred no reminders of the past.

Amelia totally understood that. Living in the shadow of Wormwood Scrubs prison in a miserable, cold, damp house was bad enough, but her father was pure evil, and her mother pathetic for not running away the first time he had beaten her.

Amelia left home at eighteen, after a beating from her father, and since then Christine had married a man almost as bad as their father, while James and Peter were in and out of prison constantly for petty crime. Amelia left them to it for good, accepting that her family's awful behaviour was entrenched, and would never change. She found it hard to rake up any happy memories of them.

The Whelans' Chiswick address was closer to Acton than Chiswick, quite a long stretch from Turnham Green tube station, not that Amelia minded the walk. She was happy to delay the moment she'd have to knock on the Whelans' door. She just hoped they wouldn't slam it in her face.

It was a neat terraced house with a tiny front garden bright with flowers, and she paused with her hand on the gate, trying to summon the courage to go through it and walk up to the door. She imagined Lucy's mother flying at her in anger, the rest of the family accusing her of being an ambulance chaser. But she knew that if she didn't give Jack something tomorrow, he'd probably sack her.

With a heavy heart she walked slowly to the front door and rang the bell.

The woman with the red-rimmed eyes and blotchy skin who answered the door had to be Lucy's mother. Amelia took a deep breath.

'Are you Mrs Whelan, Lucy's mother?' she asked gently.

'Yes. What's it to you?' she replied, her voice cracking.

'I'm the person who found Lucy,' Amelia continued, her fingers tightly crossed that she wouldn't make a blunder. 'I haven't been able to stop thinking about her, and how it must be for you and the rest of her family, so I persuaded one of the policemen to give me your address so I could pay my respects.'

'You found her?' Mrs Whelan asked, looking surprised. 'They said it was a woman, but I expected you to be much older. You'd better come in.'

It was only once she was in the tiny hall that Amelia felt she could breathe again. She was in, and as long as she didn't sound like a journalist or ask awkward questions it should be all right.

The sitting room was small, no more than ten-foot square, which wasn't helped by a large maroon three-piece suite, a dining table and chairs all crammed into it. Four women were there – one was about seventy with a wrinkled face, and Amelia assumed she was

Lucy's grandmother. Another woman of similar age to Mrs Whelan might have been her sister, Lucy's aunt, as they were so alike, and two younger ones turned out to be Lucy's older sisters.

'I'm Amelia White. It was me who found Lucy,' she said nervously. 'I'm sorry if I'm intruding on your grief but finding her the way I did was such a shock I can't stop thinking about her. I'll leave if you don't want me here.'

'You sit down, my dear,' the oldest lady said. 'I always think when someone dies it's best to gather in a group, talk about them and share the sadness. So you are welcome.'

'I'm Nichola, Lucy's oldest sister,' one of the younger women said, as she moved up on the sofa to make room for the new arrival. 'And this is Tracy, our other sister.' She waved a hand towards the second girl.

They were both attractive blondes, like Lucy, with glowing complexions and slim figures. Amelia guessed they were in their late twenties or early thirties. 'The police haven't told us much, only that she was left on some rubbish in Shepherd's Bush. They said she was knocked out, then stabbed.'

'I didn't know how she died. They didn't tell me that,' Amelia said. 'It was her boots I noticed, sticking out the rubbish, much too nice to have been dumped. When I touched one the rubbish shifted a bit and I saw her leg.'

There was a strained silence.

Mrs Whelan brought Amelia a cup of tea and a slice of cake. 'We can't believe we aren't going to see our Lucy again,' she said, slumping into one of the armchairs, fresh tears welling up and spilling over. 'She went off to work like always the night before, but she said she'd probably sleep at her friend's place and see us the next day. She often did that so I had no reason to be anxious.'

'What did she work at?' Amelia asked. She thought it more diplomatic not to admit she already knew.

'She was an exotic dancer,' Mrs Whelan said. 'The policeman who came today to tell us she'd been found said she was a stripper. But she wasn't. She worked in a smart nightclub called the Beachcomber and did hula dancing. I didn't like the policeman. The way he spoke about her, it was like he thought she was a cheap little tart and led her killer on.'

Amelia was horrified as Mrs Whelan began to cry in earnest. Not silent tears, but roars of anguish. She reached out and took the woman's hand. 'I saw her picture when I gave my statement. She was a beautiful girl, and you mustn't take notice of a stupid policeman not knowing the difference between dancing for a living and being a stripper. As for Lucy leading her killer on, that's just more stupidity. Men always seem to claim such things when a woman is hurt.'

'Our Lucy was a ray of sunshine,' Tracy the younger sister said, her voice hoarse with emotion. 'She always saw the best in people. She was never fearful at being out at night either. The killer could've asked her the time, or where the nearest tube was, and she'd have stopped to answer him.'

Amelia sensed that the four women needed to pour out their feelings about Lucy so she just sat back and listened.

As they shared their opinions and memories of Lucy it was clear to Amelia that she had been a well-loved girl. These women didn't just know her superficially, as Amelia suspected her own siblings knew her: no, the Whelan clan had known Lucy inside out. Not just her love of dancing or the Rolling Stones and fancying Sean Connery, but that she liked walking in woods, corny Disney films, and often went to the Tate and the National Gallery to admire the paintings. She might come across as a modern, switched-on girl to other people, with her confident air, her hair and clothes always immaculate, but she really wanted to get married, have four children and live in a country cottage.

Nichola said Lucy didn't have a serious boyfriend, and that she'd jokingly claimed she'd need to kiss a lot of toads before she recognized her prince when he came along. She saved her money, played tennis and was doing a cookery course one night a week. As Nichola pointed out, this was preparation for the life she really wanted.

'She liked to show off a bit,' her grandmother said, as if to illustrate they all knew both sides of Lucy. 'That's why she liked being a hula girl. Her mother and I went to the Beachcomber one night to check it out. It was everything she said – posh, expensive, but all above-board. I suppose it's likely her killer met her there. Maybe he followed her when she left. But it would be wrong to suggest that the club is a low dive. Her killer could just as easily have followed her from the National Portrait Gallery.'

Amelia thought she had a point there. 'Did the police ask about the friend she normally stays with when she doesn't come home?'

The grandmother looked puzzled. 'No, they didn't. But we thought that was because she was killed on the way to stay with Frances.'

Amelia didn't say what she was thinking: that, as far as she knew, Lucy had been killed sometime the following day, late morning or even afternoon. She thought it very odd the police hadn't asked for Frances's address. It seemed remarkably unprofessional not to check with her before anything else.

'The police said that by tomorrow morning the press will be pounding on our door,' the grandmother said.

'Don't speak to them,' Amelia advised them. 'I work on the clerical side of one of the local papers and I know how pushy journalists can be. They'll twist your words, write half-truths and often complete lies. Just keep the door locked and the curtains drawn so they can't see in. The police sometimes send a woman officer round to be with the family in cases like this. I don't know why there isn't one here now.'

'Probably because they'd already made up their minds our Lucy was no better than a prostitute so they aren't going to bother,' Tracy spat out bitterly.

'I'm sure it's not like that,' Amelia said quickly. 'I was at the police station for three hours this morning and I didn't hear anyone saying anything like that.'

'People are always quick to believe the worst,' Mrs Whelan said. 'My Roger will be turning in his grave to hear such things said about his baby girl.'

'I didn't realize you were a widow, Mrs Whelan. I'm so sorry.' Amelia wished she'd checked about Mr Whelan before she'd set out today.

'He passed away five years since.' Mrs Whelan's eyes filled with fresh tears. 'It was cancer, and it took him so fast. If he'd still been with us, he would never have let our Lucy dance up west.'

'Dancers and musicians have no choice but to work evenings in places their families would prefer them not to be,' Amelia said. 'Even if she was dancing with the Royal Ballet, she'd still be up west!'

'That's true, Mum,' Nichola said, reaching out to squeeze her mother's hand. 'You've got to stop blaming yourself. Lucy wanted to work there – if you'd said she couldn't, she might have left home. She was that determined.'

A loud rapping on the front door made them all jump.

Amelia peeped out through the net curtains. 'Oh dear,' she exclaimed. 'It's the first bunch of reporters.'

She saw the horror on all four women's faces. 'Don't look so scared. Look, I ought to go now – I've taken up enough of your time – but I've got an idea. What if I tell them you've given me an exclusive story and you aren't going to talk to anyone else? Would that be all right with you? They'll go away then.'

'Are you going to write something in the paper you work for?' Nichola asked, her face full of suspicion.

'Not me, I'm just a junior, but I can tell one of the experienced reporters the stuff about me finding Lucy, and a little bit about your family.' She glanced at the photograph of Lucy on the mantelpiece. It was a classic ballet picture, taken perhaps when she was thirteen or fourteen, hair up in a bun, wearing a tutu. 'If it's okay with you I'll borrow that picture and get them to do a piece about her ambitions as a dancer. That'll scotch any stories about her being a stripper. I promise you I won't let them write anything I wouldn't be proud to show you. But I warn you, those hyenas out there will tell you anything to get a sensational story. They'll offer you money and hound you. This is the best way to put a stop to that.'

The banging on the door and the bell-ringing were becoming more insistent. All four women looked scared.

'Look, let me do what I said. I'll also ring the police from down the road and tell them you're being harassed. They'll send someone round to get rid of them.'

Surprisingly it was Mrs Whelan who got to her feet

and moved towards Amelia to take both her hands. 'You do that and take the photograph with you. I trust you. I know you have a kind soul.'

Amelia smiled and reached out to stroke the older woman's cheek gently. 'I can imagine how awful this is for you, Mrs Whelan, and for all your family. My heart goes out to you. I'll give you my number at work, in case you need me, and if it's all right with you I'll come back tomorrow to return the photograph and see how things are.'

The last thing Amelia said to the family before she left was 'Don't open the door to anyone tonight. Stay strong, and I'll see you tomorrow.'

Amelia knew something of how journalists and photographers hung around on doorsteps, desperate for any crumbs of information, but she hadn't realized just how many would be there and how hard it was to shout over the babble of questions they were firing at her.

Her legs turned to jelly, and for a moment or two she wanted to run away without saying anything. But she had to speak out. She'd promised she would.

'I have an exclusive contract with the Whelans for any news about the tragic murder of Lucy, their daughter and sister,' she announced, as loudly as she was able. The hubbub paused and suddenly all eyes were on her.

'I am the person who found Lucy's body, and the family have asked me to tell you all to leave. They won't be talking to anyone but me, and they ask that you respect their grief and need for privacy.'

She told them her name, and that she worked for *West London Weekly*, then pushed her way through the crowd and hurried off down the road.

The last thing she remembered seeing out of the corner of her eye was a television camera. Jack would be thrilled by that.

4

Amelia went straight back to the office, hoping Jack would still be at his desk. It was now six in the evening, but she had suspected for some time that he rarely went home.

He was still there, the customary cigarette dangling at the corner of his mouth, smoke swirling above his head. Yet it was strangely quiet for the night before the papers hit the newsstands. Every other Thursday the noise from the print room on the floor below was deafening, but tonight it was silent. It seemed that everyone had gone home.

'Well?' he asked, barely looking up from his typewriter.

'I've managed to get an exclusive,' she said nervously. 'But before we go any further, I've promised I'll write it.'

'I don't know about that,' he said, removing the cigarette from his lips and raising one eyebrow. 'You've no experience.'

'Well, let me write it now and you can see what you think. I've also got this.' She took the ballet photograph out of her bag. 'This picture should set the tone of the piece. She was a nice girl who had dreams of being a ballerina, not a tarty stripper.'

There was a long silence.

She knew he'd much prefer a tarty-stripper murder, and a dysfunctional family thrown in. He certainly wasn't wild about stories of would-be ballerinas. If he refused hers, she would have to walk out, and risk being sacked. She couldn't let the Whelan family down.

He sighed, scrutinizing her through half-closed eyes. 'Go on, write it. You've got an hour. I need to nip out, but I told them downstairs to hold the front page and they'll be sitting there twiddling their thumbs. When I get back, if I think it's good enough it can go in.'

Amelia's mouth dropped open. She had fully expected opposition and ridicule. The best she had hoped for was that he'd write it himself from her notes. She certainly hadn't counted on him letting her write it. What thrilled her most, though, was that he'd had enough faith in her to get a story and come straight back with it. So much faith that he'd halted the printing in the belief she could give him a great front page.

Now she had to deliver. Thankfully, on the journey back to the office she'd been planning the story in her head.

'Shut your gob and get started,' he said, his mouth curving into a seldom-seen smile. He might be setting her up to fail, but she was going to disappoint him on that score.

*

As he came back into the office an hour later, she was just finishing. She didn't say a word, just pulled the paper out of the typewriter and handed it to him.

She had told the story as it had happened: her finding Lucy on the rubbish, what she had learned from the police, then going to see the girl's family because she'd felt she had to. Portraying a girl with aspirations to be a ballet dancer had come easily to Amelia. As a young girl, she used to dream of it herself but had never had the chance to take ballet lessons. However, she had listened carefully to what the mother, grandmother and sisters had said about Lucy's hopes and ambitions, and her place in the family. By being in the girl's home with her family she'd also picked up on things unsaid. To her it was a heartrending story about a life cut short and a family's terrible loss, and that was how she'd written it. But Jack wasn't a fan of tender stories. He liked them hard-hitting and sensational.

He perched on the edge of a desk to read it. Amelia's heart was thumping, her legs felt weak and she was perspiring as if she had run a mile.

'Well, Amelia,' he said at length, looking up at her and pausing as if choosing his words. Her heart plummeted, thinking he was almost certainly going to say it wouldn't do.

'You've done an excellent job.'

Amelia gasped.

'It's probably beginners' luck, so don't think you're

on your way to a sparkling journalistic career. But this is good enough to go straight to print. I take it you've got all the ages and spellings of names right?'

'I think so,' she said. 'I remembered you said that was important.'

'You're aware that when this hits the streets tomorrow you'll be pestered by other journalists?'

Amelia gulped. She hadn't thought of that.

'And some of them will take your story and rewrite it for their paper, putting their spin on it.'

'Can they do that?'

'It's commonplace.' He shrugged. 'But you'll be the first off the starting blocks, so that will be remembered. Let's just hope the police find her killer soon and then they'll all move on to stories about him.'

Jack sent her out to get fish and chips for them both while the printers set up the front page with her story. Amelia was pleased he didn't send her home: he appeared to understand that she couldn't wait to see and hold the first copy off the press. If he had banished her, she might have just waited on the doorstep until daybreak when the vans arrived to collect the papers for delivery to shops.

After the fish and chips, which tasted wonderful, Jack took her downstairs to see the printing, and she was so excited she could barely stand still. The noise from the press and the smell of the ink were intoxicating, even though when she had first joined the paper the noise had given her a headache and the smell had made her feel sick. Perhaps she was born to be a journalist.

Nothing on earth could have been more thrilling than the moment the first paper was put into her hands. It was warm, the ink still a bit tacky, and the headline 'Murdered and Thrown Out With the Rubbish' was a bit tacky too. But Amelia was in no position to question her boss about that: it was the editor's prerogative to choose the headline.

'Off with you now,' Jack said, waving his hand towards the door. 'And don't be late tomorrow.'

It was half past nine, too late to call on anyone, but Amelia was so desperate she ran all the way from the bus stop to Max's place, hoping he'd be in and willing to share her excitement.

When he opened the door, she couldn't speak: all she could do was wave the newspaper. 'I almost didn't answer because I was watching *Monty Python*, and I thought it might be Jehovah's Witnesses,' he said, with a broad grin. 'But I think I might have wizard-like powers as something told me it was you.'

'Well, Mr Wizard, can you tell me who wrote tomorrow's front page?'

He put two fingers to his forehead and closed his eyes. 'Ah! Got it! Amelia White!'

He asked her in, telling her she must ignore the disgusting mess his room was in, but Amelia would have sat down in a pig-sty if she could show off her story.

In fact, his room wasn't as bad as she had expected. A

sink full of unwashed dishes, and his bed was unmade, but she'd seen worse.

'You read it while I wash up,' she said.

Max turned off the TV, put on a Marvin Gaye LP, pulled up the bedcovers and sat down to read. By the time he'd finished she was almost done at the sink. 'It's really good, and very moving,' he said at length. 'You've managed to portray her family's loss and anger so well. But sit down now, and tell me how it all came about.'

Amelia wasn't used to having anyone's undivided attention. She'd been brought up in a family where the one who shouted loudest got heard. All her past boy-friends had been more interested in telling her about themselves than in getting to know her.

But Max wasn't her boyfriend, she reminded her-self. He was just a neighbour who'd happened to come along at a crucial time. For all she knew he might have a steady girlfriend he hadn't admitted to.

An hour later, Amelia had told him the whole story. He was a good listener, only stopping her occasionally to question something.

'Gosh, it's half past ten,' she said, glancing at her watch. 'I've stopped you watching *Monty Python* and now I'm keeping you up. I must go.'

'I'd gladly be kept up by you,' he said, with the kind of sexy grin that suggested he'd like her to stay all night.

Amelia felt a little flip in her stomach, and noticed again how lovely his green eyes were, reminding her of woodland pools. 'Maybe we can do something together on Sunday,' she said, without, for once, considering rejection.

'That would be good. A picnic somewhere lovely, like Hampstead Heath?'

'A great idea. I'll make the picnic,' she agreed, her heart racing. 'Well, if it's not raining.'

'It won't be,' he said, getting up as she moved towards the door.

He leaned past her shoulder to open it, his face just inches from hers. 'Sunday can't come quickly enough for me,' he said, in little more than a whisper, and suddenly he was kissing her.

It was the most delicious kiss, sensitive yet sensual. Amelia leaned into him – she didn't want it to end.

'Goodnight, then,' he said, kissing her forehead one more time. 'Sleep tight.'

Back in her own room next door, Amelia got into bed, feeling as though she could have burst with happiness, not just at getting a story on the front page of the local paper but at the prospect of a new romance. She couldn't help but relive that kiss, wanting to rush back to Max for more.

Mostly she'd been extremely unlucky with the opposite sex. She'd watched other girls going to work on the tube with their man, strap-hanging and looking into each other's eyes. Often couples kissed and cuddled on the platforms. At lunchtime they were in the park, sharing their sandwiches, and clearly couldn't get enough of each other. At weekends Goldhawk Road market was full of loved-up people wandering along hand in hand. She'd never had that with anyone.

Men always wanted to get her into bed, but where was the courting, the interest in her as a person? She wasn't a virgin: she'd been to bed with four different men, each time thinking he might be The One, only to be disappointed.

Disappointment was a thread that ran through her life. It had followed almost everything right from when she was old enough to remember. When she'd started school a girl called Marcia Reynolds asked if she'd be her best friend. The very next day she turned her back on Amelia and went off with another girl. Her mother would say she was going to buy Amelia new shoes, and Amelia would ask for red ones. But she never got new red shoes, not even brown ones: her mother would just put cardboard inside hers over the holes in the soles, and wait until a pair that fitted her turned up in a jumble sale.

Her parents were one long round of disappointment for the shabbiness of their home, her father's nasty temper and her mother's apathy. There was never money for school trips, a haircut, or even a day out at the seaside in the summer holidays. She grew used to her mother never keeping her promises, for buying drink rather than food for the family, and her father showing no interest in her at all, unless it was to hit her. She dreamed of being taken away to live with nice people.

There had been two exceptionally inspirational teachers at school, but they had left after just one term, and it was back to the teachers who couldn't have cared less whether their pupils learned anything or not. When the youth-employment officer had come to the school to advise on careers, Amelia had told her she wanted to be a journalist. The woman said, 'It's no good aiming for something you can't possibly achieve. I could get you an interview at Woolworths.'

She didn't go to Woolworths: she refused to believe that was all she was worth. Instead she had a series of office-junior jobs, but she enrolled at night school to learn shorthand and typing and scored the highest marks in her class. Even then she got no praise. Her father pulled a face, telling her to find some rich bloke and marry him. Her mother sniffed and said she was getting above herself. It was at that point, when she'd got her first job in a typing pool, she left home.

She had believed that getting away from a family who dragged her down with their negativity and nastiness would change her life dramatically, that she'd make dozens of new friends she could ask over for supper or a drink. That would lead to invitations to parties and suddenly she'd be at the centre of everything.

Painting her room, pinning up art posters and covering her bed with a red blanket made it look so inviting. Bright cushions and lamps fashioned from Chianti bottles with gaily coloured shades created a lovely atmosphere. Yet she didn't make new friends: all the other tenants in the house kept themselves to themselves, and when she tried to invite the couple on the ground floor for a drink, they made a pathetic excuse, which left her feeling very awkward.

It was the same at work. No one socialized, and when Amelia had got brave and asked people if they fancied a drink after work, they were always in a hurry to get home.

At the height of Flower Power in 1968, when she worked three evenings a week in a pub in Holland Park, she met people who were more friendly and approachable. Some were squatting in empty properties in the area, and she was often invited to their places for impromptu parties. It was so exciting – they were all so radical, throwing overboard standard morality and beliefs. They talked about travelling to India, setting up artistic communes and changing the world.

For a long time she immersed herself in this new way of life, convinced she'd found the Truth and the Way. But as time passed she noticed it was always she who brought the wine when she was asked round. She lent money that was never paid back, and cooked meals for people who never reciprocated. Gradually she began to see that her new friends didn't care about her: all they wanted was someone to lie around with while they got stoned and listened to music.

It had been great fun for a while, especially while she still believed that her entire generation was intent on changing the world into a better, fairer place. But as the sixties ended Amelia saw that was an illusion, and the mantra 'All You Need Is Love', which she'd clung to, was as phoney as her father's drunken promises.

As the bells rang out for the New Year of 1970, Amelia was in her room in Godolphin Road, touching up scuffs on the paintwork. Alone again, as she so often was, these days, she arrived at the conclusion that she was boring, with no personality, or spirit of adventure: that was why she had no close friends, and her family had always been indifferent to her.

The only new friend she'd made was Kat Somerset. They'd met on a horrible stormy night at the launderette in Goldhawk Road. No one else was in there, and Kat had greeted Amelia with enthusiasm, saying she thought they both needed their heads seeing to, coming out on such a night.

Amelia was immediately intrigued because Kat had such an exciting life. She was the buyer for the bathrooms department in Harrods and often had to travel to Milan to look at new products. 'I'm sure you know the Italians lead the way in design,' she said. 'Many other bathroom companies buy products from China and other Far East countries, but not us.'

She was not only well travelled and knowledgeable, but she was interesting-looking – not beautiful or even pretty, but striking. She had long, thick, wavy dark brown hair and was very tall, perhaps five foot ten, with a statuesque body. Her nose was a little too Roman, and her dark eyes rather small and beady, but she had the kind of presence Amelia wished she had.

Kat lived further down Godolphin Road on the other side. 'I'm looking to buy a small house or apartment, Amelia. I fancy Fulham, as my boyfriend, Grant, who deals in property, says it's an area on the up and up.'

'Are you getting married, then?' Amelia asked.

'Dear me, no.' Kat tossed her hair back over her shoulder. 'There's far too many interesting men out there for me to tie myself down just yet. Grant is very generous, always taking me out to the smartest restaurants and to see shows. He's a great lover, too, but I'm playing the field for now.'

It was frustrating how rarely she saw Kat: she wanted to invite her in for a meal, perhaps get to know the friends she talked about when they ran into each other down by the tube in the early evenings. On those occasions they usually went for a drink, but Kat was always rushing off to the West End or meeting someone later.

When Amelia got the job at the newspaper, she thought she might have a busier social life. Journalists were supposed to be wild, always up for a party or dragging you down to the pub with them. They did the pub thing sometimes, and Amelia had the odd date with men she met there, but most nights after one of those sessions she came home alone, a bit tipsy, and thought how shallow it all was.

Recently she had begun to think she was destined to be an old maid, that life would be one long, dreary plod towards old age.

Then, out of the blue, everything seemed to have changed. She could have done without finding a dead body practically on her doorstep, but because of it, her job was now looking decidedly promising, and Max even more so. But she wasn't going to jinx anything by getting too excited and imagining happy-ever-after.

That didn't stop her mentally planning the picnic for Sunday, though, and what she was going to wear.

The following day, as the paper hit the streets, Amelia's colleagues were remarkably interested in her and her story, stopping by her desk to chat. Frank, the top reporter, even brought her a doughnut and a cup of coffee and praised her story, which he said made 'compelling reading'. There were telephone calls too, from other newspapers, but Jack dealt with them.

Yet however impressed Jack and the other staff might be, Amelia was still expected to stay at her desk, take calls from would-be advertisers and cold-call businesses to sell them advertising space.

But on Friday afternoon, not long before she was due to go home, Jack called her into his office. 'I've had an

49

update on Lucy Whelan's death,' he said, after inviting her to sit down. 'I thought you had a right to know first, but I don't want you bandying it around. Is that clear?'

'Perfectly.' She nodded. She assumed he'd got this information from a police source and had been told to keep it under his hat for now. Just that he was prepared to share it with her was a real compliment.

'Her body wasn't driven to the site where you found her. She was killed there, in broad daylight,' he said, almost jubilantly. 'It seems she was struck hard on the back of her head. The post-mortem revealed traces of lead in the head wound, so most likely she was hit with a length of piping. Then, when she fell backwards, she was stabbed through her side. It seems she may have fallen directly onto the rubbish, which was why there was no blood on the path. The killer then moved some bags on top of her.'

'Good heavens,' Amelia exclaimed. 'I can't believe anyone would kill someone in broad daylight with so many houses close by.'

'My source referred to him as "a creeper" – creeping up on his victim. But so far they don't have any leads on him.'

'Did they check with Lucy's friend Frances, the girl she usually stays with?'

'Oh, yes. Lucy was with her overnight. Frances was still in bed after her pal had left, but Lucy left a note thanking her. The woman downstairs spoke to her as she left – that was around twelve noon. She told the neighbour she was going to Goldhawk Road market before she went home.'

The market was only a short walk from Amelia's home and from where she had found Lucy.

'But that suggests it was an entirely random killing. If she was followed back from work, it's unlikely the killer would have waited all night for her to surface again.'

'She got a taxi to Frances's anyway,' Jack said. He looked a bit perplexed. 'Unless, of course, he'd followed her to Frances's place another day and knew what time she'd surface the following morning. He could've been waiting there and followed her when she came out.'

'But why would she go into Godolphin Road and Scotts Road where I found her? It's not the way back to Chiswick.'

'Her friend said she'd mentioned checking out a hairdresser's in Uxbridge Road. If that was where she was heading it would've made a lot more sense to cut through Lime Grove. But maybe she missed that turning. The point is, was the killer following her all the time? And what was it about her that made him want to kill her?'

'An old boyfriend?' Amelia suggested. 'Someone she rejected?'

'If I killed everyone who rejected me,' Jack joked, 'the bodies would stretch from Shepherd's Bush to Marble Arch.'

Amelia laughed. Yet although that was funny here in the safety of an office, it made her think along another track. 'If he's killing because he was rejected, there'll be others,' she said.

'You're right. In that case, we'll have to wait until another body turns up. Then police can look for common denominators.'

A shiver ran down Amelia's spine. She had a feeling that was exactly what was going to happen.

5

Amelia woke early on Sunday to find the sun shining and not a cloud in the sky. She leaped out of bed fizzing with excitement. She'd bought the picnic food the previous day, even though she was afraid it would pour with rain and they wouldn't be able to go to Hampstead Heath.

Max said he'd call for her at eleven, but at six in the morning that seemed an eternity away.

By ten she had cleaned her room, changed the sheets, and was ready, bathed, hair washed, and wearing her newest dress. It was a copy of a Mary Quant sleeveless shift, white but with a flash of scarlet down one side. Flat sandals, as heels on Hampstead Heath would be folly, and she had a red cardigan in case it turned chilly later. She had used the last of her Madame Rochas perfume, but Max was worth it.

The picnic was all packed into a basket: pork pie, hard-boiled eggs, ham and cucumber rolls, some peaches and plums, a bottle of lemonade and a bar of chocolate. She'd wanted to add more but it was already heavy to carry.

She looked in the mirror to tweak her hair. Mostly when she studied her appearance a small voice in her head whispered that she was fat, plain, her nose too big, or her eyes too small. She was certain such thoughts were her father's doing as she'd grown up with his continual nasty, barbed remarks, which, she knew, were intended to undermine her confidence.

However, today she was about 90 per cent certain she looked fine, even pretty. Her bobbed hair was shiny chestnut, her legs were good, she had a golden tan and she certainly didn't look fat. Today's positivity was all down to her success in writing the story about Lucy. She'd bought all the daily newspapers yesterday to see how they had chosen to write up the murder, and she'd been delighted to see small elements of her story in each. That at least meant all those big-name journalists had read hers. It was interesting to see the different slants they'd put on the facts. The *Daily Telegraph* and *The Times* were the most truthful, and they had used the photograph Amelia had borrowed from the Whelans. They had cut it down to a head shot, though, and didn't mention ballet. There was a quote from a neighbour, who said, 'Lucy was a pleasant girl, but a bit headstrong.' At least that wasn't really damning.

The *Daily Mail* and the *Express* had used another photograph in which Lucy looked drunk, wearing a very low-cut dress. Amelia wondered who had given it to them. Both portrayed her as a young woman who had been lured to the clubs of Soho to make a somewhat sordid living. They didn't say she was a stripper, but certainly implied it, along with a subtle message about the dangers for young women in London's West End.

Amelia was glad she'd advised the Whelans not to speak to the press. Even without contact with the family, those journalists had decided Lucy was a wild girl who had done as she liked and paid the ultimate price for it. Had they spoken to the family and twisted any unguarded comments they might have made, goodness knows what they would have added.

Amelia glanced out of the window at a quarter to eleven and saw Max standing by the steps to his house. She had a feeling he was excited, like her, but afraid to call on her early. That pleased her so she decided to go down.

'Hello, Max,' she said, pretending surprise when she opened the front door to see him standing at the bottom of the steps. 'I didn't hear the bell. I just thought I'd better come down and check as quite often it doesn't work.'

'I've only just got here. You look nice,' he said, with a smile, holding up a rolled-up tartan rug. 'I borrowed this from my neighbour. Good job I did – you wouldn't want to get grass stains on that smart dress.'

He was wearing jeans, an open-necked checked shirt and desert boots. He looked so different from how he did in a suit, and she liked it. It fitted better with him liking rock-climbing. 'I hope I've packed enough food,' she said. 'The basket got heavy, so I stopped putting things into it.'

'Then we'll eat it quickly to make it lighter.' He laughed. 'I'm starving already.'

Even before they got to the tube station Amelia had entirely forgotten how nervous she was. Max had such a lovely dry sense of humour, making little acerbic observations about the crummy shops they passed. Shepherd's Bush shared nothing with Holland Park and Chiswick, its glamorous neighbours, but however run down it was, they both liked it.

Once on the tube they discussed Saturday's reports in the dailies on the murder.

'You've got your five minutes of fame as "the Girl who Found the Body",' Max said, his eyes twinkling. 'That sounds like one of those cheap thrillers. But I love the *Mirror*'s pious "Her family are broken with shock and grief", yet in the next sentence it's saying she went to a friend's home late at night, instead of going home, wearing skimpy hot pants. They might as well have said she was a girl of dubious morals and had it coming to her.'

Max had bought today's *News of the World*, which had stated she was a stripper in a sleazy Soho bar. It had sickened him to read that, he said. 'It beggars belief,' he added, shaking his head. 'She was murdered, for Heaven's sake. And she danced in an exclusive Mayfair nightclub. Even if she was on the game in the alleys of Soho, she still wouldn't have deserved to be killed. I can't imagine how devastated her family must be to see her portrayed in that way.'

'Let's not talk about it any more,' Amelia suggested. 'It's too nice a day to dwell on sad stuff.'

'A wise plan,' Max said. 'So, tell me what's in the picnic basket.'

Amelia laughed. 'Nothing terribly exciting. I had a friend, Julia, whose mum made us picnics to take to the park. She was a proper mum, one that made cakes, sewed buttons on school blouses and was always there on sports day. Her picnics were amazing. She used to make us little trifles in jam jars. There were cold sausages and chicken legs too. I could never wait till lunchtime. I'd be drooling by ten in the morning, thinking about what might be in the bag.'

Max smiled. 'My mum made good picnics too, not as posh as trifles in jam jars, but thick slices of corned beef with Branston pickle in the sandwiches, and always nice cake. I take it you didn't see yours as a proper mum.'

'She was useless in every way,' Amelia admitted. 'I don't know if it was Dad bullying her that made her so spineless, or if she was just made that way. She couldn't control my brothers, she never got on top of cleaning or washing clothes and as for cooking! By the time I was twelve I was doing it all for her.'

'So that's why your room is so neat and pretty,' he said. 'All the girls I've known from organized homes live like slobs.'

Amelia had surprised herself by talking about her mother. She normally avoided conversations about her background for fear of revealing how wretched it was.

But perhaps it was good to have it out the way before their relationship got going. In the past she'd dreaded boyfriends suggesting she took them home to meet her parents. One look at the house from outside told the whole story: a front door that had been kicked open and a board nailed over it; the garden like a waste tip; filthy and torn net curtains at windows that hadn't been cleaned for years.

'I left home at eighteen never to return,' she said.

She wasn't going to tell him she'd left because her father had beaten her up for refusing to hand over her pay packet. She'd been so badly hurt that she'd only reached the end of the road before she collapsed. A neighbour had seen her and called an ambulance. While she was in hospital the almoner had pulled some strings to get her the room in Godolphin Road, and persuaded a charity to help her buy the basics she'd need, living on her own. That was a time in her life she didn't want to remember.

'It's a very strange thing, Max, but I never felt I belonged in that family,' she said, feeling some explanation was in order. 'When I was small I used to imagine I'd been left with them, and one day a classy couple would come and reclaim me.'

'I suspect there's a great deal more to the story than that! But maybe you'll tell me when you know me better.'

She shrugged, surprised by his intuition, but not willing to reveal more of herself today. 'Tell me about your parents. You said they were farmers but now they've retired to Sidmouth.'

'They're kind, loving people, who've worked hard all their lives,' he said thoughtfully. 'As a kid I thought they were the fount of all knowledge. And they were, in their world. To run a moorland farm requires strength and stamina, patience and fortitude. Not to mention veterinary skills, knowledge of animal husbandry and how to grow crops successfully. But since they sold up and retired to Sidmouth, they seem so much smaller, duller and bigoted. Is that an awful thing to say?'

'Not to me. I know you're only trying to explain the difference you see in them now from how you saw them as a child. That's not awful, just realistic.'

He nodded. 'They got married young and farmed in a remote part of Devon. Their world was us four boys and the farm. We had a brilliant childhood. But they've no experience of big cities – even little Sidmouth seems very urban to Mum, and she says ridiculous things to me like "Watch it when you go out that someone doesn't stick a needle in your arm and turn you into a drug addict."'

Amelia spluttered with laughter. 'Such naivety is rather sweet,' she said.

Max grinned. 'As if an addict would waste his heroin on a stranger! I just wish Mum would ask me about stuff instead of making crass statements that make her sound stupid. I told her it takes more than one fix to become addicted, and immediately she flew into a panic thinking I'd tried it.'

'She's just being protective.'

'Maybe. She and Dad have joined a bowling club in Sidmouth. When she told me, I was tempted to say she shouldn't bend over to bowl in case someone stuck a needle in her bum.'

'Oh, Max!' Amelia laughed. 'That's just cruel.'

By the time they got to Hampstead station they were laughing helplessly. Max had moved on to tell her some funny stories about old clients. One man had three 'wives'. He was married to one but insisted on contacting the Inland Revenue to claim an allowance for each of them and the five children they had between them. He was indignant when a tax inspector turned him down.

Amelia asked if he'd met the wives, and Max said he'd met two of them, and they'd seemed extraordinarily normal. 'All living in one house! Can you imagine? It's not as if he's a heartthrob. He's weedy and nearly bald.'

Flocks of people were making their way to the Heath from the station, and Amelia thought that maybe they should have picked somewhere less popular for their picnic. But when they got up to Whitestone Pond and saw the Heath spread in front of them, it didn't look crowded at all. They walked for a while and found a nice secluded spot to spread out the blanket and sit down.

Max dived into the picnic basket with boyish enthusiasm, delighted with everything.

'You're amazingly easy to please,' Amelia remarked.

His boyishness really appealed to her. Past men in her life were always trying to be 'cool', never showing enthusiasm for anything. 'It's nice being here in the sun, with such good company.'

'I'd marry you on the strength of that picnic alone.' He laughed and blushed. 'Oh, gosh! Talk about the need to engage the brain before opening the mouth! That wasn't a real proposal, but I'm sure you know what I mean. I can't believe we've lived so close to each other for so long but only got talking because of a murder.'

'I can hardly believe I spotted a dead body. Normally people who discover one are out in the countryside with their dog.'

'Confession time,' he said, with a grin. 'I've got to admit I always fancied you. The first time I saw you, and it must be two years ago or more, you had longer hair and a beaded band round your forehead. You were wearing an embroidered cheesecloth dress, and I christened you Pocahontas. I have to say you don't look like a Red Indian squaw now.'

Amelia giggled. 'We all wore some mad stuff back then. I saw you once in purple flares.'

'Don't remind me of that fashion disaster,' he replied, looking mortified. 'I bought them in Carnaby Street, and a pair of platform Chelsea boots. The first time I wore the boots I fell over, and it was a miracle I didn't break my ankle.'

'It was fun in 'sixty-eight and 'sixty-nine,' Amelia said wistfully. 'I loved the free rock concerts in Hyde Park, the fabulous music and the freedom to be whatever you wanted to be. But we were left with a lot of people who had drug problems. Did you get into the druggy thing?'

'I smoked a few joints, had a bit of speed, once tried LSD, but that scene wasn't for me,' he said. 'It all seemed a bit phoney. People suggested we should share everything, but the truth was that they wanted blokes like me, who had a job, to supplement them so they could lie around all day.'

Amelia's experience had been so similar. 'So we were both failed flower children,' she said impishly. 'Something else we have in common.'

'So how do you imagine yourself – I mean, where do you want to be in a couple of years' time?' he asked.

Amelia lay back on the blanket, tucking her cardigan under her head. 'It's not something I've really thought much about,' she said. 'Well, not until the murder happened – it's opened up possibilities. I might be promoted at work, but I like to fantasize that I'll be head-hunted by one of the nationals. It's also made me think I need to get my book finished and try to get it published. But there is another possibility, which you'll think is mad.'

'Go on, tell me.'

'I'd like to try and solve this murder.'

Max leaned over her and, with one finger, smoothed back a lock of hair that was close to her eyes. 'It's mad, but entirely understandable. I thought the same myself.'

'You did?' She was surprised at such an admission. He seemed such a grounded person.

'Yes, I did. Not that I've got the first idea how to go about it. But I did wonder if you could get the Whelans to give you Lucy's friend's address. Maybe we could go and see her. She works at the Beachcomber, too. She might agree to get us in.'

During the day Max told her lots more amusing stories, some from when he was a kid in Devon, others from when he'd first come to London and shared a flat with four friends. Amelia told him about working at the newspaper and the characters there, Jack being the main one. She admitted she was a loner. 'I don't make much of an effort to find friends any more,' she said. 'I suppose I've got a bit of an inferiority complex. I just assume people won't be interested in me. That's pathetic, isn't it?'

'Not at all. From what little you've said about your family it's not surprising.' He kissed her nose. 'But I promise you, Amelia, you aren't some sad little girl who needs to hide away. You're pretty, bright, amusing and very caring. The depth of feeling you clearly had for the Whelans brought a lump to my throat.'

Amelia's eyes prickled with unshed tears. She knew exactly why she didn't try to make friends, and when that had started, but she didn't think she could tell Max.

It was when she'd first got the room at Godolphin Road. She was still in physical pain from her father's beating and felt terribly alone and scared. Yet when she went into that room and locked the door behind her, she felt safe for the first time she could remember. It wasn't much of a place then – nasty old dark-wood furniture, grubby walls and a threadbare carpet. As soon as her cuts and bruises had stopped hurting, she had set to work to paint the room white. Each week when she got her wages, she bought something: a pot of paint for a piece of furniture, some vivid material, a lamp, a cushion. She scoured the junk shops in Shepherd's Bush looking for bargains. The carpet was the best one, three pounds for a dark green piece big enough to cover the threadbare one.

Transforming the dismal room to a bright, clean, colourful sanctuary had become a passion. She didn't want other people in it: it was her place of safety where she could forget the mother who cared more about a bottle of cider and a packet of fags than her daughter, or her bully of a father who had made her believe she was useless at everything.

She had a few dates in the first three years she lived there. One had led to a relationship that lasted an entire year. Paul was a few years older than her, an articled clerk at the firm of solicitors where she worked as a typist. He was religious and believed it was wrong to have sex outside marriage. She liked that he wanted her to go to church with him, and didn't pester her for sex as other men had done before him. While she didn't think she was in love with him, he was decent, and she hoped real love would grow. But when the mini-skirt hit the magazines and shops in Oxford Street, Paul was horrified when she met him one evening wearing one. He sent her home to change, and it was then she realized he was controlling her. He would sulk if she didn't want to go to church every Sunday morning, he monitored what she wore, and he picked every film they went to see. He was appalled when he caught her reading a novel by Harold Robbins, because it was well known for graphic sex scenes. She knew if she didn't end it with him, she'd be trapped before long in a narrow, cold marriage.

He took it badly. He said she should be grateful he'd wanted to marry her – after all, she was hardly out of the 'top drawer'. She had to find another job, too, so she didn't have to see his chilly, disapproving expression any more.

The experience with Paul cemented the idea in her head that she must stay free. But soon loneliness emboldened her to try again, mostly with men she met through working for a temping agency. None of the dates led to anything worthwhile, and she knew she was at fault because she tried too hard to please, just as she'd always done with her father.

It was difficult to make girlfriends, too: they always seemed to be in little cliques and didn't want anyone new joining them. So, she drew back into her room on a programme of self-improvement, reading books on that subject, then the classics, and magazines, so she was up to date with fashions and current trends. She listened to classical music on the radio, imitating the

BBC voices she heard. Sometimes it occurred to her that her room had become like a caterpillar's cocoon, and that one day, when she was completely ready, she'd shed the cocoon and emerge a complete and perfect person.

She'd thought that moment had come when she'd run into Emily, an old school friend, three years ago. Emily had always been an extrovert, and popular with everyone at school. She'd given her fair hair an Afro perm and wanted to set the world alight.

Amelia got her hair permed too, and together they went to clubs in Soho, festivals in parks and love-ins at Alexandra Palace. Amelia lost most of her inhibitions, with hippie men, who were not bossy, mostly good lovers, fun and imaginative. She and Emily had a blast until Amelia began to notice that people were always dossing on her floor, eating food she'd bought and cooked, and when they drifted off to Cornwall or to Spain, they never invited her to come too.

Then in early 1970, Emily drifted off too, to a commune in Scotland, without as much as a goodbye. All that was left of those heady fun times was a lingering smell of patchouli oil, a mark on her neck from hippie love beads and a big scratch across the Beatles' *Abbey Road* album.

Amelia realized it was time to pull back into her cocoon, to update her image and to find a job with some hope of promotion or she would drift aimlessly, like so many others she knew. She had been temping all along, but now she was determined to find a job with a future. In March 1970, when she was twenty-five, the *West London Weekly* took her on.

Now, since finding Lucy Whelan, she felt she had plunged head first off a diving board into a new pool. Meeting the Whelan family and getting respect from Jack and other journalists was good, as was meeting Max. She felt she'd finally found her niche, not clinging to the comfort and safety of her room but marching boldly out into the world.

'What are you thinking about?' Max asked. He was propped up on his elbow next to her, looking down at her.

'Just how long it's taken me to find out what I really want,' she said, with a smile. 'Seven years, in fact.'

'So are you going to tell me what that is?'

She lifted her hands to cup his face, smiling up at him. 'No, I can't put it into words. But I'd like to be kissed.'

His head came down towards hers, but he stopped just a couple of inches from her face. 'I've been thinking that since we left home. But you've got a knack of disappearing inside yourself, which makes a chap like me anxious.'

Unable to think of an answer to that, she pulled him closer and kissed him. He responded eagerly, his hands sliding beneath her to take her in his arms. It was the kind of kiss she'd imagined a hundred times, but never actually experienced. Slow, sensual and sensitive, sparking waves of desire that made her arch her whole body into his, and the world around them to disappear.

'Gosh,' was all she could say, when he moved away slightly. 'That was . . .' She paused, unable to find the right words.

'It made me wish we were back in your pretty room and I could make love to you,' he murmured, against her cheek. 'Is it too soon for that?'

'Possibly.' She wanted to say she wasn't on the Pill, but that sounded too mechanical. She certainly couldn't ask if he had any Durex. Yet even under the sleepy spell of sweet seduction she knew she couldn't risk unprotected sex: she'd seen too many other girls panicking at an unwanted pregnancy.

'So if it's "possibly" too early, does that mean you aren't averse to the idea?'

His eyes were twinkling and the corners of his mouth looked like he was trying not to laugh.

'In books people can have sex seamlessly. They don't seem to concern themselves with time, place or consequences.'

'Did you mean you'd like to do it on Hampstead Heath without anyone noticing?'

Amelia laughed. He had put on a very innocent questioning expression and she knew he was teasing her. 'I'm sure you know exactly what I mean. Sex without all the usual hang-ups, the fear of seeming too easy, of becoming pregnant et cetera . . .'

'So are you afraid of being "too easy", or of becoming

pregnant? Or is it one of the et ceteras, which I'm not familiar with?'

She looked into his lovely woodland-pool eyes and knew she'd finally met an intelligent man who could be trusted. 'Both I guess,' she said, putting one hand over her eyes, feeling self-conscious.

He took her hand away. 'Amelia, I really like you, not for a one-night stand, but with the hope that we've got something special, because that's the way it feels to me. Does it to you?'

'Yes,' she whispered.

'Well, in that case we need to be adults about it and discuss what we want, or don't want. So do you want me?'

'Yes, but I'm not on the Pill,' she said, blushing furiously as no man had ever said anything like that to her before.

'Then I'll take control until you can get on it. But for now let's have some more kissing.'

6

'I've got to go,' Max whispered, as he kissed Amelia's neck and cupped his hands round her breasts.

'Surely not already,' she said sleepily. 'It's not even light yet.'

'It's nearly seven and I've got to shower, shave and get to Uxbridge by nine. You go back to sleep and I'll see you tomorrow evening.'

It was weeks since the day they'd found Lucy's body and become friends. A week on from that, when they'd had the picnic on Hampstead Heath, their love affair had started. They'd got so sunburned that they didn't go to bed together then, and Max had had to go away to see a client in Brighton where he stayed for the remainder of that week.

Amelia went to the doctor and got the Pill, but it would be a further two weeks before she was fully protected. She was shocked by how much she wanted Max: he was on her mind all day, and at night she tossed and turned, thinking of him. But he'd gone off on another business trip to Birmingham, so she couldn't even tell him.

It was early on a Saturday morning when it finally happened. She awoke at six thirty to the sound of Max throwing gravel at her window. 'I got the first train back from Birmingham to be with you because I couldn't bear it any longer,' he said, as she let him in. 'I even gave up the hotel's full breakfast!'

They fell into the bed she'd just got out of and made love. It was extra special and passionate because of the spontaneity and even more so when Max told her he loved her.

'I think I knew I'd fallen for you the night you came around with your story about Lucy Whelan,' he said, leaning up on his elbow to look at her. 'But I told myself it was too soon to be sure. I know I want you for ever now – I just hope you feel the same way.'

'I do.' She sighed, hardly able to believe that he felt as she did. 'I feel as if I've waited my entire life for you to come along. But you were just two doors down.'

He'd bought her the latest LP from the American soft-rock band Bread, and when she heard the track 'I Wanna Make It With You', she cried because he sang along to it.

It had been a rollercoaster ride ever since that day – lovemaking so beautiful it made her cry, so much laughter. Even a walk to the market with him was an adventure. Max often had to go to clients' business premises around the country, which meant he had to stay in a hotel overnight. Before they met, he'd always revelled in the luxury and a big breakfast the next day, but now he said he missed Amelia too much to enjoy it.

She counted the hours till he returned and wished he didn't have to go away so often.

When he was at home they stayed in Amelia's room as it was bigger and she had a double bed. Max suggested they look for a proper flat together, but she thought it was too soon to make long-term plans.

It wasn't that she didn't want a permanent home with Max, but memories of her parents' miserable marriage, and that this room had been her sanctuary for so long, made her cautious. But she tended to smile and say, 'Let's see how it goes,' each time Max mentioned it. She was as nervous about saying no as she was about saying yes.

As Max got out of bed, Amelia roused herself enough to sit up. 'Don't forget we're going to see Frances tomorrow at seven,' she reminded him.

Frances was Lucy Whelan's friend. The funeral had been held a month ago, but still the police hadn't found her killer and the newspapers had long since lost interest. Amelia was right back selling advertising space, as if nothing serious had happened, and poor Frances had been persecuted by journalists in the first couple of weeks. Back then she had refused to speak to Amelia, which was entirely understandable. But Amelia had since written to her, hammering home the point that she wasn't after publicity and wasn't going to write a word about it, just wanted to do some private investigating to see if she could find some lead that had eluded the police.

Frances must have sensed her sincerity as she'd finally agreed to this meeting.

Max pulled on his clothes, and when the kettle boiled he made tea for Amelia. He put the mug on the bedside table next to her, bent over to kiss her again and left. She listened to his footsteps on the stairs, and the careful way he opened and closed the front door without the banging that all the other tenants did.

Propping up her pillow behind her, she sat with her tea, marvelling that he always made it for her. The first man in her life who'd ever done that. But, then, he was adorable in every way. Funny, kind, helpful, interested and wonderful in bed. She smiled, amazed that she'd got to six weeks and still hadn't found a downside to him.

She had expected to be irritated that he went to his amateur dramatics club every Wednesday – he was rehearsing for a production they would perform during the first week in December – but she wasn't. In fact it was nice to have a bit of time to herself because he always stayed at his place on Wednesday nights. Thursday nights he would regale her with all the intrigue in the club. He made it so funny she felt as if she knew snooty Vera Parkside, who got very cross if anyone dared to criticize her. Then there was the hapless Ronald Dowry who was completely under the thumb of his wife, Doreen. The play was billed as a comedy, but Max said it was a farce, the kind Brian Rix had perfected. It was called *The Dinner Party* and Max was the

74

obsequious butler, keeping up his servile manner and lofty standards even when the guests were behaving outrageously. He quoted a few lines from it sometimes and they always made her laugh.

There was an autumnal nip in the air as Amelia left the house to go to work, and she noticed the leaves on the trees all along the street had turned golden. She was glad she'd thought to wear her coat over her plain black office dress.

She'd gone just a few yards when she heard someone call her name and turned to see Kat running to catch her up. She was wearing a long black coat, with a mini skirt beneath it, and her hair in a big plait over her shoulder.

'Long time no see!' Amelia exclaimed, as Kat fell into step with her. 'How have you been?'

'Busy,' Kat said. 'Off to Milan again, and New York. There've been so many after-hours meetings at work, too, and, of course, various men I had to be wined and dined by!' She laughed as she said this. 'No time to look for a house. But you! Fancy you finding the murdered girl in the rubbish. The whole street was agog.'

Amelia blushed. While the newspapers might have forgotten the story, in local shops and at work she was still known as 'the Girl who Found the Body in the Rubbish'. It was all they wanted to talk about. 'Yes, poor girl,' she said. 'But quite honestly I'd like to forget about it.'

'But you wrote that marvellous piece in the local rag,' Kat said. 'You told me you were just a gofer, not a journalist. That piece could've been written by someone on *The Times*.'

'Well, thank you,' Amelia said, hoping Kat would drop the subject. 'Not as exciting as your life, though. Tell me, what was New York like?'

She wished her job was as exciting as Kat's – she'd give anything to go to New York, Paris or Rome. She often daydreamed of travelling, and had even tried to persuade Max they should book a holiday somewhere exotic instead of finding a flat to share. His response had been that he was too busy at work to take a holiday.

'New York is frantic, noisy, exhausting. Everyone seems to do things at a hundred miles an hour,' Kat said. 'But going back to the murder, how did you get so much information about the girl? I'd have thought her relatives would be very cagey.'

'They didn't mind talking to me as I'd found Lucy and felt a kind of bond with her. I went back to them a few times – I even went to her funeral, which was terribly sad. But in some strange way her mother seems to find my visits helpful. She feels she can talk to me about Lucy, now that her neighbours and many of her friends want her to stop. I just wish the police would catch the killer. That would really help her family.'

'Changing the subject,' Kat said, with a wide grin, 'I saw you go past the other day with a man. Don't tell me he's just a friend! You looked all loved up. How long have you been seeing him?'

Amelia smiled. 'Yes, that's my lovely Max. I've been

seeing him for about six weeks. Ever since I found Lucy Whelan's body. He helped me and called the police.'

'I thought I'd seen him somewhere before. Does he live close by?'

'Two doors down from me,' Amelia said. 'I can't really believe I'd never spoken to him in two years of living so close to each other. But what about you? Out of all those admirers, is there anyone special?'

Kat wrinkled her nose. 'Rich men can be a bit boring. But I've got used to nice meals and presents. Not sure I want to go back to deadbeats. But, tell me, have the police made any headway finding the killer?'

Amelia couldn't believe Kat was so keen to talk about the murder and not reveal more about her exciting dates and trips to other countries. 'I don't think they have, but I haven't spoken to them since I had to give them a statement. My boss likes to keep tabs on the case, he has friends at the police station, but they don't tell the general public what lines of enquiry they're working on.'

The girls parted at the tube station, as Kat had to catch a train and Amelia had only a short walk from there.

'Let's have a drink soon!' Kat called, as she moved into the crowd going into the station. 'It's been too long.'

As Amelia walked on towards the office her thoughts turned again to the Whelans. Each time she'd seen them she had felt more determined that Lucy's killer must be found. Jack had admitted his friend in the police force had told him they had no leads at all. There didn't appear to be any motive for the killing, not sexual, robbery or a family dispute. His friend had said that a killer who struck at random was always the hardest to find because – the old cliché – you were looking for a needle in a haystack.

But Amelia was sure there had to be some motive. The killer must have been watching Lucy for some time. They had to have had a connection, even if it was only a tenuous one. A jilted boyfriend? An older man at the nightclub who had become fixated on her? A man she'd turned down for a date? But everything she'd learned about Lucy so far confirmed she was a sunny-natured, easy-going girl. Nothing she'd been told had suggested she was capable of upsetting anyone.

The moment Amelia walked through the doors of the office she sensed something and glanced towards Jack's office. He was pacing the room, which he always did when something dramatic had happened.

'What is it?' she asked Frank, the senior journalist.

'Go in and see Jack. He'll tell you,' Frank said. 'Seems the Creeper has struck again.'

Amelia felt a cold shudder run down her spine, yet as awful as that was, it was exciting too. 'Another murder, sir?' she asked, as she opened Jack's office door. 'When? Where?'

'Her body was found just a couple of hours ago in Ravenscroft Park, close to you again,' Jack said. He stopped pacing and perched on the edge of his desk. 'Seems she was killed late last night. Another pretty blonde. Same age, same MO – whacked on the back of her head, then stabbed. He'd partially covered her with fallen leaves. A dog-walker found her.'

Amelia sank onto a chair, horror taking over the first flush of excitement. 'Oh, my goodness! Are the police sure it's the same person?'

'Absolutely. Again, no sexual interference. Like Lucy, there was no bag, but again they think it was taken to delay them in finding out who she is.'

'Or it could be a trophy?' Amelia said. 'I read that killers like to keep something.'

Amelia was too shocked to ask any further questions. One murder so close to her home was frightening enough, but two suggested that the killer lived nearby, or that the area meant something to him.

'Until the police know who she is and where she lives, we've got nothing much to write about,' Jack said despondently. 'It's not as if I have any good excuse to send you to see the girl's folks either. Even when we find out who she is.'

'Maybe I could brazen it out in a cold call,' Amelia suggested. 'That is, if your friend in the police could tell us who she is before the information goes on general release.'

Jack's face brightened. 'What would you say?'

Even though Amelia didn't fancy the idea of calling on a grieving family when she had absolutely no reason for it, Jack looked so eager and trusting that she wanted to please him. 'I'm not sure yet, but I'm going to see Frances, Lucy's friend, tonight. She might tell me something that could link the girls together.'

'I honestly think you're the only person who might be able to get a foot in the door of the new victim,' Jack said. 'There's something about you that instils trust.'

Amelia suspected he'd claimed the same thing to many young journalists over the years. But she wanted to believe he was sincere.

Max telephoned her at the office close to four o'clock. 'I'm really sorry, Mimi,' he said, using the pet name he'd given her. 'I have to stay in Luton tonight. There are major problems with the books, and I'll be working on them till late, and probably tomorrow too. Can you postpone the meeting with Frances?'

'I could but I don't want to,' she said. 'It's okay, Max, I'll go on my own. If I postponed, she might not arrange another day. I'll see you tomorrow.'

Amelia was disappointed. She'd wanted Max's opinion on the questions she was intending to put to Frances. And he might have thought of some that hadn't occurred to her. But it couldn't be helped: his work had to come first. She didn't even tell him about the second murder because she knew he'd worry about her with another so close by.

*

Frances Ware shared a flat in Bayswater Road with two other girls. It was a wide tree-lined thoroughfare, the main route from Shepherd's Bush past Holland Park to the centre of town. There were huge, mid-Victorian once very grand mansions. Most were divided into flats now.

Amelia found the house easily – Frances had said it was just a few doors up from Holland Park tube station. Flat four was on the ground floor, its front door round the side of the house.

Frances answered the door so quickly that Amelia guessed she'd been pacing up and down, waiting for the bell to ring.

'I'm really fed up,' she said, before she'd even greeted Amelia properly. 'The police came around again this morning and woke me up. I can't tell them anything new – I don't know anything. It's probably a waste of your time coming too.'

Frances was exotic-looking, with dark hair that shone like wet tar and just touched her narrow shoulders. Her dark eyes and olive skin suggested she had Italian or Spanish ancestry, but she sounded private-school posh. She was wearing jeans and a sweater, and even without makeup, she was beautiful.

'I don't want to pester you,' Amelia assured her. 'I can understand what it must be like for you. But, as I said in my letter, I found Lucy's body, and hope that by looking at things from a different angle, I might find a connection between Lucy and the man who killed her.'

'Come on in, then,' Frances said.

She led Amelia into a shabby, untidy sitting room. Amelia, who had seen inside dozens of flats and bed-sits over the years, was never surprised or shocked by mess. She had observed that girls who came from good homes, with a first-class education, were the messi-est. Amelia knew she gave away her origins by keeping her room so tidy and clean.

She picked up a heap of magazines from the sofa, straightened them into a tidy pile and placed them on a coffee-table that held a half-eaten plate of egg and chips, two overflowing ashtrays and four coffee mugs.

'Have each of you girls got your own bedroom?' she asked.

'No, Susan and Wendy share,' Frances said, picking up the plate and mugs. Rather than take them to the kitchen, she just moved them onto the floor. 'I've got the smaller room, but there are two beds in it, which is why Lucy could stay the night. Quite honestly, Amelia, I can't imagine what I can tell you that would be any possible use to you. I'm really all talked out on it.'

Amelia sensed the girl was regretting allowing her to come over. She hadn't intended to tell her about the second victim, but it seemed the only thing to do now. 'You might feel differently when I tell you that another girl was found dead today, in the park near to where I found Lucy.'

Frances's face drained of colour. 'No!' she exclaimed, incredulous. 'Do the police think it's the same man?'

'Yes, they do. No details yet, they're trying to find out who she was as she had nothing on her to identify her. But this makes it even more vital to get as much information about Lucy as possible so that when the second girl is named checks can be made to see if there is a connection between them, and maybe to the killer.'

'I don't know that I can tell you any more than I told the police,' Frances said, her lip trembling.

'It's the minute details – places she liked, people she didn't. Any weird incidents she told you about, things that seemed unimportant at the time. Boyfriends, men who fancied her or were a bit of a pest. A taxi driver who was a bit creepy.'

'I can't think of anyone like that.'

'That's okay – it might pop into your head later, even after I've gone. Will you tell me if it does?'

Frances nodded.

'I'm sure the police have already asked you whether you saw anyone hanging around here before she was killed. As the Bayswater Road is so busy with traffic and pedestrians, I know you probably never notice anyone. But just try to imagine looking at the road and visualize anyone hanging around outside. Day or evening.'

'I didn't notice anything. But getting back to any- thing Lucy might have said, she rarely made remarks about other people. She just wasn't judgemental. Susan and Wendy are both terribly messy, but Lucy never said a word about them. She'd often tidy and wash up after they'd gone to work, even though I told her not to.'

Amelia didn't want to hear that Lucy was a saint. She couldn't have been, surely. Was anyone? 'What about at work? She was very pretty. Were other girls mean to her? And did men chat her up?'

'All the girls liked her – she was just one of those golden girls. I'm sure you had some like that at your school. They're always pretty, good at sport, liked by the teachers. Butter-wouldn't-melt types. I was never one of them, but Lucy was. As for men, well, all of us girls at the Beachcomber, whether waitresses like me or dancers like Lucy, get our fair share of men chatting us up. It's against the rules to date anyone we meet there anyway. But Lucy was good at deflecting them – she'd say she had a boyfriend as an excuse, reasoning that they wouldn't think she might have agreed to a date if it was allowed.'

'Lots of men don't take no for an answer, though, do they?'

'Too right. I've had my share of pests.' She smiled at that. 'But, like I said, Lucy was good at deflecting.'

'Did you always come straight home after work when Lucy was with you, or did you sometimes go somewhere else? Another club? A Wimpy Bar?'

'No, we never did. Occasionally we'd get the taxi to stop at the chip shop, if it was still open, but that was it. After a night in a club, all the smoke, noise and being

84

nice to people, you really don't want anything more than your bed.'

'Did you get chips that last night?'

'No – my feet were killing me. I was wearing new shoes. We came straight back, and we both went to bed within ten minutes of getting in.'

Amelia tried another tack. 'So what were Lucy's interests?'

'Dancing, obviously. She'd given up on being a ballerina – she was getting too old. She was toying with the idea of applying to be a Redcoat at Butlins. I did my best to talk her out of it – I've heard ghastly stories about Butlins. But I suppose I was being selfish, I liked having her at the club with me. She'd been very sporty, tennis, netball and gymnastics, but I think she felt dancing was enough exercise now. She practised for at least two hours a day as well as doing three sets in the evening.'

'Anything else?'

'She loved board games – she was extremely competitive and took them seriously. She once told me that at a Girl Guides camp they were playing Monopoly and there was a girl cheating. She said she told on her because she was horrified. I thought nearly everyone cheats at Monopoly – it's such a long-winded game you have to so it ends.'

Amelia laughed. She'd cheated many times when round at friends' houses after school. 'So she was in the Girl Guides? Did she take that seriously?'

'Oh, yes! "Be Prepared" was her motto. I saw a photo of her once in her Guides uniform – she had an armful of badges. I never got more than three. They despaired of me.'

Frances made Amelia some coffee, and it seemed she had now run out of steam.

'I think it's best if I leave you in peace,' Amelia said. She could see how stained the cups were and didn't fancying drinking from one. 'But if you think of anything else, could you drop me a line or ring me at work?' She jotted down the address and her work phone number. 'Before I go, you said she pretended to have a boyfriend to stop men pestering her. But did she have one? Or who was the last and what happened to him?'

'She was seeing Dan – that was a good six months ago. He dumped her because she was always working at weekends. She wasn't bitter. She said she liked him but wasn't in love with him. Since then she hadn't bothered. Dancing filled her life, really. There wasn't much room for anything else.'

Amelia sensed Frances had nothing more to say. 'Just one more thing,' she said as she got up. 'Could I come with my boyfriend to the Beachcomber? Just to get a feel for the place?'

'Of course you can! Anyone can come in as long as they're smartly dressed and can afford the hefty drink prices.' She paused and looked at Amelia. 'I'll tell you what, I'll explain to the manager, and I'm sure he'll keep you a table, maybe throw in a few drinks or waive the entrance fee. After all, everyone, including him, was very fond of Lucy.'

'That would be wonderful,' Amelia said. 'So kind of you. Could we come on Saturday?'

'Yes, that'll be fine. I'll leave your name on the door. Come about eight, before it gets frantic. Don't bank on Mr Edwards the manager being overly generous – he blows hot and cold – but I'll do my best for you.'

Amelia took both of Frances's forearms. 'Thank you for seeing me. It must've been hard when you've just lost your friend.'

'I miss her so much.' Frances's eyes filled with tears. 'But if I can help in some small way to get her killer caught and locked away, that will be something.'

The only nightclubs Amelia had visited were smoky dives in Soho, like the Bag o' Nails, and they were usually in cellars. The main music venues, like Wardour Street's Marquee, or the Flamingo, were called clubs but they were all about the music, with live up-and-coming bands. They usually closed by half past eleven, and there was no glamour, just a big space where people mostly stood around to listen.

There were discos too, but in the main they were cramped, expensive and something of a meat market. Amelia often wondered how girls expected to find the man of their dreams in a place so noisy you couldn't hold a conversation.

The thought of going somewhere ritzy like the Beach-comber was exciting. It was a chance to dress up too. She had a red crêpe dress trimmed with marabou feathers. It was gorgeous, had cost nearly a week's wages and she'd only worn it once. She had a feeling Max would be just as excited.

7

'Her name is – or, rather, was – Carol Meadows,' Jack said, the moment Amelia stepped through the door the next morning. 'And I've already rung her mother and asked if you can go and see her this morning.'

Amelia noticed other members of staff further back in the open-plan office watching Jack and listening to him. She could almost smell the hostility that he was singling out one of the younger members of his staff. 'They agreed just like that?' she exclaimed. While she felt awkward that he was favouring her, she was also stunned that he had the ability to arrange such a meeting. She knew Jack had a silver tongue when he chose to use it, but this seemed far too invasive. 'Surely her parents have only just been told she's dead. Aren't the police still with them?'

'There's no dad, just a mother,' he said. 'I telephoned her an hour ago, and the police had already left. She needs someone there with her – she even said as much. When I explained about you finding Lucy, I told her she'd find it comforting talking to you and she agreed immediately. There'll be a press release at eleven this morning, so get there now and pull out all the stops before the press hounds descend on her. Do what you did before and fend them off. Stay all day, if necessary, but bring me back a sizzling story.

'Peanut is waiting downstairs with the car to take you there. It's really close to where you live.'

Peanut was the sports reporter, an ex-professional footballer. He'd earned his nickname from the shape of his head. With straggling sandy hair doing little to disguise it, white eyelashes and badly pockmarked skin, he was unfortunate in his looks, but he was a kind and popular man, with an attractive wife and two sons. He was also a great sports journalist and had written three successful biographies on sportsmen.

Amelia had always liked him and, in her view, he had it all. She was glad he'd be taking her to Mrs Meadows as it was a chance to air her anxieties about this job and get his advice. Grabbing a notebook from her desk, she ran out of the door. If Mrs Meadows was expecting her that was half the battle, but she knew she must brace herself for high emotion.

'Jack's taken quite a shine to you,' Peanut said, as he drove underneath the Hammersmith flyover. 'You must have really impressed him with how you tackled the Whelans. He's also got the police to hold off questioning this woman further until later in the day. That was quite a feat.'

'I'm a bit scared he was too pushy,' she admitted. 'Don't you think it smacks of taking advantage when a woman is at her lowest ebb?'

'I might have been horrified if he'd sent one of the

other reporters, who act like rampaging bulls. But not you, Amelia. I know you'll be sensitive and kind.'

Amelia smiled weakly. It was a lovely compliment, but she wasn't entirely convinced.

'I hope so. I think it's a shame the police don't always appreciate how terrible it is to have questions fired at you when you've only just heard your child has been murdered. It's a miracle they can even string a sentence together. The Whelans told me they felt as if they were under suspicion themselves. And they said that one of the policewomen kept on asking creepy questions about Lucy's sex life, as if she'd done something mucky and that was why she was killed.'

'The police have to get in quick because they say the first twenty-four hours is the window of opportunity when they're most likely to catch the killer. But, hopefully, you'll be able to give this poor mother a bit of support and comfort,' Peanut said soothingly. 'All of us on the paper were touched by what you wrote about Lucy Whelan.'

'It's kind of you to say that, but I got the impression earlier everyone was angry I was getting the breaks.'

The traffic was unusually heavy today: it was stop and start constantly. Amelia fiddled with her handbag on her lap. She didn't want to bleat to Peanut, but he was the one person who had his finger on the pulse of the office and would know how her workmates were feeling.

'They'll soon get over it.' Peanut smiled at her. 'There's always a bit of initial jealousy when someone gets singled out. But they know you're the person to handle Mrs Meadows, and it's not a job any of them really wants. You'll see when you get back. They'll all be fine again.'

'I hope you're right – and let's hope the police can find this maniac before he captures a third girl.'

'Good luck,' Peanut said, as he dropped her at number fourteen Atwood Road, near Ravenscourt Park. 'You'll be fine. Of that I'm sure.'

Amelia waved as he drove off, but her heart was thumping, and her legs felt like rubber.

There were many substantial houses in the area, but the Meadowses' was a small terraced one and a bit neglected. The woman who opened the door was clearly Mrs Meadows: her eyes were red and puffy from crying. She was a dumpy woman, with a round face and a tight old-lady perm. Amelia was shocked that she appeared to be entirely alone in the house.

'I'm so glad you've come,' she said, in a weak voice, and her eyes filled with fresh tears.

Amelia went in, shut the door behind her and enfolded the older woman in her arms. 'I'm so sorry, Mrs Meadows. This is just the worst thing in the world that can be thrown at a mother. But I'm going to stay and look after you, until you can tell me who you'd like here, and we'll ring them.'

She held the sobbing woman for some minutes. When her tears had slowed to sniffs, she led her into the sitting room and directed her to the sofa.

'Tell me about Carol,' Amelia asked, once Mrs

Meadows had lit the gas fire and they had a cup of tea in their hands.

'She worked as a waitress in the King's Road, in Chelsea,' Mrs Meadows said. 'She liked to be there – she said it was where everything happened. If it wasn't for me, I think she would've moved into a flat there with other girls. I didn't mean to hold her back, but when her father left us, I couldn't cope. He went off with a younger woman.'

'That's so sad,' Amelia said. 'How did Carol take it? And how old was she then?'

'Eighteen. He said he'd waited that long so she wouldn't be affected by it. Stupid man, children are always affected however old they are. Carol hated him, and Melissa, his woman. But I think Carol hated me more because I was so dependent on her.'

Amelia was surprised she'd already slipped into the past tense. Was that acceptance, or did she feel she'd lost Carol some time ago? 'I'm sure that isn't true,' she said firmly. 'She wouldn't have stayed living here if that was how she felt.'

'She's all I had. No brothers or sisters, no parents any longer, and no real friends. Carol once said that I had no personality, and that was why I had no friends. She could be cruel, like her father. But when I married Edward, a wife was supposed to stay at home, cook and clean, make everywhere nice for her husband and children. I didn't have enough time during the day to make friends.'

'Carol was a lucky girl to have such a devoted mother,' Amelia said. However sorry she felt for Mrs Meadows, she was well able to see what a strain it was for a young woman to have a mother who relied on her for everything.

'She wanted to be a gymnast,' Mrs Meadows volunteered. 'But I said, "That isn't a proper job, that's just a hobby. You should get yourself down the council offices and get a job for life."'

'Was she a good gymnast?'

'I suppose she must've been – she won cups and rosettes. But I didn't go to the competitions because I had to get Edward's tea.'

'He could've got his own tea! Carol must have felt very alone without you cheering her on.' Amelia couldn't help but speak out because, like her own mother, this silly woman appeared to have no understanding that children, even the most confident ones, needed support. But no sooner had the words left her lips than she was sorry she'd been so sharp with a grieving mother.

'You see? You're turning against me now,' Mrs Meadows said, and began crying again.

'I'm not,' she said, and went to sit next to the older woman and put her arms round her. She thought Mrs Meadows had been living in a kind of bubble, never realizing that her husband and her daughter had needed her to be more than just a housekeeper.

The woman began to cry harder, huge racking sobs. Amelia held her, rubbing her back and making comforting noises, until at last she began to come out of it.

'What we need to do now is try and see if there was any connection between Carol and Lucy Whelan, the other girl who was killed near here,' she said. 'Maybe that will help the police find their killer.'

'Why do you think there has to be a connection?'

Amelia picked up a framed photograph of Carol from the sofa table. Like Lucy, she was remarkably pretty, with long straight blonde hair, prominent wide blue eyes and full lips. In the picture she was wearing a checked mini-dress, which barely covered her bottom, and long, tight boots that showed off her shapely slender legs.

'Some people might say the girls were picked by the killer because they were the same age, slim, blonde and pretty. But I believe there's something more between these two girls and the killer. It might be the smallest of small connections, like they were both in the same train carriage as him one day. Or he saw them both in the park, the swimming pool, a nightclub. I don't know, but we need to try and find that common denominator.'

'Carol didn't go swimming, except on holidays, and she didn't want to have holidays with me in Broadstairs any more. She went with a friend she worked with to Lloret de Mar in Spain this year.'

'What nightclubs did she go to?'

The older woman shrugged. 'I don't know that she ever went to one.'

'What about one called the Beachcomber? Does that ring a bell?'

Mrs Meadows looked blank. Clearly it didn't, and Amelia was beginning to see that Carol probably led a life she never let her mother into. She needed to talk to the girls she'd worked with and the friend she'd gone to Spain with to get the full picture.

'Might Carol have known Lucy Whelan?' She got the photograph of Lucy from her bag. 'Look at it carefully, please, and try to think back.'

Mrs Meadows studied the picture for some time. 'I don't think I ever saw this girl, not at school, the park or anywhere. And Carol would surely have said she knew her, wouldn't she? This girl's face was in all the papers.' She paused for a minute or two. 'Mind you, she wasn't much of a one for reading the papers or watching the news. If she was here, she'd be upstairs playing her records and doing her nails.'

'What other interests did she have? Any sports, games? Did she join any clubs, singing, dancing, anything like that?'

'She liked netball at school, as well as gymnastics, and she sang in the school choir, but she'd stopped taking part in any sport since she left school. She sang in her room and she liked dancing. She wanted to be a model. The police had a look in her room and they found some photographs I'd never seen. I wish they hadn't showed me them. She was in her underwear.'

'Did they take them away?'

'Some of them.'

'Could I see them? I'm not interested in the content, only the photographer.'

'That's what the police said too.' Mrs Meadows sounded as if she was about to cry again. 'I couldn't believe my beautiful girl would cheapen herself like some common floozy.'

'To get into modelling, they expect you to have pictures,' Amelia said. She had to make this up as she knew nothing about modelling, but she didn't want to leave Mrs Meadows with bad images in her head. 'Those photos were probably the start of her portfolio. You might just as easily have found ones of her in a wedding dress, in a tweed suit or a ballgown. Now, may I go and look?'

'All right. I left them on the dressing-table.'

'Would you mind if I looked around a bit more in her room? You never know, I might see something relevant to other interests.'

'Yes, you can, but please don't disturb it. She hated me touching anything in there. It's the bedroom at the front of the house.'

Amelia couldn't help but feel guilty as she walked up the stairs. She knew she ought to feel nothing more than sympathy for a poor mother who had lost her only child, but she was excited at the possibility of finding skeletons in Carol's cupboard.

The first thing that struck her about Carol's room was that it was far bigger than the other two bedrooms upstairs, with a view of the park. Another pointer, perhaps, to the possibility that Carol had ruled the roost since her father had left and insisted on having the best room. It was also impersonal: there was nothing to say that a young woman had spent a great deal of time in there recently. The cups and rosettes for gymnastics were on a shelf in the alcove by the chimney breast but, like almost everything else in the room, they appeared to date from her schooldays.

The photographs in a folder on the dressing-table were far more recent and were what was commonly known as glamour photography. Not pornography but very saucy, like the page-three girls in the daily papers.

Amelia half smiled as she looked at them. Carol was striking the most seductive poses, wearing the skimpiest underwear and a come-hither smile. There was no doubt that she was extremely pretty and had a lovely figure, but Amelia thought she had hard, calculating eyes. She didn't feel the girl would ever have wanted a holiday in Broadstairs with her mother. She was probably vain and selfish, on the hunt for a millionaire husband.

Tearing herself away from the photographs, she did a quick search around the room. It didn't reveal much more than Carol's taste for expensive clothes and shoes. There were a couple of Ossie Clark dresses in the wardrobe, both of which must have cost more than Amelia earned in a month. A white kid coat, too, with the label Skin. Amelia had seen adverts for that shop in the King's Road.

There were no letters or diaries, just a few old photographs stuck onto the glass of a picture. Beneath them was a print of Rupert Bear on a toboggan. That made Amelia smile as Rupert books were the very first she had read, and she'd always wanted yellow checked trousers like his. She assumed that, at some time, Carol's tastes had run to simple things too.

The photographs were of Carol with six girlfriends, when she was twelve or thirteen, and appeared to have been taken in a park. They were all in school uniform, but they'd taken off their ties and blazers. She didn't think they'd had an adult with them because it seemed that each of the girls took a turn to be the photographer. They had all pulled their pleated skirts up to show a great deal of leg – she remembered doing the same – and they were posing like fashion models. If there had been an adult with them, they would have tried to make them look more natural and suggested they took at least one complete group picture.

Amelia took two of the photos, making sure she had all the girls in them, put them into her bag and stuck the rest back onto the picture.

There was little else to look at: a few books, of the sensational bestseller sort, like *Forever Amber*, *Mandingo* and some Harold Robbins novels. A Beatles poster hung on the wall, and there was one of Elvis Presley in his army uniform, which was fading with age. There was a Dansette record player too, pale blue imitation leather. She lifted the lid and found several singles on the spigot: the Everly Brothers, Elvis, Bobby Vee and Adam Faith. As these were all hits from the early sixties, she assumed Carol had another more up-to-date record collection elsewhere.

In fact, Amelia sensed that Carol had taken all her favourite things from this room, leaving a few bits, like her winter coat, some other clothes, shoes and makeup to satisfy her mother that she still thought of it as home.

When she got back downstairs Mrs Meadows was crying again. 'I'm so alone,' she said, through her tears. 'I don't know if I can stand it.'

'It will get easier,' Amelia said, once again moving to sit next to the woman and taking her in her arms. 'Maybe when all this is out of the way you could get a paying guest. You'd have someone else in the house and some money coming in. If you cooked for them, too, that would keep you busy.'

There was no response to that suggestion and Amelia found herself wishing the police would come back so she could slip away.

'Did Carol come home every night?' she asked. 'Or did she stay over with a friend?'

'She said the tubes had stopped running by the time she finished work.' Mrs Meadows sniffed back her tears and wiped her eyes on her cardigan sleeve. 'So she stayed with a friend. I think it might have been a man friend, but she wouldn't admit it. She knew I didn't approve of sex before marriage.'

'What was the name of the restaurant she worked

at?' Amelia thought it best not to comment on the possibility of a man friend. She felt it was extremely likely Carol had been with a man. But if she could meet the staff at the restaurant she might find out for sure.

'The Bistro in King's Road,' Mrs Meadows said. 'It's near Sloane Square tube station and Peter Jones. She took me there once, but the food was too fancy for my taste.'

'I'll need to go soon,' Amelia said, looking at her watch. It was nearly eleven, and once the other newspapers heard the press release about the murder, they'd be here in their droves. 'Now I have to tell you something, Mrs Meadows. Very soon now, all the daily papers will know about Carol and they'll come here. It's not nice – they'll bang on your door, ring you and even rap on windows to get a story. What I want you to do is to ignore them. Don't let them in. Maybe go up to your bedroom and stay there. Put the phone down if it's one of them, and only speak to the police if they ring. Can you do that?'

The poor woman looked terrified and Amelia's heart went out to her. 'I know it's scary, but they'll wear you down if you speak to them, twist your words, and may even print things that aren't true.' She paused as a bright idea came to her. 'I can stay a bit longer and tell them you've given me an exclusive story, if that would help? If they think you really won't or can't speak to them, they'll go away.'

'If you could, my dear,' she said in a wavering voice. 'I can't take any more.'

'I know. You're in an impossible situation. All I can do is try and make it a little less awful. Now is there anyone I can ring for you to ask them to come?'

She shook her head in sorrow, and Amelia's eyes welled with tears. No one should have to go through something like this without a friend or family member for support.

'What about your neighbours? I can pop along and ask one to come and be with you. Who is nice?'

The woman sat with her head bowed for the longest minute. 'There's Miss Dawes. She lives at number thirty – she invites me in for tea sometimes. She's kind, never says anything bad about anyone.'

'Then I'm going to get her,' Amelia said. 'Now give me the key so I can let myself back in.'

It was nearly twelve before Amelia finally got away. Miss Dawes was a kind, forthright and religious woman, with holy pictures and a crucifix on the wall. She was at least sixty-five, with white hair, a very lined face but the kind of soft blue eyes that suggested she'd seen a great deal in her time.

She was, of course, horrified to hear Carol had been murdered.

'That poor woman. Carol was the centre of her life, her only interest too. I can't imagine how she'll cope with this.'

'As you know, she hasn't got anyone. I was hoping you could spare some time to be with her. At least until the police come back.'

'Of course I will,' Miss Dawes said, without a second thought. 'No one should be alone at such a time.'

Amelia explained the situation with the press, and reiterated that it was best not to answer the door to them.

'I quite understand. They can be like a pack of jackals,' she said, with surprising vehemence, as if from personal experience. She took off her apron, put on her coat, picked up a cake tin, which contained a Victoria sponge she'd just made, and said she was ready.

Amelia smiled at her. 'I hope if I'm ever in a tough situation there's someone like you around to help,' she said.

'My dear, you look the sort who could cope with anything.'

Amelia had only just taken her in to Mrs Meadows when the first journalists arrived.

'I'll go out there and see them off,' she told the two older women. 'I have to go back to work now, but remember what I said. Don't open the door to anyone but the police. Miss Dawes, will you answer the phone? If it's journalists, just tell them Mrs Meadows can't speak to anyone. They'll try to ask you questions but be firm and refuse to answer them, then put the phone down. We can't take it off the hook in case the police need to ask something.'

'You go back to work, dear,' she said. 'I'll look after Mrs Meadows. Don't worry about her.'

'You're so kind.' Amelia felt as if a weight had been

taken from her shoulders. 'I'll ring later to see how things are. But it might be a smart plan to go upstairs.'

The banging on the door was growing more insistent. Amelia shut the two women into the sitting room – with thick lace curtains at the window no one could see in, but to the occupants it would be like living under siege.

Bracing herself, Amelia opened the front door and as the group of journalists surged forward, she closed it behind her.

'Go away,' she said, in a loud, clear voice. 'Mrs Meadows is not going to speak to anyone else today. She is distraught, as I'm sure you can imagine. Please don't make her pain worse by knocking on her door or windows.'

'Who are you?' one of the crowd called out. They were mostly men – she saw only two women.

'Amelia White,' she said. 'I work for the *West London Weekly*. I was asked to come and be with Mrs Meadows because I found Lucy Whelan six weeks ago. Mrs Meadows has given me an exclusive on the tragic story and, as I've said, she doesn't wish to speak to anyone else about it. The police will be here very soon. I'm sure they will issue a further bulletin later. Now, if you would kindly go and allow Mrs Meadows to rest . . .'

They didn't want to. Amelia felt as if she was standing in front of a herd of cows, trying to make them move. She walked towards them, holding her arms out slightly to indicate they were to back up. For a second or two she thought they wouldn't – she could hear murmurings of dissent – but suddenly they began to move. She walked through the front gate and shut it behind her.

A camera was pushed close to her face, but she moved on regardless. She heard some cars start behind her, and three drove past before she got to the end of the road. As she turned the corner she glanced back: there was still a small coven gathered outside the gate.

Jack charged out of his office as soon as she came through the door. His face was alight with excitement. 'Well?'

'That poor woman is so alone.' She sighed. 'I didn't get the same pure-little-girl vibe I got from Lucy's family. I hope some bad press doesn't push Mrs Meadows over the edge. If you're thinking I'll churn out some of that, you're mistaken.' The moment her last words left her lips she was afraid she'd gone too far. Jack never liked anyone standing up to him.

He perched on a desk and folded his arms, looking stern. 'If you want to be a journalist you have to write what you see and hear. We don't write fairy stories.'

'I didn't hear or see anything bad. I've just got a feeling. I can't and won't write my feelings because I could be wrong. If you want, I'll write that Carol was the only child of a lone mother. That she worked in a King's Road restaurant and wanted to be a model.'

She wasn't going to tell Jack about the saucy pictures

because he'd get his teeth into that and never let go. 'I'll write a piece now for the paper tomorrow, and then I'll go over to King's Road to where Carol worked and see what I can find out there.'

Jack crossed his arms and stared at her, as if he was considering whether or not to push her further. 'Fair enough,' he said eventually. 'If you find anything interesting, ring me. I can slot it into the paper without you coming back here.'

It took Amelia nearly an hour to write up the story as she found it hard not to allow her personal feelings about Carol and her mother to spill onto the page. 'Tragic Widowed Mother and Resentful Wayward Daughter' would delight Jack but hurt Mrs Meadows still more.

Once it was done she handed it in and rushed off to the King's Road.

Mrs Meadows had said Carol believed Chelsea was the place to be, and Amelia agreed with that. Each time she went there she wished she could afford to live there. The amazing shops, fun pubs, great restaurants and clubs all added up to Wonderland. She had once spotted Scott Walker of the Walker Brothers walking down King's Road. She'd thought he was the most beautiful man she'd ever seen and followed him for some time, trying to pluck up the courage to speak to him. She never did.

The Bistro was by the Chelsea Antiques Market. It was a medium-sized eatery, which was surprisingly quiet considering it was two in the afternoon. Amelia went up to the man behind the bar. He was in his late thirties, slender, and looked Italian, with jet-black hair and a deep suntan.

She introduced herself and discovered he was the manager, Antonio Perez. He spoke English without an accent, so she assumed he'd been born in England. She asked if he had been told about Carol's death.

'Yes, the police called on me this morning to question me,' he said. 'We are all so shocked.'

Amelia then explained her part in this, but as she was talking about Mrs Meadows, something about his expression didn't seem right. He looked anxious about something, wanting to say what it was, but hesitating.

'Is there something more you could tell me about Carol? You look troubled.'

'I don't like to speak ill of the dead,' he said, and beckoned her to a table in a corner at the back, signalling to a waitress to take over behind the bar, 'but I have to tell you this as the police know so it'll all come out. First, we called her Jazz here, and I sacked her the afternoon before she died. For theft.'

8

When Antonio saw Amelia was in shock he called the waitress to get her a coffee. He said later she looked like she'd just seen her granny run over by a bus.

'I left her mother absolutely heartbroken,' Amelia said, her voice trembling. 'What on earth is this going to do to her?'

He pursed his lips and shrugged. 'Jazz had been stealing from me for months,' he said. 'But that wasn't all. She was also manipulative, vain, greedy, a bully and a liar.'

'My goodness!' Amelia exclaimed, shaken to her core. She'd realized Carol hadn't exactly been Daughter of the Year, but she hadn't expected to find out from her employer that she was a thief and thoroughly reprehensible.

Antonio looked upset. 'I have to admit I was totally taken in by her. I thought she was wonderful at first.' He paused, as if trying to decide whether he should reveal more. 'It's no good, I have to admit it,' he said eventually, colouring as if embarrassed. 'We had an affair. I thought I was in love with her. I even suspected another girl working here of being the thief.' He hung his head in shame. 'I realize now that Jazz strung me along to enable her to get away with it. She used to tell me about her sick mother who needed her home every night, but later I discovered she hardly ever went home, staying over with this man or that. Always looking for the main chance.'

'Did the police reckon you might have killed her?' She was sure he would be considered a prime suspect.

'Oh, yes. They were here when I arrived this morning to open up. Fortunately I had an iron-clad alibi. The day before yesterday, just after the lunchtime rush, I was holding Jazz here, intending to call the police to arrest her. I rang my accountant to come over too. I thought he could explain to the police what Jazz had been doing far more clearly than I could. But stupidly I had entrusted my staff to keep her locked in the staff room upstairs. Jazz, being as wily as a fox, realized this. She managed to fool one of the girls and slip out the back way.

'Ken, my accountant, stayed sitting here at this table all afternoon talking to me and going through the books. I closed the Bistro at six – I had no stomach for greeting people or feeding them – and I went home with Ken to his house in Twickenham. I had dinner with him and his family and stayed the night.'

'How awful for you.' Amelia really felt for him. He was clearly a kind, decent man. 'I came here to speak to some of your waitresses – I thought they might know more about Carol's life. You see I think there's a connection between her and Lucy Whelan, the other recently murdered girl. If I can work it out, it might make it easier to find her killer.'

'Was she a conniving thief too?' he asked bitterly.

'No, she seemed a nice girl, but she did resemble Carol in looks.' She got the picture of Lucy out of her bag and showed him. 'Have you ever seen her? Did she come in here or might any of your staff have known her?'

He studied the picture carefully. 'I don't think I've ever seen her. The trouble is she's got that Jean Shrimpton appearance, long hair, wide eyes. It's so fashionable that lots of girls copy it, especially here in Chelsea.'

Amelia wanted to know so much more, such as how Carol had managed to steal from him for so long and how she'd done it. Was she taking money from the till, or getting it in some other way? Who were the men she stayed over with when she wasn't with Antonio? She simply had to talk to the other waitresses . . . But all she could think of now was how devastated Mrs Meadows was going to be when the stealing came out. And it was certain to be revealed, given that Antonio had told the police he had tried to detain the girl to have her arrested for theft. In fact, it was likely that it had already been part of a press release, and that by tomorrow it would be front-page news.

She said much of this to Antonio, and explained that she thought she should go back to Mrs Meadows to warn her.

'I think you'll find the police will have told her already, the poor woman.' Antonio sighed. 'I can't grieve for Jazz. I'm just angry with myself that I got so infatuated with her I didn't see what she was doing. I'm old enough to know better. But it is strange that when she escaped from here she ran for home. For someone as quick-witted as she was, that was folly – it would be the first place the police would look. So was it just a random killing? A man who likes her type and lives in that area? Or had the killer selected her some time ago, for reasons known only to him, and followed her from here? Or had she done something nasty to him and this was her punishment?'

'I doubt it was something she'd done to him – at least, if she was killed by the same man who killed Lucy. From what I've heard about her, Lucy was angelic. He could've been here in the restaurant, though. Did you have words with her here where people could hear?'

He looked sheepish. 'I shouted at her, called her a dirty little thief and a liar. That was before I marched her upstairs and locked her in. I was so angry it was a miracle I didn't hit her. I think that is why it's so quiet today. My regulars haven't come in. They don't come here for a sideshow.'

'I'm so sorry, Antonio. It's an awful situation for you. Could I come back another day and talk to you again? Not to write anything about it, just to see if I can piece this whole thing together.'

'I wish you luck with that but, yes, you can come

back. Just give me a ring to tell me when you want to come.'

Amelia found a phone box and rang Jack to let him know of the latest developments. She told him everything because she felt she had to.

'I feel so bad for Mrs Meadows,' she said, her eyes starting with tears. 'It's terrible her daughter was killed, but then to be told she was a thief too.'

'We can't help that,' Jack said firmly. 'The police will have told her by now, and Mum is collateral damage, I'm afraid. Don't go back there, Amelia. She isn't your problem and you can't make it better for her. Go home now. You've had a harrowing day. I'll add this to the piece you wrote but, for the sake of your conscience, I'll back-pedal on the sensationalism.'

Amelia managed a weak smirk at that last statement. She doubted he would. But he was right: the theft would come out, as would the glamour modelling and everything else. Once something like this hit the papers there were always those willing to share their memories or grievances, and the story could keep on running. Sadly no one could save Mrs Meadows from humiliation.

As she came out of Shepherd's Bush tube station, Amelia saw Kat and rushed to catch up with her. She really needed a diversion or even a shoulder to cry on.

'You look tense,' Kat said, after she'd greeted her. 'Had a difficult day at work?'

'The worst,' Amelia agreed. 'Have you got time for a drink?'

Kat looked at her watch. 'I've got a date later but listening to a friend's woes is more important than making a man wait. Let's go in the Black Dog – it's rough but, then, most of the pubs round here are.'

Once they were sitting down with a double Bacardi and Coke each, Amelia told Kat about the second murder and that Carol had been sacked for theft. Kat looked astounded. 'You promise you won't bandy this around?' Amelia begged her. 'I shouldn't really be telling anyone about it.'

'There's times when we all need someone to confide in,' Kat said, squeezing her hand in sympathy. 'I won't breathe a word to anyone, you have my word on that. But do you know what the police are doing to find this killer? Have they got any new leads?'

'I wouldn't know. I haven't spoken to them. But my boss seems to think they're as much in the dark as they were with Lucy Whelan's death. They do think it was the same man – no sexual interference, her bag taken more to slow down identification rather than as part of a robbery. She wasn't a sweet girl, though, like Lucy. She was mean to her mum, used men, and generally seems to have been a conniving bitch. But it's her mum who worries me most, Kat. She had nothing in her life but her daughter. What's this going to do to her?'

'Maybe her mum made her like that,' Kat suggested.

'You do hear that sometimes. Not that I'd know, my mother was so wonderful, kind and loving.'

That was the first time Kat had ever mentioned family, and Amelia felt bad she'd never thought to ask her about them.

'Was? I'm sorry, Kat, have you lost her?'

Kat did a little shake of her head to imply that this was something she didn't want to discuss. 'Yes, several years ago, but let's not talk about me. You need to get all this off your chest – you're clearly deeply concerned.'

Amelia thought it was so nice that Kat cared about what she'd been through. So many people were too wrapped up in themselves to take on board how others felt and what had happened to them. Even Max didn't seem very interested in Amelia's family. Since the day on Hampstead Heath he hadn't asked her any more questions.

'Well, her mother appeared to be blind to Carol taking advantage of her. It seemed to me that she'd tried hard to be the perfect wife to the detriment of her daughter. Then, of course, her husband left her anyway.'

'Well, Amelia, I don't want to leave you but I must go now,' Kat said, knocking back the last of her drink and getting to her feet. 'You've got a big heart, but you can't take on everyone else's problems. Go home to your man – Max, isn't it? – and leave the sleuthing to the police.'

'I'm so glad I ran into you,' Amelia said, and got up too. 'You've been a tonic, letting me air all this. I feel so much better now. We ought to get together more often, though I suppose with your job you don't get much free time.'

'No, but I can always find time for a friend,' Kat said. 'You just say when.'

Max didn't come in till nearly eight. Amelia had dropped off to sleep when she got home: her day had proved exhausting. Max flopped down on the bed beside her and put his arms around her. 'What have you been doing today?' he asked.

'A long story,' she said wearily. 'I meant to make something to eat, but I was too tired, so I think it'll have to be fish and chips.'

'I'll nip out and get it,' he said, kissing her nose. 'Then you can tell me this long story.'

An hour later, the fish and chips eaten, the bottle of wine Max had bought empty and Amelia's shortened version of the day's events relayed, Max took her hands in his across the table.

'I think you must back off,' he said. 'The killer must have followed Carol, knew where she lived and every-thing else about her. It was the same with Lucy, so it stands to reason he'll be aware of you and your involve-ment, which means you could be in danger too.'

That idea hadn't occurred to Amelia, and she looked aghast at Max.

'Surely not. He's got a thing about blondes – he wouldn't want a girl with dark brown hair. I won't count for anything. But it's nice of you to be concerned.' She patted his cheek affectionately.

'You do count for something. He'll have worked out by now that you've been trying to find out who he is. He might think you're getting close. Back off now, Mimi, let the police handle the investigation.'

'Now you're scaring me.'

'Better to scare you than let you be complacent. People who kill don't follow rules or set patterns.'

Amelia sighed. She guessed he was right, but she wanted to delve into all this and find out more. 'Let's just go to the Beachcomber Club tomorrow night and get an idea of Lucy's working life. Then no more.'

Max frowned. 'But that won't be it, will it? You'll be back in Chelsea asking questions. Carol sounds like a horrible girl, and the people she hung around with are probably horrible too. I wish you wouldn't.'

'Just the Beachcomber, please! I've never been to a ritzy nightclub, and as the manager is likely to give us a free drink or two, shouldn't we grab the opportunity with both hands?'

'Okay, but please back off then, Mimi?'

She nodded. That wasn't the same as promising.

The Beachcomber club under the Mayfair Hotel was beyond belief to both Amelia and Max. Designed to resemble a tropical island, small streams meandered through the club, with rustic-looking bridges that led to tables under straw umbrellas. The waiter pointed out that in the pools there were live baby crocodiles, and real parrots flew among the abundant tropical foliage or perched in cages. A film playing on a screen of waving palm trees, crystal blue sea and white sand added to the illusion that they were far away from London. The music was South Sea Island, too, and the members of the four-piece band were not, perhaps, actually Hawaiian but they looked the part.

They had no sooner sat down than a waitress dressed in a grass skirt, flower garland in her hair, and another covering her bikini top, came to their table. 'Compliments of the manager,' she said, with a broad smile, putting down a bottle of champagne in a silver bucket. 'Have a lovely evening.'

She was gone before Amelia could ask her anything about Lucy, but it was so thrilling to be in such a fabulous nightclub all dressed up, with free champagne, and Max at her side looking very handsome, that Lucy's death was eclipsed.

The sky in the film darkened and it began to rain. The palm trees bent over in the hurricane-like wind, and forked lightning lit up the dark sky. But slowly the rain and wind slowed, the sky gradually grew light again and the sun came back.

'It's miraculous,' Max murmured. 'What a place!' He took Amelia's hand and kissed it. 'You look beautiful tonight. Maybe we should make a habit of going to places like this.'

'I don't think we could afford it,' she said, loving that he was being so attentive. 'I've looked at the menu and the drink prices are astronomical.'

'I've got a few plans up my sleeve that could bring in some big money,' he said, fixing her with his lovely green eyes and still holding her hand. 'I can't tell you about it yet, as it might not come off, but I think we're going places, darling.'

Amelia felt a glorious fizz of excitement welling up inside her. When hula girls came onstage and danced, Amelia felt she actually was in the South Seas, so much so that she half expected a coconut to fall at her feet. She wondered which of the four dancers had replaced Lucy. And which of the girls had been her closest friend.

'Hello, Amelia.' A voice at her elbow startled her and, to her surprise, she saw it belonged to Frances. She'd looked for her earlier but assumed she wasn't working when she couldn't spot her.

'What an amazing club this is!' Amelia exclaimed, then introduced her to Max.

'So you can see it's all above board here,' Frances said, perching on a spare seat beside them. She was wearing the uniform of grass skirt and flower garlands and looked stunning. 'From what I've read in the papers today, though, the new victim sounds like a real bitch.'

'So it seems,' Amelia said, reluctant to speak ill of the dead. 'A quite different kind of girl from Lucy, which makes it even harder to imagine what they had in common. Is there anyone here I should speak to? Someone who knew more about Lucy?'

Frances shook her head. 'We're all quite close, but Lucy spent more time with me than anyone else. Besides, it's a Saturday night, the club is filling up and no one has the time to chat. I must go too. But you've got my phone number – ring me if you want to.'

She disappeared, and as Amelia looked around the club, she could see all the tables were taken now. There were mink and fox stoles over evening dresses, sparkling diamonds at throats and on ears. This wasn't a place where she and Max could afford to spend an evening.

'I think we should go when we've finished the bottle,' she whispered to him. 'We're out of our league.'

He grinned. 'I was thinking the same, but it was good practice for when my ship comes in. I'd like to see you with a diamond necklace and a fur stole.'

'Well, I'm glad we came,' Max said, as they walked up the road hand in hand towards Park Lane. 'I didn't expect it to be as classy as that.'

'Nor me,' Amelia agreed. 'I wonder if the killer used to go in there to watch her dance. Was it just because he wanted to get close to a girl he fancied? But if that was the case, it's strange that he didn't try to rape her.'

'I'd say it was all about rage, not lust,' Max said. 'He may have tried to talk to Lucy and Carol, but they ignored him, which fired him up.'

'But if he wanted to talk to them why was he armed with a lead pipe and a knife?'

Max put his arm around her tightly. 'I don't know. I don't think about murdering people. You said you were going to let it go,' he said, 'so let's find something else to talk about.'

As they walked out of the tube at Shepherd's Bush, Kat suddenly appeared beside them. She looked none too steady on her feet, and when Amelia said hello, for a moment she didn't appear to recognize her.

'Oh, of course, it's Amelia, my neighbour and fellow launderette chum,' she said, slurring her words. She was wearing her usual black maxi coat, with a mini-skirt beneath it, and as she walked there was a flash of her long legs. On most girls this type of outfit looked good, but for some reason it didn't flatter her.

Amelia introduced Max. 'We've been up west for a change. Where have you been tonight?'

'A pub in Portobello Road,' she said, as they began walking together. 'I met a couple of colleagues from work. They were going on to a club, but it wasn't really my thing, so I came home.'

'Any more work trips lined up?' Amelia asked, and explained to Max that Kat was a buyer for Harrods' bathroom department.

'Nothing on the immediate horizon,' she said. 'To tell the truth, I'm a bit bored with Harrods right now. I'm thinking of moving on. Too many posh housewives up from the country, and senior management who talk down to me as if I'm half-witted. Not like you, Miss Hot Shot Reporter. I read your latest on the new victim of the Creeper. You really didn't like her!'

'Kat, I didn't know either of them. I could only write what I was told.'

'But you've got such a good instinct about people and, anyway, you told me the other day what a bitch she was.'

'I don't think I actually said that,' Amelia corrected her. She wished she hadn't told Kat quite so much. To her relief, Max butted in, asking Kat a question about Harrods. She seemed as reluctant to answer as Amelia was to discuss her journalism. Fortunately Shepherd's Bush was very busy, it being a Saturday night, and what with dodging the drunks, and avoiding falling into trenches the Water Board had dug nearly the entire length of Goldhawk Road, conversation wasn't necessary.

'I heard the other morning the owner of the Greek fruit and veg shop found a drunken Irishman asleep in the trench in front of his shop. He wasn't hurt – he didn't even remember falling in,' Max said, with a chuckle. 'The Water Board should put up better barriers. Someone could seriously injure themselves.'

'Good place to leave a body,' Kat said, and laughed. When she saw Amelia wasn't amused, she turned to her. 'Cheer up! No one could drop a body off along here – it's too busy, day and night.'

'Mind how you go now,' Max said to Kat, as they reached their turning.

'I'll be fine,' she said and, staggering a little, continued along the road towards her own home.

'For one horrible moment I thought you were going to ask her in,' Amelia said, as they went into her house and up the stairs to her room. 'I thought she was a bit weird tonight, or was it just that she was drunk?'

'I think she wanted me to walk her home,' Max said. 'Her intention might have been to drag me into her lair. She was giving me the glad eye.'

Amelia looked sharply at him. 'You don't fancy her, do you?'

Max sniggered. 'Not likely. She's too tall and strong for me. I bet she'd get a man in a half-nelson as soon as look at him.'

Max had arranged to meet one of his rock-climbing friends on Sunday lunchtime, something that had been planned weeks before.

'We'd discussed going to the Himalayas to climb next spring,' he said, as he buttoned up his shirt that morning. 'But I'm not so keen now.'

'Why?'

Max shrugged. 'Because I'd have to train hard, and I suppose I don't want to be away from you.'

'That's pathetic,' she said, but was secretly touched he felt that way. 'I wouldn't mind you going.'

Max put his arms around her. 'I don't think you realize that when a chap falls in love, he doesn't want to leave his lady even for a day,' he said.

Amelia giggled. 'That's silly! But I have to admit a day without you around is too long.'

'Really?'

'Absolutely,' she said. She had a sudden pang in her heart that she couldn't live without him, and she had to tell him. 'I love you, Max, for ever and ever.'

He looked as if he was welling up. 'I'd begun to think love was for other guys and not me,' he said. 'That first day when we met by Lucy's body and I put my arms round you, I felt something right then, but it seemed so weird and inappropriate I would never have admitted it.'

Amelia wasn't good at coping with raw emotion. 'I would've thought it weird,' she said. 'I'd probably have run away screaming.'

Max gave her a smile that could have lit up the room. 'I don't want to go out now. But I must. What are you going to do?'

'Possibly nothing, maybe read, go for a little walk. But you have fun with your friends. I'll see you later.'

Max had been gone about half an hour when Amelia thought of visiting Miss Dawes, the elderly neighbour of Mrs Meadows. Jack had added quite a bit to her piece on Carol and it must have upset her mother. She thought if she saw Miss Dawes she could pass on that she hadn't been the one to dish the real dirt, and also find out if Mrs Meadows was coping.

The sky was black and threatening, and it was also

very cold. Amelia noticed that most of the trees in Ravenscourt Park had lost their leaves. There was still a police cordon around the area where Carol's body had been found, but no police any longer.

Miss Dawes was slow to answer her front door and, assuming she was afraid of journalists, Amelia called through the letterbox to her.

'I'm sorry if I'm disturbing you,' she said, when the older woman finally opened the door. 'I just felt I had to talk to you and explain that none of that nastiness in the newspapers had anything to do with me.'

'Come in, my dear,' she said. 'I wouldn't have blamed you if it had, but the police told me that they'd made a statement to the press.'

As Amelia followed Miss Dawes in, she noticed she was walking very slowly, and her voice seemed weak and hesitant.

Once they were in the sitting room, Miss Dawes sat down, and it was only then that Amelia saw how pale and shaky she was. 'You don't look too good,' Amelia said. 'Can I make you some tea, or get you anything?'

'No, my dear . . . It's just the shock. You see, Mrs Meadows took her own life this morning. She rang 999 to say she'd taken an overdose, but by the time they got to her, she was dead. I went along there when I saw the ambulance and they were just bringing her out.'

'Oh, my goodness, how terrible!' Amelia gasped, clapping a hand over her mouth.

'Yes, it is. I did my best to comfort her when you

asked me to go along there, but she was something of a lost soul. Carol was all she had, and that girl wasn't kind to her mother.'

'I feel responsible,' Amelia said, tears welling in her eyes. 'I may have made things worse.'

'You certainly didn't, and you mustn't feel responsible. You were the one person who was kind and supportive. That poor woman was reaping what she'd sown. Carol was always trouble – she had been since her early teens, cruel to her mother, demanding, a little hussy. A weak mum who never says no is a recipe for disaster. Do you know that when Mrs Meadows found money missing from her purse she refused to consider that the thief might have been her own daughter? Once she even suggested that the woman from next door had come in the back way when she was upstairs! How blinkered can a mother be?'

'I suppose it's hard to think your own child would do that.'

Miss Dawes shook her head sadly. 'She became a martyr to that girl. Heaven only knows what else went on behind closed doors. I don't like to speak ill of the dead, but Carol was bad through and through.'

It was a shock to hear this sweet-faced, religious woman speak against Carol, but clearly she'd had to spill it out to someone.

'Terrible.' Amelia sighed. 'I'm so sorry you got caught up in it.'

'My dear, I'll be fine. Shock wears off, and by

tomorrow I'll be my usual self. But I wonder if Carol had done something wicked to the man who killed her.'

Amelia stayed for an hour. She made Miss Dawes some tea, and let her talk. It transpired she'd often taken care of Carol after school when her mother had had a part-time job in a shop. She said Carol had stolen from her too, and eventually she refused to allow her into the house.

'She was as hard as nails, even at nine or ten. A beautiful child, but her eyes were cold and calculating.'

'I noticed that in the pictures of her,' Amelia said. 'At the time I thought I was seeing things that weren't there.'

Miss Dawes sighed and wiped tears from her eyes. 'Some said she turned bad when her father left, but it began long before that. Is it true about her stealing money from the restaurant?'

'I'm afraid so. Funny that she ran back to her mother, though.'

'She always did. Her mother never saw any wrong in her, not when she bullied other children, stole money from the collection box in church, set fire to rubbish in the park or shouted rude things at the neighbours. It was always someone else's fault. Never Carol's.'

As she left, Amelia hugged the older woman and gave her the office phone number in case she needed anything.

'Don't you worry about me,' Miss Dawes said, smiling for the first time that afternoon. 'I shall go to the evening service tonight and pray for Mrs Meadows. In a way I think she's in the best place. She wouldn't be able to deal with the truth about her daughter.'

As Amelia walked home, she was crying for the woman who had bred a monster by being too kind, too giving, and for the Whelans who hadn't in any way deserved to lose their lovely daughter. What was the connection between the two girls? Despite them being poles apart in temperament, and not a scrap of evidence yet that there had been a connection, she had a gut feeling there was. Whatever Max felt about it, she wasn't going to give up on this.

9

'Just call me Ant – everyone else does,' Antonio said, when Amelia sat down with him in the Bistro.

She had telephoned him during the day to arrange a meeting and he'd suggested that she come over and have supper with him.

The Bistro was noticeably quiet, but that was more because it was Monday night, very cold and windy, rather than anything to do with Carol. Antonio had heard that morning about Mrs Meadows's suicide and, like Amelia, was shocked.

'Jazz would never take me to meet her mother. She said she was a semi-invalid,' he remarked glumly, clearly aware now of how many lies he'd been told during their relationship. 'She wasn't, was she?'

'No,' Amelia said. 'A sad, bewildered woman, I'd say, but nothing physically wrong with her.'

Antonio recommended a chicken pasta dish, and the house white wine, and as they waited to be served, Amelia told him what Mrs Dawes had said. 'But I don't wish to dish the dirt on Jazz,' she finished. 'However she lived, whatever she did or didn't do, she was murdered, and no one deserves that. All I want is to find a connection between her and Lucy. I know there is one.'

'I don't know that I can tell you anything useful. There were many men who came in here and flirted with Jazz,' Antonio said, with a shrug. 'She was like a flower to bees and she could never resist egging them on, then slamming them down good and hard. A couple wouldn't take no for an answer – they'd come back again and again to ask her out.'

'If Lucy had also turned down one of those men, that might have been the connection, but Lucy wasn't that kind of girl.'

'I'm glad to hear it.' Antonio half smiled. 'One tease is enough. But as your old lady told you, Jazz could be so cruel. She'd flirt and play with men for a while, but once she was bored with them, she could cut them off with a spiteful comment. She always knew the right button to push – some of the other waitresses dissolved into tears with things she'd said to them.'

'But you didn't see this at first?'

He shrugged. 'I fell for her and she could do no wrong. I admit I was a fool, but she bewitched me. I lost two first-class waitresses through her. Happily one has come back to me. She's going to pop in a bit later to talk to you.'

'So can you tell me if any of the men she was cruel to still come in here? Could they have followed her and killed her?'

Antonio laughed lightly. 'No. If those men were guilty of anything, it was of being too soft and not rich enough for her. I did notice when I came to my senses it was the rich ones she really sucked up to. I'd love to know just how many of them she fleeced. When Jane gets here, she'll tell you that Jazz named her price for going to bed with them. And it wasn't cheap.'

'Any of those men angry enough to want to kill her?'

'Maybe. But Chelsea is like a village. I would've heard on the grapevine if she'd seriously pissed anyone off. As for you hoping to find a connection between Jazz and the other girl, it sounds to me that they couldn't have been further apart in character. The only similarity I can see is the way they looked.'

'Possibly. But there is something else,' Amelia said thoughtfully. 'Not just their appearance but both were physically fit. With Lucy it was dance, and Carol gymnastics. I'm thinking the connection may lie there.'

'Jazz didn't keep up her gymnastics,' Antonio said. 'She went to a keep-fit class, though. She once smugly told another waitress that her perfect body was her trump card.'

'She actually said that?' Amelia winced. 'I think I would've hated her.'

Antonio laughed. 'Join the queue. There won't be many people around here who'll mourn her.'

They had just finished their pasta and were on a second glass of wine when Jane arrived.

Amelia liked her on sight. She had a country-girl pink-and-white complexion and strawberry-blonde curly hair. Her only makeup was mascara. She was wearing a vintage grey fox coat, lace-up knee-high boots and a wide smile.

'I'm delighted you're talking to Ant about that vile girl,' she said. 'I can't discuss her with him without getting angry. But I'll say it now, I'm glad she's dead. Thank God she can't hurt anyone ever again.'

Amelia was a little taken aback at such vitriol, but she had to admire Jane for speaking her mind.

Antonio poured Jane a glass of wine, she said she didn't want any food, and the three of them carried on talking.

'Let's not beat around the bush. She was a hooker,' Jane said bluntly. 'She told me once she saw no point in going to bed with a man for nothing when she could get a hundred pounds for it. I think she believed that taking money from Ant was her due, for services rendered, not stealing.'

Ant looked hurt. 'If only I'd managed to keep her here that day, she wouldn't have been killed,' he said. 'Maybe I would've found out why she stole from me. Perhaps she was giving money to her mother.'

'Don't be a prat,' Jane said dismissively. 'She was robbing you blind and putting it into her own pocket. If you'd turned her over to the police, I expect she'd have found something evil to say about you that would've got you into trouble. I say we should celebrate her death. So, Amelia, you're a journalist, hang her out to dry. Don't pull your punches.'

Amelia was realizing she had some real dynamite. Jack was going to be thrilled. With Mrs Meadows dead, there was no one who would be hurt by the truth.

Except, perhaps, Carol's father, but he'd swanned off years ago.

Before she wrote a sensational story, though, she needed to remember that she was trying to find a link between the murdered girls, not just furthering her career.

She asked Jane to look at the picture of Lucy to see if she recognized her.

Jane stared at it for some time. 'No, I don't think I've ever seen her. And, no, I can't think of anyone who would chase Jazz over to Hammersmith to bump her off. The people around here she'd pissed off would have tripped her up, thrown paint or dog shit at her, but they wouldn't have followed her to get their revenge. Besides, from what I've read about Lucy, in that article you wrote, she wouldn't have wanted to live in the same country as Jazz, never mind be friends.'

'So it seems, but I feel I'm missing something,' Amelia said. 'Like, if I just knew the magic word that links these two girls, the whole thing would be solved.'

'I'm sure the police think that all the time,' Antonio said.

They moved on then to talk about living in Chelsea and how expensive it was getting.

'The trouble is all these droves of posh prats,' Jane said. 'They get their daddies to pay for a flat for them, which pushes the prices up, and the rest of us poor girls have to make do with a bedsitter in the Fulham Road. Still, they're an entertainment, thick as bricks most of them, those loud braying voices, and their belief they're God's Chosen.'

She regaled Amelia with hysterically funny tales of such girls she knew well. 'But they're generous, I'll admit that,' she finished up. 'I had nowhere to live a while ago and Carmella, Queen of King's Road, let me stay in her spare room. She didn't even want rent. In return I did the cleaning and, believe me, that flat needed it. She had a cat that crapped anywhere.'

Amelia had to go. She thanked Antonio for the supper and Jane for the entertainment and hurried off. It was disappointing she hadn't got any leads, but the story she was going to write about Carol would get Jack's juices flowing.

It took hours to write the piece. It would've been easy to write a vindictive muck-spreading article, and perhaps that was all Carol deserved, as Amelia certainly hadn't heard anything to suggest the girl had a softer, kinder side. But she had been murdered, and she felt she had to find a way of showing why she had been so mercenary and calculating. To do that Amelia had to sheathe her claws and remember this was a girl who wanted to be a gymnast, and latterly a fashion model.

It wasn't right to look back on her own bleak childhood and think that if she'd had a loving mother, like Mrs Meadows, she might never have spent months alone in a rented room, trying to create a world she wanted to live in. Yet a voice kept yelling that, even with her miserable childhood, she hadn't stooped to stealing, or making men pay for her company. Why should she paint Carol in a kinder light than she deserved?

She told herself she was a journalist. Let the true gutter press do a complete character assassination: after all, they hadn't spoken to the woman who had given birth to Carol. They couldn't imagine what it was to hold your baby in your arms and dream of a golden future for that child. Mrs Meadows might have been a weak woman, maybe she'd let her husband control her, but there was no doubt she'd loved her daughter. Amelia could almost feel the pain the poor woman must have experienced to take her own life. No doubt she had blamed herself for Carol's faults.

Amelia remembered that when she was about sixteen a neighbour called Beryl Bentley had taken her in for a cup of tea when she'd found her crying, her face swelling and turning purple after a punch from her father.

'I can't make your father a kinder man, or your mother strong enough to stand up to him,' Beryl said, and put a little brandy in her tea to help the pain. 'But if it's any consolation to you, Amelia, I'll bet your mum felt she'd been punched too, knowing what he'd done to you. That's the curse of being a mother. You think that everything your child does wrong is somehow your fault. You didn't love them enough, you loved them too much. You failed to notice changes. You hoped that everything would turn out for the best.

'It's a bugger, Amelia, but a mother always takes the

blame. That's the reason your mum gets drunk. She needs to make herself numb. If she didn't, she'd go crazy with her own powerlessness to stand up to your dad, her inability to look after you kids, and the terrible guilt that she allowed herself to be sucked into marriage with that bastard.'

'What do I do, then?' Amelia had asked, crying then because it was the first time someone had seriously acknowledged what she was going through, or what a brute her father was.

'You leave home and you make the kind of life you want,' Beryl said. 'That won't come easy. You've grown up used to slaps and punches, and that could turn you into a victim of a sweet-talking bastard offering to "take care" of you. Men like that home in on vulnerable women, and before you know it, they're bullying and controlling you.'

'I wouldn't let that happen,' Amelia insisted.

'Yes, you will, because you've been so long without love or tenderness that, one kind word, you'll be putty in their hands. Better to stay alone until you're stronger. And, believe me, being alone is so much better than being with a cruel or heartless man.'

'But I don't want to be alone,' Amelia cried. Beryl was frightening her and giving her the idea that all her future held was an abusive man, or a life of utter loneliness.

'You're too special to be left long on the shelf,' Beryl said, with a little chuckle. 'You just need time to find

136

out who you are and what you want. One day when you least expect it, a man will come along and you'll sense his good soul. He won't be flash or boastful. He'll be happy to walk in the park with you or help you in the launderette. He'll fill your little world, share everything he has. He'll encourage you to do what's good for you, and you'll know he's Mr Right.'

Remembering Beryl's wise words made Amelia feel that Max was the man with the good soul. He had filled her world and shared all he had. Even if he did have to go away on rather mysterious jobs, she should trust him.

It was also time that she forgave her mother for being so pathetic, even if she still couldn't forgive her father. Maybe their brand of child-rearing had given her strengths that girls like Carol Meadows didn't have.

Jack loved her article. He said half jokingly that he'd have liked three-in-a-bed tales, drug-taking and embezzlement, too, but in a more generous moment he patted her on the back and told her she'd done well.

As the weeks crept by towards Christmas, the police appeared to be no nearer finding the murderer and people stopped talking about it. But otherwise things had got better and better for Amelia. After she'd written about Carol Meadows, Jack gave her a rise of two pounds a week, and she was contacted by *Style*, a leading glossy magazine for women. They were impressed by the factual yet sensitive way she wrote, and asked if she'd like to interview some ordinary women who had achieved amazing things.

Nothing had ever thrilled her as much as that did. It was acknowledgement that she could write well, and she couldn't think of anything she'd like better than writing about inspirational women. She read through the profiles she'd been sent and was impressed as most of the women, some of whom had small children, had had only rudimentary education, and no help financially from anyone, but had somehow qualified professionally or started up businesses. Two had gone to night school to get O and A levels so that they could go on to university; one planned to become a doctor, the other a scientist.

Another woman was cutting out dresses on a door balanced on two trestles because she had no table in her tiny flat. She was working around the clock to sew them and had an order from a chain of boutiques for a hundred in all sizes. Once she'd been paid, her plan was to rent a workshop and employ another seamstress to work with her.

The beauty of the job Amelia had been offered was that she could do it in her spare time as they wanted just one story a week. Astoundingly the sum of seventy pounds for each article had been suggested. She didn't earn that much in a month at the *West London Weekly*.

Max was as excited as she was and went out straight away to buy her a second-hand electric typewriter. Amelia felt all her Christmases had come at once.

*

Christmas was so cosy. Max's parents had asked him to come home, but he excused himself on the grounds that he was working right up to Christmas Eve. Amelia decorated her room so it looked like Santa's grotto, with lights and more lights, a Christmas tree and artificial snowflakes on the window.

She had made a stocking for Max, but she thought he must either have been poking about and found it, or just guessed, because he made her one too. She'd put silly joke things in his: a false stick-on moustache, a pig's snout held on with elastic, a light-up tie-pin and a pair of socks that played 'While Shepherds Watched' when pressed.

Max had majored on pretty things for her: tiny soaps, glitzy hair clips, a scarf with robins and a jewelled pen. To Amelia it was wonderful. As a child, her stocking had never held more than an orange and a few sweets. But, then, Christmas had been a time for her father to get crazy drunk: he broke doors down, smashed a window and her mother's face. It had never been happy or even peaceful.

With Max it was everything she'd ever wanted. A room full of love, warmth, comfort, good things to eat and the promise of the best year ever ahead of them. It crossed Amelia's mind that she could write a good magazine article on what people hoped for at Christmas set against the reality of what they could expect.

'To us,' Max said, raising a glass of sparkling wine to

her. 'Maybe we'll look back in twenty years' time and realize that Christmas 1970 was our most magical.'

'We'll still be together, then?' Amelia said, as she clinked his glass.

He didn't answer her for a bit: he appeared to be rummaging for something near the Christmas tree.

'Yes, but only if you agree to marry me now,' he said suddenly, and when she looked at him, he was wearing the pig's snout and the false moustache. 'I didn't think to buy a ring. But I've got these.'

Amelia shrieked with laughter. She hadn't expected a proposal – and certainly not when he was wearing a pig's nose. 'Just as long as you lose that thing before we get married.' She could hardly get the words out she was laughing so much.

'More seriously,' he said, whipping off the nose and moustache, 'I love you, Amelia. Nothing in my entire life has felt as right as having you for my wife.'

Later that evening, when Max had dropped off to sleep, Amelia smiled to herself. For the first time in her life she felt she had what Beryl Bentley had said she should aim for. She was in control, and she knew she wasn't blundering into a nightmare. It was such a good feeling.

But the happy and joy-filled Christmas vanished on 27 December when Max said he must leave the next day to spend New Year with his parents.

'They couldn't understand why I didn't go to them for Christmas and now I need to tell them about you and how I feel, and I can't do that adequately with you there. I'm sure you can see that.'

She said she could but she was hurt that he'd even think of leaving her to see in the New Year alone. They both had the whole week off between Christmas and New Year, and she had thought they could go to the Victoria and Albert Museum one day, maybe to the pictures or to see a play in a theatre up west. It would be no fun doing any of that on her own.

Amelia went to see him off at Shepherd's Bush tube the next morning. She wanted to go up to Paddington with him, but he said he hated goodbyes, and at a mainline station it would feel much worse.

'I'm sorry,' he said, turning to kiss her just before he went through the barrier. 'I know you're hurt, even though you've done your best to hide it. But it'll be good for you to have some time alone. You've got to write one of those articles, haven't you?'

'I'm not hurt,' she lied. 'And, yes, I have got the article to do. Maybe I'll ring the woman and ask if I can come and talk face to face with her. She's only in Kew.'

Max disappeared into the crowd, and she had to bite back tears. He hadn't said he loved her before he left.

It was very cold, and it felt as if it might snow. Amelia had never felt so forlorn and alone. She thought of calling on Kat for company, but then she remembered she'd be working, so her friend wouldn't be at home.

She telephoned Grace Meredith, the young woman she was going to write about, from a phone box in

Shepherd's Bush, hoping against hope she might ask her to come over to Kew straight away.

However, Grace was busy, and suggested four o'clock the following day. Amelia agreed but the appointment was so late in the afternoon: she would have liked it to be earlier. She didn't know Kew well, it would be dark by then, and it left her with nothing to do for most of the day.

The next morning Amelia pulled herself together and decided to set out for Kew early. The shops there were interesting, and she would find a café to read her notes about Grace again, so she was sure of her subject.

She first checked where Grace lived. To her surprise, it was a turn-of-the-century red-brick rather grand apartment block, not at all what she'd expected. Grace had been put into care at the age of ten when her mother died of cancer. Her parents were divorced, and her father's new wife said she couldn't cope with her. That was why Amelia had imagined Grace would live somewhere humble.

Whether or not Grace had liked the children's home wasn't stated, but it had clearly had a profound effect on her, as she became a nursery nurse. She had also trained to counsel bereaved children. The main thrust of Amelia's article would be about her counselling work.

Amelia knew nothing about counselling, especially for children. She had read a bit about child guidance, which was basically a psychiatrist trying to find out why a child was disruptive, violent or withdrawn, purely because of her own bleak childhood. But Grace's work appeared to be more specific. Furthermore she was working towards getting other people into this field: at *Style* magazine they had said she was passionate on the subject.

The café she chose to wait in was just across the road from the apartment block, and as she sat with a pot of tea and a couple of hot teacakes, she watched for people coming in and out.

She found it quite amusing that she'd imagined Grace to be a bit down-at-heel, a woman who had been treated badly as a child and wanted to rescue children in a similar situation. A rather dull and earnest person. Yet everyone she saw coming out of the apartment block looked elegant and well-dressed. It made her see that she should never make assumptions about anyone.

At five to four it was dark, and she made her way across to the apartment block. As she approached the short path flanked by privet hedges, she had the oddest feeling that someone was close behind her. But when she turned no one was there.

Flat six was on the first floor so she didn't take the ancient wrought-iron lift, which was in the stairwell, the stairs going up round it. The first floor had four highly varnished front doors with equally well polished brass letterboxes and knockers. Number six was on the street side of the block.

'I have an appointment with Grace Meredith,' Amelia said, to the attractive and slender dark-haired woman who answered the door, assuming this was Grace's landlady.

'Hello, Amelia,' she said. 'I'm Grace. Do come in.'

Within half an hour Amelia knew she'd made a major mistake in imagining Grace and she had a great deal in common. In fact, they had had very different experiences. Understandably Grace had grieved for her mother when she died, and was sad her father hadn't cared enough to stay or look after her. But she had really liked the children's home she had been sent to and was happy there. Grace had observed as she got older that many of the children who arrived there had had problems that needed to be talked out, which had resulted in her interest in child counselling. Even the lovely mansion apartment, with furniture that could have come from Heal's, was hers, left to her by her maternal grandmother.

'She was dead long before my mother went,' Grace explained. 'I didn't know her because she was angry that Mother had married a man she considered beneath her. She left this apartment in trust for me because she didn't want my father to get his hands on it. I was fifteen when I first heard I had an inheritance, though I had to wait till I was twenty-one to claim it.'

'That was a lucky break. How kind of your grandmother.'

'It was. I just wish I'd known her. She was clearly a strong, intelligent woman. Shame she died before my mother or I might have lived with her. But, then, had

I done that, I doubt I'd have thought child counselling was necessary. It also struck me even then that it's no wonder so many children are screwed up – it all comes from their parents. That was my reason and motivation to go into child counselling.'

It was extremely interesting to learn how Grace structured her sessions, and of the high success rates. But while Amelia was listening hard, and taking shorthand notes, she wondered whether giving some of these disturbed children a cuddle would achieve the same result. Grace didn't look like she cuddled anyone. Her straight back, her almost ballerina-like stance and her sharp, dark eyes, which appeared to miss nothing, were a little chilling.

Style magazine had already been to photograph her, so when Amelia had finished her questions, she thanked the woman for bearing with her and said the magazine would send her a copy of the article. Grace closed the front door the second Amelia was through it. Another disconcerting glimpse into her lack of warmth.

Out on the street again it was dark and cold. Amelia hurried along to the tube station, her shoulders hunched, and her thick wool scarf tied tightly around her neck. Once again, she had the strange feeling that she was being followed, but when she turned no one was there, except a couple of housewives with their hands full of shopping bags.

She got out at Ravenscourt Park tube to save changing trains and made her way down Ravenscourt Road towards Goldhawk Road. Sleet started to fall, and she got her umbrella out of her bag, her teeth chattering with the cold, her mind turning longingly to the French onion soup she'd made the previous evening.

Out of nowhere there was a blow to her head, and she was falling to the pavement . . .

'Don't move!' a male voice cut through the darkness. 'My wife has run to a neighbour to call an ambulance. Can you hear me? Do you know what happened?'

'I think someone hit my head.' Amelia tried to lift her arm to touch it.

'Don't get up. I saw someone running away from you as we turned the corner. I thought they'd gone to get help,' he said. 'Can you tell me your name?'

'Amelia White. I need to get home.'

'Not yet, my dear. You need checking out first by a doctor. It's too dark to see properly but I think that's blood on the pavement. Ah, here's my wife now! How long will they be?' he called.

'On their way they said,' the female voice called back. 'Is she conscious?'

Amelia felt she might be sick, and her head hurt so much she was sure there must be a huge gash. Also, she was terribly cold. The woman leaned over her and smoothed her hair back from her face.

'Her name is Amelia and she thinks she was struck,' the man informed her. 'Must have been the man we saw running off.'

'You poor girl, you'll soon be tucked up in the ambulance. Can we telephone anyone for you when we get home?'

Max's face swam in front of her, but as bad as she felt and however much she wanted him, she couldn't get them to ring him. He hadn't given her his parents' number. Besides, even if she knew it, it was too late in the evening to get a train back and he'd be panic-stricken.

'No, it's okay. I'll be fine.'

She heard the ambulance coming. She felt that if she had to spend another ten minutes on the cold ground, sleet striking her face like razor blades, she might just die.

10

'Who hit you?' the young policeman asked.

Amelia rolled her eyes with impatience. She had been asked the same question by different policemen five times already. She might be on a trolley in Casualty, but that didn't mean she'd lost her marbles. 'If I knew who'd hit me and why, don't you think I would've told you by now? I heard nothing. I was given a crack over the head and I felt myself falling. I think I lost consciousness but I came to as I remember a man speaking to me. I think his wife called 999 and he said something about seeing a man rushing away. They assumed at first he was running to get help.'

'Yes, but did you see what this person looked like?'

'How could I? He came up behind me. But if it's any help I had a feeling someone was following me at Kew. I couldn't see anyone, and I didn't sense anything at Ravenscourt Park station. I'm concerned now that it might be the person who killed the two girls locally. You see, I found the first body and I wrote articles for the local paper on both girls.'

'So that's why your name seemed familiar,' the young policeman said, grinning inanely. 'Do you think it was the same attacker?'

'You're the bloody policeman,' she snapped. 'Do your job.'

Her head ached so much, yet despite the pain she was very aware that her attacker might have killed her, too, if the kindly older couple, whose names she didn't know, hadn't come on the scene.

A nurse had said the wound only needed three stitches, but to Amelia it felt as if her head was split right open. She was still cold, even though the nurses had brought her more blankets. They'd told her she'd soon be moved to a ward upstairs.

Amelia was positive it was the Creeper who'd hit her. She was so glad that the couple had arrived in the nick of time or she might have been stabbed too.

The next morning, after a sleepless night – they kept waking her to check her blood pressure and such – Amelia was allowed home. She took a taxi to the newspaper office to tell Jack what had happened because she wanted some sympathy and she was nervous about going home alone. Her whole head hurt, not just the wound. It was literally the headache from Hell.

She wished she could speak to Max: she so much wanted his reassurance and love. But she'd just have to wait till he got home on New Year's Day.

'Oh dear, Amelia,' Jack said, shaking his head, when she explained what had happened. 'Your face is very pale – it must've given you a terrible fright.'

'It's made me feel vulnerable. I'll be looking over my shoulder all the time now.'

He took her into his office and got her a cup of coffee. 'I'll ask Peanut to take you home in a minute, and I suggest you don't go out at night again without your boyfriend.'

'It wasn't late when it happened,' she said plaintively. 'How did this man know I was going to Kew? Or did he follow me from home and back again? If that's the case I'm not going to be safe there, am I?'

'Have you asked your boyfriend to come home?' Jack asked.

'I can't. I don't know the number,' she said, beginning to cry.

'What sort of a boyfriend goes off at this time of year and doesn't leave you some way of contacting him?'

'Neither of us thought of that,' she said defensively: Jack was implying that Max was careless with her. 'Neither of us has a phone at home. We just don't think of it.'

'Well, the police should be watching your place,' Jack said. 'I feel responsible for encouraging you to write about the two murders. It looks as if this killer reckons you're getting close to him.'

'But I'm not. I'm as much in the dark as I was at the start,' she said, crying in earnest now because she was overwrought from so little sleep.

'Now, now,' he said, patting her shoulder with unusual gentleness. 'I'm going to ring the police myself and see that they station someone at your address. While they're there, they can check the door locks too. But my instinct tells me he won't be back. He'll know he's scared you and that's probably enough.'

It was good to get home. Peanut came in with her and checked the lock on her door was secure. He lit her gas fire and made her a pot of tea and some toast.

'You just curl up in the warm and rest. If Jack said he was going to make the police put a man outside, he'll do that. I expect they'll change the locks too. We'd both feel happier if you were on the phone, but no one is in Bedsitter Land. I'm going to leave notes under the other tenants' doors explaining they need to be observant, and not to leave the downstairs door open at any time.'

Amelia smiled weakly at Peanut. He had managed to make her feel safe again. She scribbled a note for Kat, telling her what had happened, and asked if she'd come over if she wasn't too busy. Peanut said he'd put it through her letterbox on his way back to the office. Before he left, the police arrived to tell Amelia they were putting an officer outside, and that a locksmith was on his way.

In the morning, Kat came over, bringing with her some magazines and a big bar of chocolate. 'I didn't get in till late last night, too late to call then. I've got to go into work now, but if Max is away I could come again when I get home tonight.'

'No, Kat,' Amelia said. 'I'm all right now. I'm not scared with the police outside. I shouldn't really have sent you that message, but I was feeling scared and alone yesterday.'

'That's what friends are for,' Kat said, and bent over to give her a hug. 'You've had a horrible fright, and it's going to take a little while to get over it. I was attacked once a few years ago in Hyde Park. They knocked me down, kicked me about and were obviously going to rape me. Luckily two other men shouted at them, so they just snatched my bag and ran away. I had broken ribs and concussion from the blow to my head so I know how you feel.'

'How awful,' Amelia said. 'We always tend to think we're the only one who's ever been hurt. I'm glad you've made me see it's not just me.'

'If you want some advice, don't try to find out anything more about these murders. It might be the killer warning you off. Listen to that warning. If you need me to get you any shopping, or go to the launderette, just ask the policeman outside to drop a note through my door. Meanwhile, rest.'

Amelia was in bed before the New Year of 1971 came in. She could hear music down the street from someone's party. At the stroke of midnight people went out onto the street to bang trays and sing 'Auld Lang Syne'. She sniffed back a few tears because she felt so alone.

*

Max arrived home on 2 January while she was having her stitches taken out. He was unable to get in as the locks had been changed so he'd gone back to his own room. Later, when he saw her get out of a police car, he came along to see her.

'The key wouldn't work,' he said angrily, when she let him in. 'Couldn't you have told me in person that you didn't want to see me any more? And what's with the police anyway?'

Amelia was hurt that his first thought was for himself. She pointed to the dressing on her head, which he hadn't even noticed, and was tempted to shut the door on him. But she was so relieved he was back she told him what had happened. 'If you'd given me your parents' telephone number, I could've rung you,' she added sharply. 'The police are here to stay until they know whoever attacked me isn't coming here.'

He was contrite then, said he'd meant to give her the number but had forgotten. But he was oddly reticent about his stay in Devon, just said it had been 'all right' when she wanted to know his parents' reaction to his news about her. He hadn't wanted to talk about what he'd spent the days doing, whom he'd seen or any of the usual topics of conversation.

Max was also weird about the police being outside. He kept peeping round the curtain to see if the car was still there and said a guard was unnecessary now he was home.

Amelia felt sorry for the series of policemen who

stayed in shifts overnight. They had to be terribly bored and cold – the weather had turned Arctic with intermittent flurries of snow. When she started back at work, the officer on guard drove her there and another collected her to bring her home. She rather liked having her own private chauffeur, but she wished she could take walks and go shopping, and wondered how much longer she'd have to live like that.

There was a pall of gloom everywhere, and though Amelia knew hers was understandable, everyone at work was much the same. They kept going on about the decimalization, which was due to start in February. No one wanted it, and most were convinced it would put prices up. But that was a little way off. Right now, there were the power cuts to grumble about. Every afternoon for at least two hours, the electricity went off. Hospitals, hotels and large factories mostly had generators to fall back on, but garages and other businesses couldn't function at all. A shop without lights made it impossible for shoppers, but paradise for thieves.

Housewives complained they couldn't do the ironing, or cook if they had electric cookers, and an all-electric home meant no heating, TV or cups of tea. Mothers couldn't even make up a baby's bottle. At the newspaper the phones were still in use so Amelia could carry on with ringing the advertisers, but for the duration of the power cut, typing had to be done on the two old manual machines. With the power off, the office was soon freezing, and everyone started coming to work wearing several jumpers and usually added a coat once the electricity went off.

Max's accounting work wasn't suffering so much: the ledgers he worked on were all handwritten, but he said it was hard to see figures on a dull grey day without a desk light.

'Life's not a lot of fun right now,' Max remarked one cold Saturday afternoon when once again the lights had gone out. 'But I suppose I should be grateful we've got a gas fire.'

'You certainly should,' Amelia said. 'I spoke to Ted and Barbara upstairs yesterday. They've only got an electric heater, and they said they get into bed when the power goes off. I don't care about the lights or anything else much, not now they've taken my stitches out and I can wash my hair again.'

Max just looked sharply at her, as if what she'd said was selfish. She'd had a lot of those looks from him lately. She wondered if he was jealous that she was driven to work and home again, while he had to do the shopping and go to the launderette. She hadn't asked him how he felt because that might mean she had to disclose her own feelings. The truth was she was scared. Not just of the Creeper, but of Max growing tired of her.

Just when it seemed everyone had lost interest in the Creeper, on 18 January he struck again, killing a third girl.

This one was left behind a tree on the green by Turnham Green station. It had been an exceptionally wintry night, with thick frost, and perhaps that explained why no one spotted the girl's body until seven the next morning.

Amelia heard the news from Jack when she went into work and was so shocked she felt faint.

The new victim was Rosie Lark, a model, close in age to the others, but this time with chestnut brown hair. Jack said he'd been told by his source she was well known in the fashion world and had been on the cover of *She* magazine last summer. Her name was linked with that of a Chelsea footballer, Matt Parkin.

'If he let her go home on the tube alone, he'll take a lot of flak,' Jack said cheerfully. He had an unerring knack for nosing out a secondary story.

'Does she live in Chiswick?' Amelia asked, ignoring his previous remark.

'Yes, in Bedford Park. Her parents are loaded.'

'But if she'd come back by tube, why was she on the green? Surely she'd go straight down the road.'

'I don't know.' Jack looked startled. 'The workings of the female mind are a mystery to me. Maybe she didn't come back on the tube. She could've been somewhere on Chiswick High Road and cut down the back streets.'

'I know if I was out when it's dark and frosty, I'd go the well-lit route where people are.'

'Let's wait for more news – no point in surmising stuff. Anyway, the father of this girl is the managing director of Larks Engineering, out Slough way. It's a phenomenally successful company so I expect the police will pull out all the stops to find the killer this time.'

'Are you saying they didn't bother much before because the girls weren't from wealthy homes? That's a hideous assumption.'

Jack gave her a lopsided grin. 'You know me, Amelia, I say it how it is. This girl's father will flex his muscles and suddenly the police will be combing every blade of grass, dragging all sorts in for questioning. You wait and see. Meanwhile another murder in the area is going to cause panic. As if things aren't bad enough with the power cuts.'

By the same evening the murder was front-page news and on the television, and they knew it would be splashed over tomorrow's dailies across the country. Amelia sensed Jack wanted to get some special handle on this, as he had with her help before, but he didn't suggest involving her – if he had, she would have turned him down. He had had to be satisfied with using one of his other reporters and writing a rather scaremongering front-page article himself, about the danger of younger women going out alone at night in the Chiswick area.

When she got back from work, Max was already home. 'Your friend Kat called round and brought you these.' He pointed to a bouquet in the sink. 'She said she was sorry she hadn't come over recently but, first, she got tied up late with work and then she saw I was home.'

The flowers – bright pink roses – were lovely, and Amelia was touched at Kat's kindness. Neither Jack nor Max had thought to buy her flowers. 'How sweet of her,' she said. 'I bet she asked you a million questions.'

'Not quite that many,' Max replied, and frowned. 'But she certainly wanted to know all the ins and outs about where I'd been. I thought she'd never go. I was talking to her on the doorstep and it was freezing. In the end I had to ask her in. She was so nosy too, looking at everything. I'm being mean about her, aren't I?'

'Well, a bit, when she'd brought me flowers, but I'm sure you were diplomatic and told her you were in the middle of cooking our tea.'

'I was peeling potatoes and about to grill some chops.'

'That's good! I'm starving.'

Half an hour later when they were sitting at the table eating, they talked about their respective days at work. Max said he had to go on a special course to do with the imminent decimalization.

'What do you need a course for?' she asked. 'Surely accounting will be easier with everything in tens rather than twelve pennies in a shilling et cetera.'

'That's what I thought but it seems it's more complicated. The thing is, sweetheart, I've got to go to Rugby for it, and be away for two nights. I don't want to leave you while everything is so messy, but I've got no choice.'

'I'll be perfectly fine,' Amelia said, reaching out to

take his hand. 'The police are outside and they take me to work. I'm not going anywhere else. I'm as safe as it's possible for anyone to be.'

'Okay, then, but when I get back, I think we ought to find somewhere new to live. Not just because of the Creeper but because it doesn't make any sense paying two lots of rent and us both living in here. Or we could buy a flat or a little house. I've got lots of contacts to get us a mortgage.'

Amelia loved the idea of having her own bathroom, not to mention a separate bedroom so her clothes and bedding didn't absorb cooking smells. Yet she had a feeling it wasn't a good idea to burn her bridges just yet. She was still annoyed that Max had left her alone at New Year. He hadn't been very sympathetic about her attack, and often seemed cross that he had to do the shopping. She just wanted to be absolutely certain before they began house hunting.

'Don't you think it's too soon? What if we fall out?'

'Is that likely?'

'How can I answer that? We haven't known each other that long.'

'Long enough for me to know I want to spend the rest of my life with you.'

Amelia loved that he felt that way, and so did she. But she still didn't understand why he was rushing things and pushing her into a corner.

'Wouldn't your parents think we were being a bit hasty?'

'They got married when they'd only known each other for six weeks so they can't say that to me. Besides, I told them I wanted to marry you.'

That was news to her. Surely he should be taking her to meet them before telling them he wanted to marry her. 'What on earth's fired you up like this?' she asked.

'Just loving you,' he said. He got up from the table and crouched beside her chair, putting his arms around her and leaning his head against her chest. 'You haven't told me much about your childhood, but I know it was bad – I sense the insecurity in you. I want to wipe that out, make you feel as special as I know you are.'

For some reason she heard the desire to control her in that statement, rather than to protect her. 'That's a lovely thing to say, Max, but I'd rather go on as we are for a bit longer. See how things pan out.'

He got up and went over to the window. Without seeing his face she knew he was hurt, maybe even angry. How could she make him see that she had to be 110 per cent sure before she gave up this room that had been her haven for seven years? It was the only security she'd ever known. But Max couldn't understand how she'd been when she first came here: he and his siblings had had a happy childhood, with parents who loved them. He'd never witnessed his mother being beaten to a pulp or felt the sting of a leather strap across his back as she had. And until she felt able to tell him all of that, how could they move forward to a future together?

11

Max slammed the door as he left at eight that morning and Amelia burst into angry tears. It had been their first real row, just as he was going off to Rugby for two days.

Ever since he'd suggested moving and getting married, she'd noticed a change in him. It wasn't her imagination: he was becoming controlling. So far it was all petty things that perhaps were unimportant. Suggesting she kept a notebook to jot down everything she bought, the money she put into the electric and gas meters so she could economize. He criticized her habit of buying fruit and veg from the Greek shop in the Goldhawk Road. He said it was cheaper in the market. As he'd been doing the shopping since she was attacked that hardly mattered, but to Amelia, Demetri in the Greek shop was a friend – she'd talked to him almost daily for seven years – and she hated Max referring to the place as the Wop Shop.

He said she was to stop buying cleaning materials to use in the bathrooms and other common parts of the house, and indeed stop cleaning until the other tenants agreed to pay her to do it.

Amelia had no intention of doing that. Maybe that

was the way it should work, but she'd taken it upon herself to do the cleaning seven years ago. It was a bit late now to change the order of things and, anyway, she quite liked doing it. If they said they'd take turns to clean and then didn't do it, she'd be unhappy about it.

Max had also begun to tell her what to wear: her checked skirt was too short; she looked 'brassy' in her red jumper. Some people would say it was just his way of showing how much he cared about her. But a little voice in Amelia's head was telling her to be cautious. She wasn't going to ignore it.

Last Sunday they were going to a pub in Shepherd's Bush that did a good Sunday lunch and he told her to put on her blue wool dress. She didn't like herself in it: she felt it was too tight and made her tummy look fat. He said that was silly and he liked her in it so she must put it on.

That same day after lunch she stopped to speak to a man she knew from the market. He'd been taken into hospital with a heart attack recently and she asked him if he was better now and whether he was going back to his china stall. She spoke to him for just a few moments, but Max asked why she wanted to speak to a deadbeat like him. It was true, he did look a bit rough in a woolly hat and a shabby donkey jacket, but it was very cold and, anyway, what difference did his appearance make? She'd bought mugs, plates and other items from him over the last seven years — what sort of person would it make her if she didn't ask how he was?

On Tuesday night he said he wanted sausage and mash for dinner when she'd planned to make a new pasta dish. 'You can do that tomorrow,' he said dismissively. 'I don't fancy pasta tonight.'

She told herself she was being hypersensitive, but she kept noting more and more of these incidents. Each one was nothing to get worked up about on its own, but put together, she could see he was undermining her decisions.

The row this morning had begun when he'd said she must ring some estate agents while she was at work. He wanted details of houses selling for up to fifty thousand pounds in the Chiswick and Ravenscourt Park areas. 'Two bedrooms and a garden,' he said, not even looking at her.

'Max, I did say I thought it was too soon,' she said quietly.

'Nonsense,' he said, as if she was a naughty child. 'I want to get onto the property ladder now while prices are low because of the state of the economy. It's madness to wait. By the time you've made up your mind, the prices will have leaped up.'

She didn't like his tone when he said 'by the time you've made up your mind', the implication being that she was unable to make decisions quickly. She remembered the many times her father had belittled her mother in that way. In the end her mother couldn't make decisions because he'd convinced her she was too stupid.

'If you want to get on the property ladder you do so,' she snapped. 'Just don't drag me into it.'

'Are you wearing blinkers?' he shouted at her. 'Do you really want to stay in this crummy room for another year or two?'

That did it.

'Crummy room?' she exclaimed. 'I love this place, and if you don't like it, don't bother to come here any more. Get back to your own room, which is infinitely crummier than this one.'

She saw a new expression on his face. His eyes darkened, he scowled, and he looked frighteningly angry.

Backing away from him she caught her leg on the coffee-table and fell.

'See what I mean? So much bloody rubbish in here you can barely move,' he said.

She asked how he dared to criticize her home and he said it was like a hippie junk shop.

At that she told him to get out, picked up some clothes he'd left on a chair and threw them at him. 'Take that "junk" with you too,' she snarled.

He grabbed his stuff and left, banging the door as he went.

She was proud that she'd held back her tears till he'd gone. But now she felt as if she'd be crying all day. All this time she'd believed he was The One, daydreaming of a rosy future, having children, and growing old together, fulfilling all each other's needs. But now she could see the flaws in their relationship. She'd fallen for a man who wanted and needed to be in charge. He wasn't cruel, not the way her father was, but might he become so in time?

Before she'd met and fallen for Max, if any friend had asked her what to do about a controller in her life, she would have advised her to get out of the relationship, as men do not change, even when they promise they will.

But she couldn't end it with Max: she loved him too much. The attack on her had meant she was unable to go out and interview any more women for *Style* magazine, and Jack had put her back on selling advertising space, saying she could write articles again when he thought she was fit for it. So Max had become her entire world.

What was she to do?

She had to pull herself together because at any moment her police guard would be knocking on the door ready to take her to work. She wiped her face with a damp flannel, ran a comb through her hair and put on some lipstick.

Right on cue the front doorbell rang three times, the police's signal. She put on her coat, picked up her handbag and went down to open the door.

It was PC Sam Hamilton, young, fresh-faced and boyish, with blond hair and blue eyes. He had told her on a previous occasion he was twenty-eight, but he looked more like twenty-one.

'How are you today?' he asked. 'I'm stiff with cold and starving.'

'I'm so sorry,' she said. 'It must be awful being out there in the car. I'm beginning to think it's pointless and the Creeper's lost interest in me.' Sam opened the car door for her. 'It's all part of the job,' he said, with an easy smile. 'I'll be fine after a bacon sandwich and a mug of coffee. Let's hope whatever made you cry this morning can be fixed as easily.'

Amelia was embarrassed that he'd noticed her puffy eyes. She'd thought she'd calmed them down. As he pulled away, he looked round at her. 'Sorry, I shouldn't have said that. But I've got a sister, so I know when someone's been crying.'

'I hope you're as good at detecting crime,' she said, and smiled at him because he looked crestfallen.

'I read your articles about the murdered girls,' he said. 'You write really well – I felt I knew them. Lucy seemed lovely, but reading between the lines, Carol sounded a real piece of work.'

'I'd have put it in stronger terms, but it didn't seem right to come out and say it. Now there's another dead girl, and my theory about there being some connection between them doesn't seem to hold water any longer. This one's got dark hair.' She paused for a moment and sighed. 'Sadly I don't think I'll get a chance to stick my beak into Rosie and her family.'

'Never mind about that. I'm only glad you weren't another victim,' he said. 'You were lucky that couple came along when they did.' He fell silent for a couple of minutes, then turned to her again when he stopped at the traffic lights. 'Did you fight with your boyfriend? He came out of the house with a face like thunder.'

'I can see why you joined the police, questioning everything.'

'I'm not always like that.' He laughed. 'But when I read your articles, I felt something special about you. Not many journalists seem to care the way you obviously do. And I noticed you understand the forces that make people react as they do. So when they put me on this job, I hoped I'd get the chance to talk to you. So tell me about your boyfriend.'

'He was a bit nasty, that's all, and I told him to get out.'

'Permanently?'

'I didn't think that far ahead.' She smiled sheepishly at him. 'But he seems to be becoming a bit of a controller. That worries me.'

Sam looked at her for a minute or two without speaking. His blue eyes had clouded over to become grey, the way the sky often did. 'It should worry you,' he said. 'We see some nasty stuff between married couples on this job. What you must remember, Amelia, is that some men find a perfectly lovely woman and then, because they have problems themselves, try to mould that woman into whatever they think they need to make them happier. Don't you ever let that happen.'

Sam's words made her feel protected, but also told her she had to be realistic where Max was concerned. As she walked up the stairs to the office, she recalled something her mother had said once. Amelia was nine or ten at the time and her father had given her mum yet another black eye and wrenched her arm so badly she could barely hold the teapot at breakfast.

'Never fall for a man, Amelia, who thinks you're lucky he even looked at you. He'll only ever see you as his slave and punchbag.'

Amelia didn't think Max thought she was lucky to have him, and neither was he likely to use her as a punchbag, but he'd made many remarks that suggested he believed he was the clever one. The good catch.

It was good to be at work, busy with phone calls to advertisers: it took her mind off Max. She'd been at her desk for about an hour when Jack appeared. 'Come into my office,' he said.

Mystified, Amelia followed him. His usual way of summoning anyone was to roar at the top of his voice.

'Shut the door,' he said. 'And sit down.'

Amelia obeyed. 'Did I do something wrong?' she asked.

He smiled. 'Why is it you always assume you're in the wrong?' he asked. 'Keep it up and that boyfriend will blame you for everything. That's how it works.'

Such wisdom on a day when it was kind of relevant seemed nothing short of miraculous to her.

'I spoke to Mr Lark, the father of the latest murdered girl, late last night. He isn't impressed by the police inquiry. He thinks they're sitting on their hands. He's read your two articles about the other girls and the one thing that struck him was that you believe there was a connection between the girls. Then he'd heard you'd been attacked. He said, and I quote, "If the killer wants to silence her, I think she might have got something."'

'Bloody hell!' Amelia exclaimed. 'I didn't expect that!'

'Nor me, but Mr Lark is a highly intelligent man, and one of those people who believes that if you want something done, do it yourself. He wants to talk to you, Amelia, as he put it, "to thrash a few ideas around". He's grieving. He can't believe his beautiful daughter has been taken from him, and his wife is almost a basket case.'

'Surely he wouldn't want to see me now when it's all so raw.'

'That is exactly why he wants to see you now. He needs to pour out all he feels, his stories of when Rosie was little, her boy- and girlfriends, the things she cared about. He could talk to a counsellor, a priest, a friend or a colleague but, as he said, "There was something about those articles that makes me think she's the one to talk to. Maybe together we can find a way to the truth." So, Amelia, what do you think? Want to give it a shot?'

Amelia felt like smiling to see Jack's face. He was lit up from inside, she could see, convinced he'd got the golden goose right here on his newspaper and she would lay the golden egg today and on many other days too. He was, of course, hoping for an exclusive story, though knew he wouldn't have it straight away. But by getting Amelia in with the murdered girls' families, he felt certain he'd have what he wanted once the killer was caught.

He was something of a reprobate, but at heart he was honest and brave. He also cared about getting to the truth, though he went to great pains to make out he didn't.

Did she want to give it a shot? Of course she did. This was no time for acting bashful.

'Well, how can I refuse? When do I start this thrashing out?'

'Immediately. I'll get Peanut to drive you there. Mr Lark will see you're brought home later in the day. Depending on how it goes he might want you there tomorrow too.'

Amelia was still surprised that Mr Lark wanted to do it right now, but it was fine with her. It might even take her mind off Max. 'Who else will be there?'

'I think you'll be alone with him. He said his wife had been taken to her sister's. Rosie was an only child.'

Ten minutes later Amelia was sitting in Peanut's car on the way to Bedford Park in Chiswick. She remembered that back in the sixties the local council had wanted to tear down the beautiful old Arts and Crafts houses, because so many had been neglected and divided into bedsitters. The council had wanted to replace them with blocks of flats. But a few staunch locals had fought to get the houses listed, and now they were being bought up and renovated to bring them back to their original beauty.

'Mr Lark was one of the people who fought to save Bedford Park,' Peanut informed her. 'Some will say he did it to feather his own nest – he'd already bought three properties there. But I for one applaud his actions. Beautiful buildings shouldn't be torn down to be replaced by blocks of flats. We all need beauty around us to inspire, whether that's parks, buildings, theatres or art galleries.'

'I couldn't agree more,' Amelia said. She'd often walked around Bedford Park, looking at the houses that had been restored and dreaming of living in such a place one day.

The Larks' house was very imposing, one of the three-storey semi-detached ones, the gate and railings white-painted wrought iron. Its warm red brick looked so inviting in the pale winter sunshine, she could hardly wait to see what it was like inside.

Mr Lark opened the front door before they reached it. He was a big man, at least six foot two, with broad shoulders and a mop of thick grey hair. She guessed him to be in his late fifties, but he looked younger, strong and fit. 'You must be Amelia,' he said. 'Do come in.'

Peanut backed away. He'd done his duty in getting her to the front door. Amelia glanced back and saw he looked a little anxious. She wondered why.

The house smelt of polish, and as the hall had the original parquet flooring it was clear someone was looking after it. She had a glimpse of a grand sitting room, with midnight blue sofas and a Chinese rug, but Mr Lark led her to a far smaller room towards the back of the house. 'We call this the snug,' he said, 'because it's much cosier on a cold evening, and I use it as an office if I need to work at home.'

'It's lovely,' Amelia said. The walls were painted a very dark green, which set off a white marble fireplace to perfection. 'So many books,' she added. One whole wall was covered with them, from floor to ceiling.

There was a glazed door onto a small yard and beyond that the garden. She could see a great many conifers at the end, making it private.

Amelia took a buttoned leather seat by the fire and got out her notepad and pen. 'I won't be taking notes, Mr Lark. This is for the names of places, schools, or something like that, which I might want to check later.'

He had a stern face, and although no one would have expected him to be laughing today, Amelia had the impression that he was always serious, maybe even dour. His eyes were grey, like his hair, and the lids drooped. He had deep frown lines on his forehead.

'Call me Henry,' he said.

'Well, Henry, first may I offer my condolences. What happened to Rosie was terrible and it must be the very worst nightmare for you and your wife.'

'Thank you.' He nodded as he took the seat opposite her by the fire. 'We still can't really believe that's it, that we'll never see her again. We were always worried that we'd go while she was still young enough to need us, but it never entered our heads she might go first.'

'Can you tell me where she went that last evening?'

'To her friend Mabel Livingstone's. She's another model, living further up Chiswick High Road. They went to the Golden Orchid Chinese restaurant, which I believe is close to Mabel's home. They had made plans to go to a club afterwards, but it was so cold they decided against it and parted outside the restaurant.'

'You've obviously spoken to Mabel. Did she say if anyone was hanging around outside?'

'She didn't notice anyone. She said there wasn't much traffic . . . but someone wasn't put off by the cold.'

'So Rosie walked home alone?'

'She's done that walk hundreds of times in all weathers, just as her friend would walk from here back to her home. When the last girl was killed in Ravenscourt Park, I did try to stop Rosie going out alone after dark. I said I'd take her anywhere she wanted to go, but my protests fell on deaf ears.'

'I'm sure parents all over the world have that problem,' Amelia said in sympathy. 'It was suggested I got a taxi to Kew and back the evening I was attacked, but I didn't want to spend money on a taxi when the tube was so close.'

That wasn't true – no one had suggested a taxi – but she thought it might make Henry feel a little better.

'What time were you expecting Rosie home?'

'I never knew when she was coming in. It was

something I used to nag her about. She'd say she'd be in by eleven, then go on somewhere else and come back at three in the morning. I'd given up, though. She was twenty-six, and you can't keep your kids wrapped in cotton wool for ever.'

'No, you can't,' she agreed. 'You went to bed and it wasn't until morning that you found she wasn't at home?'

'That's right, and even then I didn't think any harm had come to her. I thought she'd just stayed the night with Mabel. She often did. Just after eight I walked along to Turnham Green Terrace to buy a paper and I saw all the police activity on the green. I spoke to a policeman, who said they'd found another girl. I felt queasy then and asked what colour coat she was wearing. When he said red, I nearly collapsed.'

'How awful for you, Henry.' Amelia could see he was shaking as he relived that terrible moment. 'That must have been worse than a policeman coming to your door.'

'He didn't realize straight away what was wrong with me – I think he thought I'd had a seizure and needed to go to hospital. I swore at him when he kept fussing, and screamed out that it was Rosie.'

Henry closed his eyes and wiped his hand across his forehead, a gesture Amelia thought meant he wanted to get rid of the pictures in his head. Her heart went out to him. She felt he was on the verge of breaking down and howling like a child, but he was holding it in because he believed that was what men should do.

'It's okay to cry, Henry,' she said softly. 'It might help release the anger and hurt inside you.'

He looked at her, and briefly she thought he was going to shout at her.

'I got the feeling when I read your articles that you'd been in a dark place too,' he said, his voice shaking.

'Not as dark as you're going through, but bad enough for me to understand. Would you like to be alone for a bit? Let me make you some tea or coffee, or we can carry on and you can tell me what Rosie was like when she was younger.'

He didn't answer for a moment, sitting forward in his chair, his whole body sagging.

'Tea would be nice,' he said, after a bit. 'A neighbour brought round some homemade chocolate cake. Rosie used to say that chocolate was the cure for everything.'

Amelia smiled. 'I think that too. So tea and cake it is.'

The kitchen was galley-style, with a pine refectory table and benches right at the end by doors that opened onto the garden. Amelia thought it was the nicest she'd ever seen, with its pale green cupboards and white Formica work surfaces, so fresh and modern-looking. She liked the way saucepans were hung on a brass rail and the doormat by the back door said, 'Lots of Larks to be had here'. Someone must have had it made for them.

She found the tea things, and the chocolate cake in a tin on the work surface. While she waited for the kettle to boil, she arranged everything on a tray.

177

Talking to the Whelans had been tough, Mrs Meadows even worse, but Henry Lark was in a league of his own. She thought he must normally be like a bull elephant, charging through life with ruthless efficiency, scattering all those who didn't fit in with his plans. But, with her suspicion of his true character, it was so sad to see him crushed and defeated.

The kettle boiled, she made the tea and put the pot on the tray, then carried it into the snug.

As she put it down on a coffee-table, she saw he'd pulled out some photo albums.

'That's good thinking, Henry,' she said. 'It will help me to visualize Rosie and get to know her. I haven't seen any pictures of her yet.'

Henry handed her a large black-and-white photograph.

Amelia almost gasped. Rosie was a classic beauty, a perfect oval face, prominent cheekbones, wide brown eyes and long, silky chestnut hair. In this picture she was wearing a slinky white evening dress studded with sequins. 'Was this from one of her modelling assignments?' she asked.

'Yes. It was in the Christmas issue of *Tatler*. She was advertising the watch.'

'I was so caught up in her beautiful face I hardly noticed that,' Amelia said. It was white gold with diamonds and probably cost a king's ransom.

'Most of our friends said something similar,' Henry said. 'But, of course, in the magazine the details of the watch are emblazoned on the page. Rosie wasn't a beautiful child, though. She was remarkably plain. Crooked teeth we had to get straightened and puppy fat too. We thought she was lovely, of course, but she suffered from bullying at school. Children can be very cruel.'

'I bet the kids who bullied her felt very ugly themselves when later they saw her in magazines. How did she get to be a model?'

'She was approached by a woman who worked for an agency. We were on holiday at the time in Wales – Rosie was coming up for eighteen. I thought the woman was a chancer – you know the sort, target the kid with stars in her eyes and talk her into paying for an expensive portfolio of photographs.'

'But this woman was genuine?'

'Yes. In fact she made us see how beautiful our daughter had become. You don't really notice change when you see someone every day. Rosie was so shy, she didn't show off, didn't wear makeup, didn't have much confidence either. But Caitlin, that was her name, saw what was there and eventually convinced my wife and me of it. It was Rosie who took the most persuading.'

He showed Amelia several other glossy fashion pictures, in all of which Rosie looked fabulous. But then Henry put an ordinary snapshot into her hand. This was Rosie on a beach when she was about seven. She'd lost her front teeth, her hair was plaited, and she was wearing an unflattering ruched swimsuit. Amelia had

had an almost identical one. She remembered that when she got into the paddling pool at the park it filled with water and she'd had to press it out or risk looking as if she had a weird big bottom.

Henry was right: she was plain. What Americans called 'homely'. She'd read that word in *What Katy Did* and liked that it didn't sound cruel. At seven there wasn't so much as a hint of what Rosie was to become.

Amelia couldn't bring herself to describe any child as plain, so she asked where the picture had been taken.

Henry showed her many more over the tea and a slice of the delicious chocolate cake. There were lots of little stories, and through them Amelia saw Rosie at private school, at sports day in the egg-and-spoon race, in the swimming gala, in the back row of angels in the nativity play. Then one in the Guides.

'She was in the Guides?' Amelia said.

'She loved it. She did so many badges, used to talk to us about being kinder to our neighbours and helping people every day.' He laughed as he said it and Amelia was able to imagine the intense young girl wanting to make the world a better place.

'Any particular friends there?'

'There was Hilary, though we were never sure she was a good influence. Bossy, you know – I saw her as typical Girl Guide material.'

'Did she keep in touch with Hilary? I mean, after she left the Guides.'

'For a short while. I always felt that Hilary was the

one who put her off Guiding. What makes you want to know about Guides?'

'As I said, I've been looking for something all three girls shared, a place they went to, or even a fourth person. So far, nothing's jumped out at me, other than all three of them being beautiful. Possibly dancing or sport, like gymnastics.'

'Rosie liked dancing, but never did gymnastics. I wouldn't call her sporty. She was the kind to curl up with a book.'

'I see, but Guides came up with Lucy, so I'm going to check again and see if Carol was a member. Which Guide troop was Rosie in?'

'One that met at our local church, St Michael and All Angels. She went to church with her mother regularly until her modelling career took off.'

'Do you think the Guide mistress who knew Rosie will still be around?'

'It's highly likely. Women like that tend to be very committed. And it wasn't so long ago, only twelve or thirteen years.'

Henry talked and talked as he got out more photographs. He told stories about Rosie being naughty or disobedient as easily as he talked about occasions when he was proud of her, for winning a prize or doing something good.

Again and again he was overcome by emotion. But he bit back his tears and carried on. 'I can't believe I've been robbed of walking her down the aisle to get married or holding a grandchild in my arms,' he said at one point, his strong voice wavering. 'My business, this lovely house and the money in my bank mean nothing now. I'd give up everything for one more day with my Rosie.'

Amelia saw from the photographs that Mrs Lark was beautiful, too. In some of the pictures she looked very much like Jacqueline Kennedy, the same elegant style and the chiselled cheekbones.

'How is Mrs Lark coping?' Amelia asked tentatively.

'Not at all well,' he said sadly. 'She's just folded in on herself, if you can understand what I mean. She isn't talking, or even crying. She's just blank, as if everything she was has gone. She's with her sister Madeline in Surrey, but Madeline told me this morning she refuses to consider any kind of counselling or psychiatric help. She says her life is over now.'

'That's absolutely awful!' Amelia exclaimed. 'But I have to say hundreds of thousands of people lose a child, and go on to do something worthwhile with their lives. What about all those people who lost their sons in the war? Their grief is just as fierce as Mrs Lark's.'

She stopped, suddenly aware her outburst was too much. 'I'm sorry, that was unkind of me,' she ventured, waiting to be shown the door.

To her surprise, he smiled. 'Not unkind, truthful,' he said. 'I agree with you entirely. But I've been fortunate to have you to talk to. You've been a shaft of light in an otherwise dark tunnel. Tell me how one so young can be so wise?'

'I didn't know I was wise, Henry,' she said. 'I understand pain because my childhood was pretty awful. I've had times I thought I would never fit in anywhere.'

'I sensed your understanding of pain in the articles you wrote. Which I might say were brilliant. You're not just a journalist, you're a lioness on the side of truth.'

Amelia wanted to punch the air in jubilation. But instead she merely smiled.

'That's a lovely thing to say. Now, I ought to contact Mabel and try to find out about the Guide mistress. But I don't want to go if you still have things you want to tell me about.'

'I think I should show you Rosie's bedroom,' he said. 'I think we've talked enough for one day. But I'm sure by the morning I'll have more to tell you, so could we meet again then? Maybe we could walk in Richmond Park and have some lunch.'

Amelia hesitated. That sounded dangerously like a date. He was alone, grieving, and he felt she understood him. What if that led him to make a pass at her?

But it was possibly more dangerous to be alone in the house with him.

'Okay – well, as long as my editor and my boyfriend are happy about it. Let me jot down Mabel's address and the Guide mistress's name and number. Then I'd like to look at Rosie's room. I expect the police have been all over it.'

Henry sighed. 'Yes. They were looking for evidence

of men she might have been seeing, and wanted to look at letters, diaries and photos.'

'Did she have a boyfriend?'

'She had many.' Henry shrugged and pulled a face. 'She was always attracted to the arty sort. Musicians, mainly. Usually they were scruffy, weak, dreamer types, but they were harmless, or I assumed so anyway. I can't think of one I could imagine lying in wait for her on a frosty night to kill her.'

'How did these relationships end?' Amelia asked.

'They usually fizzled out, nothing dramatic. Musicians travel about quite a bit, and they aren't available at weekends or evenings when they've got engagements. She liked going to gigs with them, but even that wore thin. She said once that standing around watching and waiting wasn't really for her. Sometimes she said she felt like she was just a trophy.'

'So did she ever have a serious romance, a steady boyfriend, whatever the word is to describe a feeling of permanence?'

'At sixteen to eighteen she had Albie.' Henry smiled. 'He'd been her friend since they were toddlers and lived just down the road. They did everything together until he went to Newcastle University. But then her modelling took off, Albie got into the university social life, and gradually they drifted apart. No dramas there.' Henry smiled. 'They remained friends. Rosie even went to his wedding last year. He rang us when the police announced the identity of the Creeper's latest victim.

He was terribly upset. He said you always hold a torch for your first love.'

Amelia nodded. 'Shall we go upstairs now?'

'You go alone, my dear,' Henry suggested. He looked tired and drained. 'I can't face that room now. It's the one to the right at the top of the stairs.'

Amelia was glad to be alone. Poking around in someone's bedroom was testing with someone standing by watching.

It was the kind of bedroom Amelia had daydreamed about when she was back in White City sharing a tiny grubby box-room with her sister. It was mostly green and white, but with splashes of bright pink here and there. The bed looked fit for a princess, a small double with pretty lace fabric draped from the ceiling to either side of the pink velvet headboard. There was a kidney-shaped white dressing-table with a triple mirror under the window, which overlooked the back garden. The entire surface was covered with cosmetics, hairbrushes and bottles of perfume. The small drawers beneath were full of costume jewellery, all in a jumble. Opposite the bed there were wall-to-wall wardrobes, all packed with clothes, so many that Rosie must have struggled to remember what she had.

Amelia ran her hand beneath the rails. In her experience, women tended to hide things there. Sure enough she drew out an old chocolate box with a picture of a thatched cottage, a metal cash box and a jewellery roll.

The jewellery roll was full of clearly valuable pieces, among them a plain gold necklace, a white gold one studded with diamonds, a chunky silver bracelet and some sapphire earrings. Amelia put them back where she'd found them. The cash box wasn't locked: it held fifty pounds and some loose change. She put that back, too, and opened the chocolate box. It held love letters, many from Albie. She read the one with the most recent date. It was a lovely letter. He'd clearly told her previously that he'd met someone important to him and she must have responded wishing him well with no hard feelings because he said he valued all the good times they'd had together and she'd been the very best of friends. He hoped they'd stay that way and he'd be watching her career, feeling proud that he knew her so well.

There was nothing creepy, cruel, sarcastic or nasty in his letter. Amelia was certain he was a genuinely nice young man, writing to an equally kind and caring old girlfriend. Not one word in it was reproachful or bitter.

She picked up the letters to group them together better, and underneath them she discovered a few black-and-white snapshots. She thought they were taken on a Box Brownie, as they were small and square – more modern cameras produced bigger oblong prints.

A row of bell tents, with a kind of camp kitchen in the foreground. A fire with a rack above the flames for cooking on. She had seen people camping with similar equipment.

A group of Guides and their mistresses. Amelia peered closer and saw Rosie. She looked so different then, her hair tucked up under her beret, and she was plump, but the picture was too small to see faces clearly.

She flicked through the remaining pictures and found one of three Girl Guides.

Taking it over to the window she peered at it – the faces were a bit blurred. She was certain Rosie was in the middle, but could the girls at either side of her be Carol and Lucy?

12

Deciding it was kinder not to give Henry false hope until she found out if the other two girls in the photo were Lucy and Carol, she slipped the photograph into her jacket pocket.

Back in the snug he was waiting, looking expectant.

'Anything?' he asked.

'Afraid not, nothing but the usual girls' stuff. What a lovely room.'

'It was never normally so tidy.' He half smiled. 'Rosie had a clear-up a couple of days before . . . Her mother was cross with her, saying if she wanted to live in a pig-sty, she could arrange it. Rosie only laughed, but she did tidy it. I know her mother would welcome an untidy room if we could have Rosie back.'

'I'll go to Mabel's now. Would you mind giving me her address? I'll see you in the morning, if you still want me to come.'

'Yes, I do, but you can't go walking up to Mabel's alone. I'll take you there and perhaps you can get the man who brought you here this morning to drive you home.'

Amelia had forgotten she wasn't supposed to go anywhere unescorted. 'I don't want to put you to that trouble.'

'You're going to a lot of trouble for me,' he said, and he squeezed her shoulder in an affectionate manner. 'Let me just ring Mabel first, though, to see if she's in. As for the Guide mistress, you'll have to contact the vicar for that, but I can give you his number. He's the Reverend Charles Turner. A good man.'

Mabel was at home, and twenty minutes later Amelia was in her sitting room.

Her flat was above a furniture shop in Chiswick High Road, but it was reached through a little court-yard at the back. Amelia's first reaction was surprise. It wasn't a couple of ordinary rooms but big, modern, light and bright. Newly decorated, it was filled with the kind of super-smart contemporary furniture that could only have come from Heal's on Tottenham Court Road.

Mabel was Eurasian, exceptionally beautiful, with short curly black hair. She was wearing a long, slinky red sweater dress, the kind that was unforgiving on most women.

Amelia recognized her face from fashion magazines, and she had a vague recollection that her name had been linked with the photographer David Bailey.

'I hope it isn't an imposition descending on you like this,' Amelia said, 'but Henry Lark seemed sure you'd talk to me about Rosie.'

'Do sit down,' Mabel said, indicating the black sofa strewn with zebra-striped cushions. 'Henry did explain your involvement and I'll be glad to help in any way I can. I'm still stricken with guilt that I didn't insist Rosie stay here that night, but I had a photo call at seven the next morning.'

'When did you hear what had happened?' Amelia asked, as she sat down.

'The police arrived just a few minutes after I got home that evening. It was around seven, and I'd had an awful day. I was cold and hungry, and hearing Rosie had been killed was absolutely devastating. We'd been close friends for some years, and I can't really believe she's gone.'

Amelia thought that sounded heartfelt, but she was surprised Mabel's eyes didn't well up. Were they really such close friends?

'I'm sure the police asked you absolutely everything, including about anyone who might have had a grudge against Rosie, but if there's something that perhaps you didn't want to say to them, or just didn't seem relevant, please tell me.'

Mabel shrugged. 'As models we get more than our share of odd bods hanging around trying to engage with us, over-enthusiastic fans and admirers, too. Then there's women who resent us because either they couldn't do modelling or they're one of those feminist bra-burners and despise us. But we're always care-ful with them, Rosie more so than most because she worked on wanting to please everyone.'

'Any of these people stand out more than the others?'

Mabel shook her head. 'Certainly no one nuts enough to lie in wait and kill her on her way home.'

Amelia got the pictures of Carol and Lucy out of her bag and showed them to Mabel. 'I know you'll have seen these in the papers and on the news but look again at them now and tell me if you've ever seen either of them before.'

Mabel studied them carefully. 'No, I haven't – they've both got that sixties style that so many girls copied, but I'm a hundred per cent sure they've never been any-where near me, or Rosie, for that matter. Well, while she was with me anyway.'

Amelia wasn't going to show her the old photograph of the three girls together in case she mentioned it to Henry. 'Did she ever tell you stories about her friends when she was younger? I believe she was in the Guides.'

Mabel sniggered. 'She said she was a "keener", always wanting to get more badges. By all accounts she got most of them. She used to make me laugh, telling me about the lengths she went to. I was never in the Guides, so it all sounded weird to me.'

'Did she ever speak about going camping with them? And any friends she made there?'

'There was Hilary, she often mentioned her. She used to call her Hairy Hilary sometimes. You can imagine why. Teenage girls are often a bit cruel. They went camping one summer and it rained all the time. She said the food was awful, and the toilets were the chem-ical kind. I think she gave up Guides after that.'

'This Hilary, did she live near Rosie?'

'She must've done as she was in the same Guide company, whatever they call it. But I think she must've moved away because I asked Rosie once if she was still hairy, and she said she hadn't a clue as they last saw one another when they were fourteen.'

'Any other friends she spoke about, from school, youth clubs or suchlike? I'm assuming you two didn't meet until Rosie became a model?'

'That's right. We met at an agency in Knightsbridge. She was seventeen, I was eighteen, but I'd been modelling for two years by then. I kind of took her under my wing. She didn't appear to have any real friends. But I think her parents were very picky about who she mixed with.'

'Did she tell you that? Or did you guess because of stuff she said?'

'Both, really. Back at the start of her modelling career, her dad used to drive her to jobs and wait for her. She had to escape him to go on a date or just down the pub after work. So when we were working together, or nearby, I'd tell her dad I'd bring her home. When he found out my family were rather grand, with a country seat in the Midlands, he suddenly seemed okay about her being with me.'

'Mr Lark's a snob, then?'

Mabel giggled. 'He certainly is. The kind of self-made bloke who spends his whole life trying to act like he was born with a silver spoon in his mouth. Mrs Lark was even worse – I once saw she was reading one of those books on etiquette. You know the sort, where they teach you never to say "serviette", only "napkin", and don't use words like "lounge" or "toilet".'

Amelia didn't like her being so cutting about her friend's parents. Especially as Rosie had just been killed. 'I didn't notice anything like that about Henry,' she said. 'But, then, I come from a housing estate in White City, and it was so rough there we called the lounge "the front room".'

'I didn't mean to mock,' Mabel said, looking a little embarrassed. 'But this is just between us, right?'

'Anything you say will go no further,' Amelia assured her.

'Well, if you want the truth, Rosie wasn't the angel her parents are claiming. She took speed all the time to keep her weight down, and she often told her parents she was with me when she was off screwing around. She would walk over anyone to get a good assignment. Not me – she knew she wouldn't work again if she crossed me – but everyone else was fair game. She was on the hunt for a rich husband, too, preferably someone in the film or music industry. She wanted to get into films – she did a couple of screen tests, but apparently she hadn't got what it takes.'

'So she might have really pissed someone off then.' Amelia felt a flutter of excitement in her belly. This was better than hearing that Rosie had been perfection.

'Yes, she did piss off a few people, but not enough for

them to kill her. Her dad said you believed there was a connection between the three murdered girls. Well, I can't speak about Lucy, the first one – she sounded saintly – but the description of the other was remarkably like Rosie.'

Amelia looked at Mabel for the longest moment. It dawned on her that what this girl had told her wasn't spite: she had liked Rosie, and as such she wanted her killer found and punished, so she'd decided to tell the truth, even if it put her and her friend in a bad light.

'Thank you for being honest,' Amelia said eventually. 'It's hard to admit a friend isn't quite how others see her.'

'We had a great deal of fun together,' Mabel said, and now her eyes *were* welling up. 'I'll miss her so much, but I wouldn't be helping to find her killer if I pretended she was like a Sunday-school teacher. She was after the main chance. She wanted wealth and to get away from her parents because they suffocated her. But she and I had so many laughs. I loved her company. It's hard for models to make real friends.'

'Really? I always imagined you all lived in a rarefied world of fun, being wined and dined, admired by everyone.'

Mabel shook her head sadly. 'People may tell us we're beautiful, but most of us are insecure. For instance, when I'm asked to do a swimsuit assignment, I feel physically sick because I'm too thin. None of us dares to eat what we like for fear of putting weight on. We're afraid to be seen without our makeup on and our hair perfect. Sometimes I feel I don't know what the real Mabel looks like. I know Rosie felt this too, always on show, perfection expected. It's a strain. She took speed to keep slim, then sleeping pills to come down from the speed. I drink more than I should.'

'I'm so touched that you felt you could open up to me,' Amelia said. 'It's time I went now, though. Can I use your phone to ring the office? I'm not supposed to go anywhere alone since I was attacked.'

'Of course.' Mabel pointed to the white phone on a side table.

Peanut asked no questions but said he'd be there within fifteen minutes.

'Just enough time for one drink,' Mabel said, when Amelia told her that, and before she could refuse, Mabel had disappeared through the door. 'Just a small one,' she called.

'Will you keep in touch?' Mabel asked, as she handed Amelia a glass of wine. It was small, but Mabel's was huge. 'I'd like to get to know you better. Not to talk about Rosie, just to be friends.'

Amelia looked at the girl she'd thought had everything – the looks, money, the right upbringing – but for all that she was still short of a friend. 'I'd like that,' she said, and meant it. 'I'm not on the phone at home but you can contact me at the office.' She handed her a card. 'This wine is lovely.'

*

'I wish you'd drop all this,' Peanut said, as he drove her back to the office. 'Tell Jack you've had enough. He won't pressure you to carry on.'

Amelia looked at Peanut reflectively. She admired, trusted, and liked him. 'Why are you so worried?' she asked. 'I'm touched that you care but, really, what harm can come to me when the police take me to work and bring me home? And there's you too!'

Peanut turned off the main road towards the Thames. He said he wanted to talk to her for a few minutes before he returned to the office. Amelia thought that sounded a bit ominous, but she could hardly insist he drove her straight back.

'You're young and vulnerable, and that worries me,' he said, with a big sigh as he parked by the river. The water had taken on the grey of the sky, and a stiff breeze was whipping up silvery-topped waves. 'I know you have a family, but for reasons I can only guess at you have nothing to do with them. Until you met Max you were always alone, and now, when most girls with a new love would be devoting themselves to him, you're off somewhere else.

'You've immersed yourself in all three of the murdered girls' lives. I swear you've entered their minds to try and solve the mystery of their killer. I find that deeply perturbing, my dear.'

'Don't all would-be journalists get like that with a meaty story?' She laughed.

'Only the obsessive ones,' he said. 'And don't laugh at me, this is serious.'

'How many really good opportunities come our way in a lifetime?' she asked heatedly. 'Two, three? Well, as far as I'm concerned, this is maybe the one and only opportunity for me. Besides, I'm not sure Max is right for me. He's becoming very controlling.'

'Now why doesn't that surprise me?' Peanut shook his head sadly. 'I've never told anyone on the paper this, so please keep it to yourself. But I work as a counsellor in the evenings. And you, my dear, are almost a textbook likely-to-become-abused woman. I may be speaking out of turn, but I suspect your father was a bully – was he?'

'Yes,' Amelia admitted, her face flushing with shame. 'How did you know that?'

'The way you willingly do anything Jack asks, the way you stand back and watch life from the sidelines. There are many clues if you know what to look for.'

'I thought I hid my insecurities well,' she said, in a small voice.

'You do. Most people would never guess anything was amiss, except people like me, who try to help – and, of course, men with a tendency towards controlling. They can sniff it out, like a dog can home in on a piece of meat. I suspect by trying to solve these murders you feel more powerful.'

'I don't,' she said indignantly.

'I know you do. Now if you were learning to play the piano or doing gymnastics, I'd be happy you were throwing yourself into learning something new, but I can't be happy with this. Apart from anything else, the killer is clever. He's targeted these girls, and almost certainly knows everything about them. He'll have done the same with you, Amelia. Don't kid yourself he hasn't. I don't think he intended to kill you the other week – it was a warning for you to back off. But if you persist, he may feel he has to kill you too.'

'You're scaring me now.'

'Good. Maybe you'll take my warning seriously. So, it's back to the office, I think.'

As Peanut stopped in front of the building to let her out, he took her hand. 'I'm sorry if I've made you nervous. That wasn't my intention, only to get you to drop it and leave it to the police.'

Amelia gave him a weak smile. 'I know, and I'm sure you are right. I can't promise to do as I'm told, though.'

13

That evening, Peanut's warning kept coming back to Amelia. She wasn't particularly worried by it: he was just being a bit of an old woman. After all, how would the killer know who she was visiting? He might have been following her the day she went to Kew, but unless he had mounted guard over the house in Bedford Park, he couldn't know she'd been there or that she'd visited Mabel. There was no one around, not when she got there or when she'd left. It was the same when she'd gone to Mabel's. Peanut was just a well-meaning old worry-guts.

Regardless of what he'd said, she had every intention of going out to Richmond tomorrow with Henry and she was also going to see the vicar he'd told her about.

Yet she was astounded that Peanut had known her father was a bully, and that she might be a target for similar men. She didn't think for one moment that Max would ever hit her: all she had to do was be firm with him when he did that controlling thing. She was already sorry they'd parted with bad feeling. She wished she was on the phone so she could ring him at his hotel and hear his voice. Perhaps on reflection he was talking sense about buying a house. Now that she thought about it, imagine anyone wanting to stay in a room like hers, sharing a bathroom and clearing up after other people, when they could have a house of their own.

Was she really intending to spend the rest of her life being afraid to take a step outside her familiar world?

With all these conflicting thoughts spinning in her head, she felt on edge and lonely. She made herself some cheese on toast, checked that her policeman was still outside, then undressed and got into bed. Sleeping had always been her way of dealing with problems. It didn't solve them, of course, but sometimes solutions appeared in the morning, and even if there was no solution, nothing ever looked so bad by day.

It was bright sunshine when she woke the next morning at seven. She remembered then that she didn't have to go into the office, as Jack had said Sam the policeman could take her to Chiswick at ten thirty. Jack was being amazingly kind to her, but maybe it was just a ploy to make sure she brought any good stories straight to him.

Making tea and taking it back to bed while the gas fire warmed the room was a real treat. She heard the geyser in the bathroom popping as someone turned it on to run a bath. That meant the bathroom wouldn't be quite as icy as usual, which was good. She wondered what it was like to live in a centrally heated house, to take a warm dry towel from a heated rail and be able to wallow in a bath without turning blue with cold.

Maybe it *was* time to go along with Max's plan. But

did that mean they'd get married? He hadn't made that clear. If they didn't, what security would she have? At least this place was hers. He couldn't make her leave it if they fell out. But maybe he'd taken yesterday's row seriously when she'd told him to get out. What if he didn't come back?

Aware she was making problems for herself by thinking such negative thoughts, she picked up her book by Toni Morrison, *The Bluest Eye*. As she read that the black narrator of the book thought she could be beautiful only if she had blue eyes like white people, it crossed her mind that she had a similar problem. She imagined she'd be okay if she'd been born into a different family.

What did a girl have to do to escape what she'd been born into? Was it even possible to escape your roots, or were they just that, roots that went down so far you could never pull them up?

She'd learned to speak better and dress well, had mastered shorthand and typing, and could fool most people into believing she came from a middle-class home, but when she was alone she was just Amelia White from White City, the girl who had lived at number eight, the most squalid house in Bradley Close.

'Enough of that,' she told herself aloud, as she got out of bed. 'You can be anyone you want to be. Stop wallowing in negativity.'

She switched on her radio and 'I'll Be There' by the Jackson Five was playing. She sang along as she got out the jeans and an Arran sweater she intended to wear that day. She wasn't allowed to wear jeans to work, but she didn't think walking in Richmond Park counted as work.

Aware she could be out in the cold all day, she pulled out the embroidered Afghan coat she'd bought in Kensington indoor market a few years ago. She'd felt a million dollars in it back then, the ultimate coat for a 'groovy chick', as the salesman had said.

It was looking a bit bedraggled now, but it was very warm. With her long red boots, red bobble hat, matching scarf and gloves, she felt she looked good.

'You look nice,' Sam said, when he called to pick her up. 'I always wanted a coat like that, but it wasn't quite the right image for a policeman.'

Amelia laughed. 'People would find a hippie policeman too strange.'

As they pulled out of Godolphin Road, she asked him if there had been any developments in the case.

'We've had two crackpots confessing to be the murderer.' Sam grinned. 'One lives in Manchester and couldn't even give a London address where he'd been staying when he was supposed to have killed the girls. It soon became clear he'd never even been to London. The other bloke was a Londoner, but he said he'd strangled the girls rather than stabbed them. Why on earth would anyone want to admit to a murder they didn't do?'

'For five minutes of fame perhaps.' She laughed. 'Unless they have a yen to live in prison.'

'People have come forward about seeing someone in Ravenscourt Park at the time of Carol's death. But what they saw is the same as the couple who helped you when you were attacked. Tall, wearing dark clothes. So that's not much help.'

'It seems completely impossible for anyone to kill three people in a built-up area and not be seen.'

'I know, but the way the bodies were left, with no attempt to conceal them, suggests the killer is very aware of how little notice people take of one another in London. He seems to realize that you can be almost invisible.'

'Could that be his problem? That no one has ever taken any notice of him? Someone so ordinary that he blends in with his surroundings?'

'That has to be a cast of thousands, if not millions,' Sam said. 'But it might account for why he picked those three girls. None of them would ever have been overlooked.'

'So maybe it's a kind of sex thing. They're the sort of girls he'd like to go out with, but they wouldn't look twice at him.'

'Possibly.' Sam turned into Bedford Park. 'How are you getting on with Mr Lark?'

'To be honest, I'm not quite sure what he wants of me. He asked me to go for a walk with him so we could talk, but I think we've done all the talking now. He hasn't told me one thing that I could claim was a clue.'

'Talking does help grieving people,' Sam said, as he pulled up in front of the Larks' house. 'He may suddenly remember something relevant, so hang on in there. I'll see you tomorrow, I expect.'

Amelia turned to look at him as she got out. 'It's really good seeing you every day,' she said impulsively. She liked the way he looked: take away his uniform, let his fair hair grow a bit longer, and he could have been a Beach Boy in summer. But it wasn't just his looks: she liked the way he spoke to her, as if she was important, and really listened. 'You've made me feel safer.'

'I like seeing you every day,' he said, looking at her intently. 'I want things to get better for you too.'

He drove away then, leaving her wondering if he meant better with Max, this case being solved, or if he could possibly be thinking of them dating.

She shook herself mentally, wondering what had made her think he could be interested in her that way.

'It's a shame we haven't got a dog,' Amelia said, after they'd been walking for about an hour in Richmond Park. 'This place is enormous – you wouldn't know you were so close to a huge city.'

She was trying to get Henry to talk. He seemed to be wrapped up in his thoughts and it was making her feel uncomfortable. Because it was a weekday and very cold, there were few people about. The earlier sun had disappeared behind thick grey cloud, and everything looked grey. Leafless trees, scrubby grass, not a scrap of colour anywhere, except her red hat, scarf and boots. She wished he'd call it a day and want to go home.

'What did Mabel tell you?' he asked suddenly.

'Just how she met Rosie mostly. I asked if they'd had any people hanging about watching them while they were working. Anyone who made them feel nervy.'

'She didn't work very often with Mabel,' he said sharply.

'Yes, I realized that,' Amelia said. 'But they did talk about their work, and therefore creepy people hanging around would've come up. She said Rosie was good at deflecting that kind of attention.'

'What did she mean by that?' His tone was now aggressive.

'That she had a knack of putting people in their place without being rude.' She thought Henry could do with a lesson in that himself.

'Did she tell you if Rosie had any boyfriends?'

'She didn't say. I took it to mean there was no one special enough to mention. But surely you would know if there had been someone.'

'Girls don't always tell their parents such things. Do you think Mabel told you everything?'

'I believe she told me everything that might have some bearing on what happened to Rosie. I wouldn't expect a real friend to start spilling the beans about everything they shared.'

They walked a little further in silence. She felt he was brooding on her last statement. They came to a little copse of trees on a mound, but instead of walking round it he went straight towards it.

'When Rosie was little, she used to run into these odd little copses to hide,' he said, as an explanation. 'I reckon she imagined we'd think she'd completely disappeared.'

'This one is the kind of place I would've made a camp in,' Amelia said. They were right on the edge of it now and the trees were so close together it would be hard to go right through it.

'I'm sorry if I've been a bit dour today,' Henry said, turning to her and putting his hands on her shoulders. 'You've been so understanding about what I'm going through.'

When he drew her to him, she didn't back away. She thought he was going to give her a fatherly hug. But suddenly his arms were locked around her, his mouth was on hers, his tongue forcing its way into her mouth, like a fat, disgusting slug.

She tried to wriggle from his embrace, but he was holding both her arms tightly to her sides and, even more frightening, he was nudging her backwards into the copse of trees. She wrenched her mouth from his, screamed and head-butted him, but he pushed her back against a tree and once again forced his lips over hers. His breath was heavy with excitement, but when he let go of one of her arms to push his hand into her crotch, her hand flew up to rake at his face with her nails, and at the same time she kneed him in the groin.

The surprise made him stagger back, and she took the chance to flee, tearing down the mound onto the path they'd walked along to get there. She had never been a fast runner, and her thick coat held her back, but terror drove her on at a speed she might have been proud of back at school.

All at once she understood why Peanut had looked concerned when he'd taken her to meet Henry Lark. He clearly had a sixth sense that the man wasn't safe with young women.

She could hear Henry shouting at her, but she didn't turn to look, just kept on running till she felt her heart would burst. She kept hoping to see someone to help her, but the park was deserted.

After she felt she'd covered around a quarter of the distance to where Henry had parked his car, she stopped to look back. He was a long way behind, bent over as if he had a stitch.

'I hope you die of a heart attack,' she muttered, then began to run again.

About ten minutes on, she saw two people with a large black dog coming up a path to her left and realized she didn't need to get back to the car park. With another glance behind her, she saw she'd passed trees that blocked her view of him, and vice versa. But though it was tempting to run to the people coming towards her and seek their assistance, it was too complicated a story to blurt out to strangers, and Henry might catch up with her.

She ran past the couple with the dog, reached the trees at the edge of the park and found a road behind them. Like most roads that overlooked parks, the detached houses looked like they belonged to rich, successful people. They had manicured hedges and, doubtless, in the spring and summer their gardens would be beautiful. Having no idea where she was, or which direction to go in, she decided the only course of action open to her was to knock on a door, and ask if she could use the telephone to ring the police. It was fortunate that they had given her a card with a number to ring in an emergency. She took it out of her shoulder bag and went up the garden path to the nearest house.

It was almost half an hour before the police arrived. Janet Grey, the owner of the house, had taken over. Knowing nothing more than Amelia's name and that she'd been attacked in the park, she took the card from her hand, and rang the police.

Her crisp, rather plummy voice, her beautiful home, which smelt of a cake baking, and her obvious concern reassured Amelia. She had been completely out of breath when she knocked on the door, holding her side as she had a stitch. The effort of making herself understood suddenly brought what had happened into sharp focus. She broke down in tears. Mrs Grey hugged her, told her she was safe now, and as soon as she'd got her breath back, she'd make her some tea.

The two policemen who came for her were not among the ones Amelia already knew. Sergeant Roper was in his fifties, a tall, stern-looking man, and PC Blunt, who had accompanied him, was perhaps thirty with flame-red hair and a freckled, kindly face.

It was clear they knew exactly who Amelia was, and Sergeant Roper said he would prefer to take her statement about the incident at the police station.

'She's very shaken,' Mrs Grey told them. 'I understand you need to interview her but let her finish her tea and gather herself first.'

Later that day, Amelia looked back on Janet Grey and her home as a model of how she'd like to be and to live. She was perhaps forty, and elegant, wearing a pale pink twinset and a toning pleated skirt. Her shoulder-length hair was light brown, very well cut and shiny. Her house radiated warmth, not just from the central heating but from her, and though Amelia had only seen the kitchen, she had loved the order: the red poppies on the curtains, a tea-cosy like a thatched cottage, and a row of bright green frogs looking down from the dresser.

But before she'd got to the point where she could take stock of the day, she'd had to deal with the questioning, the embarrassment of having to explain exactly what Henry Lark had done. Had she encouraged him to think she wanted him? Why did she agree to go to Richmond Park with him?

Sergeant Roper didn't mince his words with her

either. 'It seems to me, young lady, that you see your-self as a private eye! I know you're a journalist and that you found the body of Lucy Whelan, but that should've been the end of your involvement. Yet you went ahead and wormed your way into the families and friends of all three girls. Then you were attacked in Ravenscourt Park, perhaps by the man the press is calling the Creeper. Now you've allegedly been assaulted by the father of the third victim. You have got to see today's incident as the end of your delv-ing into this business. Put it aside and get on with your life.'

'What do you mean "allegedly been assaulted"? That sounds as if I made it up. Go and see him – I scratched his face. That's proof, isn't it?'

'As we speak, one of my officers is interviewing him.'

'He's a pervert. His daughter was killed, and he tried to sexually assault the one person who was trying to help by getting information to find the killer.'

'Don't you see that by agreeing to go to Richmond Park with him, you led him to believe you were inter-ested in him that way? When people are in a state of grief, they often reach out to someone for comfort, especially if they believe that person wants them.'

Amelia felt as if she might explode. 'He said he wanted to talk to me about Rosie out of doors. It never crossed my mind that he would do something like that. What is it with men? We show concern for you, listen to your problems and somehow that translates to you that we fancy you! Don't words like empathy, sympathy, concern or caring exist in the male world?'

The sergeant folded his arms and looked even sterner. 'I believe your boss is waiting for you upstairs. Go home, Amelia. I know you mean well but let the professionals do the digging and the crime-solving.'

Amelia leaped to her feet, sickened by his attitude. 'Well, good luck with that. I found a really worthwhile clue that links the three girls, but I'll sit back now and see how long it takes you to find it for yourselves.'

She slammed the door of the interview room behind her and hoped she'd managed to rile him.

Jack was waiting in the reception area. 'Bloody hell, Amelia! I got a fright when my pal down here rang and said you'd been brought in. He said you'd been assaulted. Is that right?'

'I'll tell you about it in the car,' she said, anxious to get out of the building.

'So was I stupid to agree to go to the park today? Did it sound to you like he was planning to seduce me?' she finished, as they drove to the office. Jack hadn't said a word as she'd told him what happened.

'If he thought a park in midwinter was a good place for seduction, the man's obviously lost his mind,' Jack replied, with a hint of laughter in his voice. 'But, then, I wouldn't expect a man who'd just lost his daughter to try it on with another girl of the same age. So, no, I don't think you were stupid, just being kind.'

'Thank you for that,' Amelia replied. 'The sergeant made me feel really cheap. But I've got something I didn't tell him about. Look!' She took the photograph out of her shoulder bag to show Jack.

Jack studied it carefully. Then he grinned, as if he'd finally worked out what he was looking at. 'All three girls together! God almighty, Amelia, that's dynamite.'

'I think the common denominator is the Girl Guides,' she said, and told him the name of the church in Chiswick to which Rosie's company was attached.

'I don't suppose I can write this up in the paper, though, it being part of an ongoing police investigation. But if he's charged with assaulting you, we can do something about that.'

'Oh. Jack.' She sighed. 'You know he'll never be prosecuted. I went with him to the park of my own free will, he'll say I led him on, and there are no witnesses to what he did. The most damage I could do to him is write what Mabel told me, about Rosie being like Carol in character, a gold-digger who used men. But let's see what the Guide mistress has to say about Rosie, and find out where and when that camp was. Then I'll plan what to do. Only I doubt I could really be so cruel to Rosie or her poor mum.'

'You aren't doing anything more now, sweetheart. It's all too dangerous,' he said. 'I'll find the Guide mistress and show her the picture. As for that weasel Lark, I'll let him know in no uncertain terms what I think of him. He's a disgrace. No wonder his wife has gone off to stay with her sister. I bet she knows what he is. Now let's get you home. You're white and shaky.'

'I haven't done any work for days.' She sighed. 'The others must think I'm your pet, or worse.'

'They don't. They all understand what's been going on and, believe it or not, they're rooting for you. So it's home for you. Put your feet up and forget about all this.'

14

Jack dropped Amelia at her house, warning her to stay in and not answer the door because her police guard wouldn't be along until six o'clock.

'How long are they going to keep this up?' she asked, not even opening the car door – she felt so apathetic. After the day's events she wanted normality again. She didn't even feel as if she cared who had murdered the girls.

'They'll keep it up until they think it's safe to leave you. I expect that means when they've got the Creeper in custody. What time will your boyfriend be back?'

'I don't know that he will be.' She shrugged. 'He went to Rugby for a couple of days, and as we had a row before he left, maybe he won't come back to me at all.'

'I don't think he can be that stupid,' Jack said gallantly. 'A lovely bright spark like you? They don't come along that often.'

Amelia turned to Jack. She had grown fond of him and his bulldog appearance, especially since she'd found he had a heart after all. 'I don't feel like a bright spark.'

'You will, once you've abandoned all this detective stuff,' he said. 'That bloke Lark needs a good kicking.

I'm going round there tomorrow to put the fear of God into him.'

Amelia's smile was a washed-out one. 'Well, if you do, tell him Rosie wasn't the angel he painted. She and Carol were tarred with the same brush. Not that I think you would tell him that. For all your bluff and bluster you'd be remembering he loved his daughter.'

'I'll also be remembering what he did to you, and that might get the better of me. Now clear off, sweetheart. Have an early night and I'll see you tomorrow.'

On the dot of six Amelia heard a car draw up and saw that Sam was taking the first shift. She was hungry but didn't have anything in the cupboard that she wanted to eat. She sat down and switched on the television to listen to the news. That was depressing: first some frightening footage of the carnage at Ibrox Park in Glasgow back in January when sixty-six people were killed in a crush at the football ground. Then it went on to the Vietnam war, showing women and children running from napalm fire. They said the American soldiers were going to be pulled out of Vietnam soon, and Amelia wondered why they had stuck their noses into another country's business in the first place. The news moved on to various atrocities in Belfast. She couldn't take any more misery so she switched it off.

The front doorbell rang and, as always, Amelia looked out of the window. Sam was standing on the pavement gazing up at her. He made a gesture with his hand, which she understood to be a request for tea.

'I'll go away if you're busy or your boyfriend's here,' he said, when she'd gone downstairs and opened the door to him. 'But I heard at the station what happened today, and I was worried about you.'

'I'm not busy, come in,' she said, feeling it was the first good thing to happen that day. She walked up the stairs ahead of him. 'I'm fine, just a bit fed up.'

Once he was sitting down by the fire and the kettle was boiling, Amelia said she was most upset at her powerlessness. 'Nothing will be done to Mr Lark, not even a rap on the knuckles. How dare he think he can treat me that way?'

'Several of us saw his clawed face – you left your mark good and deep there, Amelia. We all think he should be charged with assault, and if you insist on it, he will be. But, as you know, cases like this are usually more damaging for the victim. He'll get all the sympathy with his daughter murdered and his wife in a state of shock. His defence lawyer will portray you as a floozy on the make, or even worse.'

'I'm aware of all that,' she said sadly. 'It's just so unfair when I was only trying to help him.'

'He's done this before. I unearthed an old offence. Same thing, took a young lady to a park after a lunch together and assaulted her. That was four years ago, and he wasn't charged because the girl had drunk quite a lot at the lunch, and it was believed she was trying to entrap him in some way.'

'Only a man would think like that,' Amelia said.

'Well, probably not you, Sam, but the old-school judges, barristers and the like.'

'I showed it to Sarge, and you might be surprised to hear he was sympathetic to you. He said no woman would claw someone so badly unless they were really fighting to get free. But Lark is a powerful man. He'd have a top-class lawyer, and all you'd get is public humiliation.'

The door of the flat burst open then and, to Amelia's astonishment, there was Max. 'So, what's this? Personal protection?' he said sarcastically.

Amelia could see he was angry, his face flushed and tight-lipped. 'Sam's just arrived for his shift and came up to see how I was. I was attacked earlier in the day.'

'Sam is it now? Very cosy,' Max said. 'And where were the police while you were attacked?'

'Please stop this, Max,' she said quietly. 'It's been a distressing enough day already.'

'I'll go back to the car,' Sam said, getting to his feet. 'Just to set the record straight, I've been here for five minutes. I heard back at the station what had happened to Amelia and I came to ask her how she was before starting my shift. You should be concerned about her, not angry with me.'

He left then.

Max shut the door behind Sam and, leaning back on it, folded his arms and looked at her thoughtfully. 'You're a liar. There's not a mark on you. Wanted some attention, did you?'

Amelia was scared now. His voice was harsh and his eyes so cold. How could he suddenly be like this?

'I am not a liar and get out, please, Max. I won't be spoken to like that,' she said, trying not to show she feared him. 'I would've told you exactly what happened, but not now when you are being so nasty. Just go.'

He leaped forward and punched her in the face so hard her neck cricked with the force of the blow. 'I know what you are, Amelia bloody White. You play the poor little downtrodden girl with a brute of a father, but it's just a big act for attention.'

'I've never played anything, never even told you about my family,' she said, and although she was trying hard not to cry, the tears came anyway.

'You've got what you wanted, haven't you? People worrying about you, making a fuss of you and, best of all, the gullible young pig to dance attendance on you.' He took a step forward and punched her in the stomach, winding her.

Amelia screamed then, even though she was bent over in pain. 'Stop it,' she cried. 'You said you loved me! Is this how you treat someone you love?'

He grabbed her hair with his left hand and pulled her upright. 'Love you? I despise you.' He slammed his right fist into her cheek. 'I'll make you so ugly no man will want you.'

'Oh no you won't.' Sam's voice came from behind Max. He caught hold of his shoulder and spun him round, punching his face. As Max fell to the floor, Sam leaped to him, rolled him over and clamped handcuffs on him. As a last gesture of dominance he used his foot to bang Max's face on the floor. 'That's where you belong, on the floor, lower than dog shit.'

Amelia could only look on open-mouthed. She remembered she had given the police a spare set of keys, but she had imagined that Sam would be sitting in the car with his radio on, deaf to any cries.

'Max Creedy, I am arresting you for the assault on Amelia White, and for the murders of Lucy Whelan, Carol Meadows and Rosie Lark. You have the right to remain silent, but anything you do say and rely on later in court may be used against you.'

'Murders!' Amelia repeated, thinking she must have imagined it. 'Surely not. No, Sam! He might be a bully but he couldn't have murdered those girls.' She was shaking from Max's attack, and in pain, yet she still felt she had to defend him.

Sam looked round at her. 'Sit down, Amelia. I'll come back to you as soon as he's been taken away.'

'I didn't murder anyone,' Max bellowed out. 'She's a liar if she told you that.'

Sam caught hold of Max's arm and hauled him to his feet, then pushed him towards the door.

At that point Amelia heard a police siren and, looking out of the window, she saw another police car pulling up with two officers inside it.

She watched from the window as Sam handed Max over to them. They put him in the back of the car and drove off. Sam locked his car and started to walk back towards the house.

The pain in her face and stomach was awful. She had just got to the mirror over the mantelpiece when Sam came in.

'How did you get back here so fast when he told you to go?' she asked, looking in horror at her face, which was already turning purple, her eye beginning to close.

'I could see in his face he was going to hurt you,' Sam said. 'So I called it in just in case. I didn't even get into the car – I was downstairs with the door open. When you screamed, I ran up.'

'But you arrested him for the murders! Please tell me I haven't been in here with a killer!'

'We suspected him right back at the start of this,' he said. 'There was something about the way he was so close when you found Lucy. He called the police, then made a move on you. But there wasn't any evidence to charge him. Anyway, never mind that now, let me look at your poor face. Have you got any ice in your fridge?'

He made her sit down on a chair by the table, opened the ice box in the fridge and tipped the contents of one of the ice trays onto a clean tea-towel and then held it to her cheek. 'Any loose teeth?' he asked.

'I don't think so,' she said. The ice was soothing but she felt suddenly dizzy.

The next thing she knew she was on the floor, Sam

bending over her. 'You fainted,' he said. 'Good job I was right there. Now let's get you up onto your bed.'

'He punched me in the stomach too,' she said, in little more than a whisper. 'It hurts!'

Once on the bed he got her to hold the ice pack against her face, then lifted her sweater and unfastened the waist of her jeans.

'You're going to have a nasty bruise there, too, tomorrow,' he said. His hand felt cool and soothing on her stomach. 'But to be on the safe side, and check there are no internal injuries, I'd better take you to Casualty to get you looked at.'

'Why did he pretend to love me if he's a killer?' she asked, tears running down her cheeks.

'Amelia, he may turn out not to be a killer, but he isn't what you think. He isn't an accountant, and he hasn't got family in Devon.'

Amelia looked at Sam in horror. 'He's been lying to me? Didn't he ever love me?'

Sam smoothed her hair back from her face. 'I don't want to say anything that will upset you more, but I don't think people who kill have brains that work in the same way as the rest of us. He may have felt at the start it would be wise to keep you close as you were so interested in Lucy Whelan. Maybe he did fall in love with you, Amelia – you're a lovely girl.'

'How could he love me and treat me like this?' she asked, touching her swollen eye.

'I expect the violence towards you came on as it

seemed to him the web was closing around him. You must tell me everything he told you about himself, but I think we'll find a good part of it was lies.'

'And he called *me* a liar! I haven't told him any lies, not one.' She turned the good side of her face towards the wall, still holding the ice pack to her cheek, and sobbed.

'Don't cry, Amelia. I'm sorry he turned out bad, but you're young and gorgeous, even if that isn't the kind of thing a police officer is supposed to say, and you'll meet someone better, someone you deserve.'

Three hours later they were back after a trip to the police station to make a statement and have her bruises photographed, then to Casualty where an X-ray proved she had no internal injuries.

Sam bought some Chinese food on the way home – he said it wouldn't need much chewing – and came in to share it with her.

Amelia was calm now. What a fool she'd been to trust Max so implicitly, she thought. His real name wasn't even Max. It was Brian Caulderhill and he came from Southend. She still didn't know whether he was really into amateur dramatics, could sing or rock-climb, but the chances were that he had made all that up too.

'But why did he go on about buying a house?' Amelia asked Sam, who was dishing up. 'He would've been found out immediately.'

'I suspect his plan was to get the house in your name.

While we were at the hospital, they did a search in his room two doors down. They found a lot of money, acquired, no doubt, through something illegal. I got a message on my radio while you were being X-rayed. They'll be looking into that now. I think perhaps his plan was to make a big gesture by giving you the house he wanted.'

'That doesn't make sense!' she said, bewildered.

'It does, if you think about it. By putting it in your name, he avoids any awkward questions from the mortgage company. You feel secure, and grateful you've got a lovely home. But a little further down the line when things turn nasty, as they inevitably would, I expect he intended to order you to make the house over to him, which you would do.'

'But why? It sounds pointless, unless of course he just wanted to freak me out.'

'Not pointless at all. Think about it! What he's done is launder the money he got illegally. He had you sussed, Amelia. You aren't the kind to cling to a house to spite him, or for your own security. He's a devious man, and extremely jealous, and that is a recipe for a dangerous person.'

'But I didn't sense any of this when I first met him.'

Amelia had laid the table, and Sam brought over the plates of food. 'In the police we hear what you've just said all the time from women who have been beaten or conned. They say how charming, kind and generous he was. But I suppose men like that can only keep a lid on

226

their explosive side for a time. Then, whoosh, something triggers it. I suspect he imagined your enthusiasm for finding a connection between the three murdered girls would fade quickly. When it didn't, and you were talking to more powerful, intelligent people, like the woman in Kew and Henry Lark, he was afraid they'd bring up something that would alert you to him.'

'But Henry Lark turned out to be a snake too.'

Sam's mouth was full of food so he waited until he'd swallowed it to reply. 'You'd be amazed how many of those we find in any investigation.'

'This room seemed so safe and secure once,' she said sadly. 'I don't think it ever will again.'

'I'll be outside all night,' he said. 'No one will get past me.'

'But you can't be here for ever.'

He smiled, his lovely blue eyes twinkling. 'No, I suppose not, as much as I'd like to be.'

Amelia was touched by what he'd said, but unable to react.

'Not the right time to be admitting my feelings?' he said, the twinkle leaving his eyes. 'I should know better, especially as we're forbidden to have relationships with witnesses or victims. But when this is all over might there be any chance?'

Part of Amelia's head and heart wanted to say, 'Yes, every chance,' but she'd shown such a serious misjudgement with Max she was ashamed.

'I can't possibly say, Sam, not now.'

'I understand,' he said. 'But I'll leave you my address at the section house, and even if you just want a chat with a friend, drop me a line. But for now, let's finish up this food.'

At nearly eleven Sam said he must get into the car for the rest of his shift. Amelia wanted to beg him to stay, and not just for his company. Had it not been that her face and stomach felt as if they were on fire, it would have been a lovely evening. Sam hadn't sulked when she couldn't agree there might be a chance for him. He had made her laugh, and she wanted him to stay purely because she couldn't bear the thought of him being out in the cold.

'I'm due to be relieved at two,' he said, as he left. 'So don't panic if you hear me drive away. Someone else will be out there. Mind you, if Max is the killer there's nothing more to worry about.'

Amelia got into bed. The house felt too quiet, and she was afraid to turn off her bedside light for fear that all the events of the day would crowd in on her. Henry grabbing her had been bad enough: she'd trusted him, never thinking for a second that he wanted anything more than to talk to her.

But Max! She'd been with him for months, totally in his thrall, believing everything he said, trusting him, loving him. Now she realized she didn't know him at all – even his real name: Brian, not Max. It was hard to believe anyone could be as misguided as she had been. Why was she such a bad judge of character?

She thought of their lovemaking in this bed, which still had his smell on the sheets and pillow. How could he have been so loving and passionate if he'd felt nothing for her?

15

PC Sam Hamilton lowered the back of his car seat a little and got comfortable. Three hours of waiting and watching were incredibly tedious, but it was bearable because he was protecting someone he liked. On several previous witness-protection jobs he'd been guarding people he despised and then it had seemed a thankless task.

He had liked Amelia just from reading her article about Lucy Whelan. He sensed her deep understanding of people and her powers of observation. When he had met her in the flesh he was astounded to find she was younger than him, pretty and a bit shy. He had expected her to be the exact opposite.

Each time he'd talked to her, she'd revealed more of herself, albeit accidentally as she said little about her life. He guessed at a miserable childhood, with a bullying father, and a couple of police checks proved him right. He even knew that social services had found that room for her, and why. But he didn't look any further than that because by then he liked her so much he felt bad probing into her past as if she were a criminal.

She was plucky, caring, warm and intelligent. She'd made her bedsitter a bright, interesting haven, which he loved. He could imagine how grim it had been when she moved in. Since joining the police force, he'd seen so many horrible bedsitters and flats that he was glad he lived in the section house. He had been saving for a deposit on a house for the last two years: once he had passed the sergeants' exam and knew where he would be stationed, he would look for a place of his own.

When he told his father his plan, he laughed at him. 'A mortgage is a millstone around your neck,' he claimed.

Sam could understand his father's reasoning. After the war he'd been demobbed from the army to come home to a damp, cold basement flat in Lewisham. The only amenities it could boast were an indoor lavatory and all the windows still in place: most of the others in the street had been blown out by bombs and covered with timber or cardboard. Glass was hard to come by.

Sam was four that year, his baby brother Tom two, and their mother was pregnant again. The only work open to his father, Sydney, was labouring on a building site. They lived hand-to-mouth, and Sam remembered in the bitter winter of 1947 walking with his father and the old pram out to Eltham to gather wood for their fire.

It was a friend Sydney had made in the army who led him into the licensed trade, first as a barman in a pub the man owned in Lewisham. He worked there four evenings a week, which helped the family budget. A year later he was offered the job of manager at a bigger pub on Lewisham High Street, which came with living accommodation.

Sam remembered his parents' excitement at leaving the flat. The premises above the pub had a proper bathroom, three bedrooms, and were close to a school in Rushey Green. And his mother would be able to work in the bar in the evenings when the children were in bed.

It was a good move for all of them. Sam recalled how happy his father was to have a job he enjoyed and his family close to him. Sam liked his school, and a year later Tom was there too. Later Ellen, their baby sister, would join them. Ladywell swimming baths was close by, plus the library and Lewisham Hospital. Even more pleasing to Sam and Tom, Mountsfield Park was just a short walk away.

Sam could think of nothing about his childhood that was bad. He liked being in bed and hearing his father's booming voice wafting up the stairs from the bar, along with the chink of glasses, cigarette smoke and the smell of beer. To him it was a somewhat mysterious masculine world, and his father was like the ringmaster controlling everything.

He also loved seeing his mother all dressed up to work downstairs. He sensed how glad she was to have some laughs and conversation with other adults. After school it was good to be allowed a glass of lemonade and a packet of crisps to tide him over till teatime. His school friends thought he was lucky to live over a pub.

He didn't pass his eleven plus, but he still did well at his secondary school, made good friends and excelled at athletics and football. He was almost sixteen when he announced he wanted to be a policeman.

His father was against it. 'Policemen never have any friends,' he said. 'Join me in the licensed trade, and one day you'll get a pub of your own.'

Sam took his O levels and said no more about the police because his father was offered a new pub to run in Staines, near the river. It had a far more spacious and comfortable flat above it, and a garden. Tom, Ellen and his mother were all delighted with it. Sam liked it too, and he was accepted at a college in Kingston to study for A levels.

They had been at the Waterman for just six months when his mother was diagnosed with cervical cancer. Without symptoms, she was diagnosed too late and died after just four months.

Sam was glad they'd made the move to Staines, because at least for the last year of his mother's life she'd had central heating and an attractive home. Just before she died, she told him to ignore what his father had said and join the police force. 'I'm just sad I won't see you in uniform,' she added. He was amazed she'd remembered that had been, still was, his dream – he'd kept it quiet since that talk with his father.

He still missed his mum so much, the way she always listened properly and gave sound advice, how she loved to make people comfortable, remembered everyone's favourite meals and was never late. When he went back to the pub now to see Sydney he thought he could still smell Blue Grass, her perfume, and he remembered that just after she died he'd put some on a handkerchief and kept it under his pillow to smell it at night.

Tom was a stockbroker in the City and shared a flat with a colleague. Ellen was a state-registered nurse and planned to marry next year. Sydney had a new wife, Susie, who was ten years younger than him, an attractive redhead with a bubbly personality. She made no attempt to be a new mother to Sam and his siblings, but took a keen interest in the three of them. Sam was pleased to see his father happy again; he'd known how hard he'd taken Judy's death, and how he'd struggled to take care of Tom and Ellen, as well as run the pub.

There was no doubt he'd done an excellent job, and he continued to be a loving and helpful father. He didn't grumble or tease Sam when he joined the force, and said he was proud of him. He encouraged Tom and Ellen in their chosen fields too, and always found time for them all when they visited.

Sydney had been wrong, of course, about a mortgage being a millstone around the neck, but he was right about most things, and he was the best of fathers.

So what would Sydney suggest to entice Amelia? Sam smiled to himself at the thought. His dad was a bit of a caveman where women were concerned. His mum would have had more sensitive ideas, though. He could almost hear her saying, 'Don't be too soppy. Women don't like that. Just state your case, then wait to see how she reacts.'

Max attacking Amelia would make her distrust men again, he knew that. And if they couldn't find enough evidence to charge him with murder, he'd be out on the streets again in twenty-four hours, almost certainly knocking on her door. Might she fall for a grovelling apology? Possibly. Women often did.

Sam was determined to be there for her, though. After all, 'Faint heart never won fair lady.'

'What on earth!' Jack exclaimed, when Amelia arrived at work the next morning. Her right eye was almost completely closed, her cheek purple and her lip swollen.

All the staff looked up at her, their faces alight with interest.

'Can we talk in private?' Amelia said, aware she had to tell Jack the truth.

'Sure,' he said, and walked into his office, leaving her to follow. 'You didn't have that when I left you yesterday, so I'm assuming either Lark turned up at your place or it was your boyfriend.'

'Max . . . or should I say Brian? He even lied about his name,' she admitted, then went on to explain how it had come about, adding that Sam had come in to help and arrested him.

'Stone the bloody crows!' Jack exclaimed gleefully. 'They suspect him of being the Creeper?'

'Yes. But however horrible he was to me, I don't

believe that of him. And we can't put any of that in the paper until he's been charged.'

Jack pulled a disappointed face. 'We can say, "A man in his late twenties is helping the police with their enquiries." But when they charge him with your assault, we can add he's also a person of interest in the Creeper case.'

'You aren't going to mention my name,' she said. 'Any neighbours who saw him being taken away will be on the jungle drums immediately and half of West London will know in a few hours.'

'They'll look at your face and talk anyway.'

'I'm sick of all this, Jack,' she said. 'My face is sore, so's my stomach, I feel like I'm living in a goldfish bowl, and I'm hurting about Max. I really thought he was The One. What if he is the Creeper? What sort of gullible fool does that make me?'

She was surprised when Jack put his arms around her to hug her. It was uncharacteristic, but nice. But, then, it seemed everyone in her life was behaving out of character right now.

'You, my girl, must take it easy. I'd send you home on full pay until that black eye goes, but under the circumstances that would be a bad idea. You'd be lonely and cut off. So, unless you've got some friends or relations you can go and stay with, you'd better sit at your desk and sell advertising space. Something you do very well, I might add.'

'I haven't got anyone to stay with,' she said, and at

the thought of how pathetic that made her sound, she began to cry.

'Sit down in that chair,' he said, pointing to the comfortable seat by the window. 'You can bunk down in here for now, read a magazine or a paper, have a cup of tea, and try to relax a bit. I'm going to see Henry Lark.'

After a few minutes, Amelia pulled herself together. It wouldn't do to let the other staff think she had special privileges. Making her way to her desk, everyone showed concern for her. She hadn't realized that her colleagues, whom she'd always thought looked down on her – at least until she'd written the article about Lucy Whelan – were so kind.

She forced herself to laugh about her black eye. 'Wrong place, wrong time, wrong man,' she said. 'Anyway, it's back to work now, but thank you.'

Oddly Amelia had her best day ever selling advertising space. Maybe a black eye and a sore tummy were good for something. Also, being busy and involved stopped her thinking about what might be happening to Max at the police station.

Jack came in at half past four. He signalled for her to come into his office; she hoped he wasn't drunk.

He'd had a couple, she could smell the booze on his breath, but he was sober. 'Henry Lark is a despicable character, so full of himself that I nearly forgot my early training and wanted to say something cruel about his daughter,' he blurted out. It was clear he'd been dwelling on it.

Amelia didn't know whether to feel proud of Jack for defending her, or tell him off for wanting to be nasty about a victim. 'Was Henry repentant?' she asked.

'Not a bit. Denied everything, as I'd expected. But I said, "Those scratches on your cheek tell a different story." He didn't like that, tried to say his cat did it. I'm going to write something about his daughter, though, likening her to Carol Meadows.'

'Did you find the Guide mistress?'

'I've got her number and address, but I think it's best if you see her. Apparently she's quite frail, Parkinson's, but the vicar said she has a good memory. I didn't tell him what it was in connection with because I thought he'd refuse to give me her details. But you can say you're doing a follow-up piece about Lucy and you wanted to know who the other two girls in the picture are.'

'If I go looking like this, she won't want to speak to me.'

Jack looked at her intently. 'In a few days you should be fine. But I'll ask Peanut to go with you, and you can make up some fib about falling on some ice, or a car crash.'

'You think of everything,' she said, with a grin. He amused her with his effortless ways of diluting the truth. 'Just one thing, though. We should've passed that photograph to the police. They need to verify it's of the three dead girls. It could be a vital piece of evidence.'

'Perhaps, but it might let Max off the hook. I'd like to see him sweat a bit longer because of what he's done to you, just as I hope the Guide woman might have some juicy scandal about Rosie Lark to share. They can hold Max for a maximum of forty-eight hours without charging him. With luck they might find something concrete to charge him with. But another week of us holding the photo won't hurt either way.'

Amelia walked back to her desk, suppressing a desire to laugh. She liked Jack's style.

As Amelia's police guard dropped her home that evening, Kat was waiting by the steps of the house. 'Wilf, who has a room at the front of my place, said he'd seen Max being taken away by the police yesterday evening,' she said. 'What he actually said was "Your mate, the pretty one! Well, that bloke she goes with got taken away by the pigs."'

Amelia sniggered. Kat had made her neighbour sound like a Cockney villain.

'Is it true? I assume he did that to your face.'

'Come in and have a cup of tea,' Amelia suggested. 'I'll tell you all.'

After her ordeal yesterday and having been in pain all day today, it was nice to sit with Kat, eat biscuits and drink tea. She told Kat what had happened, then moved the conversation on to Kat's brown Chanel handbag. 'Is it real?' she asked in awe.

'Yes, but I get a huge discount at work.'

'You have some lovely clothes,' Amelia said. The long black coat Kat wore was cashmere, and she had an

Hermès scarf at her neck. 'Lucky you. I get my stuff in Chelsea Girl.'

'Well, you always look a million dollars,' Kat said generously. 'I love the way you've done this room up too. You have such flair. When I get my house you'll have to come along and advise me. Or you could even come and share it.'

'Thank you for that.' Amelia smiled. 'And bless you for the pink roses you brought along before. That was such a kind thought. I hope Max wasn't too rude to you.'

'He's a man,' she replied, as if that explained anything he might have said or done. 'I don't think he was ever right for you.'

'At the start I thought he was perfect,' Amelia said sadly. 'I really believed we were the ideal couple and we'd live happily ever after. But maybe I wanted that so badly I forgot to look closely. It's astonishing how many women can fool themselves when they fall in love.'

'I'm not sure I believe in falling in love. I think it's a combination of lust and liking. If we could put aside the lust and concentrate on how much we like the new man, maybe then we'd find Mr Right.'

Amelia shook her head. 'Kat, I'm beginning to think there is no such thing as Mr Right. And for the time being I don't bloody care. I'm happy to spend my evenings watching *Coronation Street*, *The Prisoner*, or even *Dixon of Dock Green*. And to catch up with some reading. But you haven't told me what's going on in your world.'

'Nothing much,' Kat said, and pulled a face. 'I got taken out the other night to dinner at the Ritz. Nice man but I think he's married. At least I had a lovely dinner.'

'I can't imagine going somewhere as grand as that,' Amelia said. 'I'd be afraid I'd give away my White City origins.'

'You'd be fine being presented to the Queen,' Kat said, reaching out to pat Amelia's cheek. 'You have a natural charm. I'm so sorry you've been in the wars – first that bang on the head and then Max turning on you.'

'You've been a good friend, Kat,' Amelia said. 'I really appreciate it. Once my face is normal again and they've caught the real Creeper, because I'm positive it isn't Max, even if his real name is Brian, we must have a night out, and I'll buy you dinner – not at the Ritz, of course, but maybe the Chinese down at Shepherd's Bush Green?'

'Fish and chips out the paper would be good with you,' Kat said. 'But why do the police think Max is the killer?'

'Appearing at the scene of the first crime, being dodgy chatting me up, evidence he's told a lot of lies about himself. I don't see that any of those things are evidence. But he was supposed to be working away at the time of the last two murders. I don't know yet if they've checked out his alibis.'

'Don't you think him turning violent with you is the really suspicious thing?' Kat said.

Amelia thought about that. If Max was guilty it must have scared him when he got home to find a policeman in the house. But surely that would stop any normal person being violent? 'I really don't know, Kat. He lashed out at me in anger. The Creeper doesn't seem angry – he does his work calmly, almost like an assassin.'

'That's a good word.' Kat sniggered. 'Perhaps he should be called the Acton Assassin. I like the sound of that, a person killing to order.'

'Don't!' Amelia shuddered. 'Creeping is bad enough. Someone killing coldly to order, like a job, is even scarier.'

'I'm going to leave you with that thought.' Kat laughed. 'I've got to get dolled up for a date tonight. If you need anything send your guard dog across to me with a message. But not tonight!'

Amelia listened to Kat's footsteps on the stairs and the front door closing behind her. She suddenly felt very alone, and nervous.

16

Each morning Amelia looked at her black eye in the hope it had disappeared overnight. But no such luck. It had gone from black to purple and now, five days later, it looked yellow. At least it no longer hurt. She wished she could say the same about her stomach. The bruise there had spread and faded. But if she moved quickly or bent over it felt like a new blow.

Max was released on bail for the assault on her and bound over so he couldn't go near her. But there was not enough evidence to hold him on triple murder, and the police were still trawling through his life to find out where all the money they'd found in his room had come from. It transpired that, rather than being an accountant, he was just a clerk in an insurance company, and the amateur dramatics society he claimed he belonged to didn't exist. Amelia realized that almost everything he'd ever told her was a lie, and that stung. Why would anyone make up such stories? Surely they knew that eventually they'd be found out. Where was he when he'd told her he'd gone to Rugby or Luton? Another girlfriend, or was he up to something criminal?

But what puzzled her more than anything else was why he'd suddenly turned so nasty. Was he just bored with her? Had something she'd done or said triggered it? Or could it be, as Peanut had suggested, that as he'd watched her becoming successful as a journalist, he'd grown increasingly jealous? After all, when they'd first met, she'd been what she described as a 'gofer', and hadn't imagined she'd rise above that station.

If he was back living in his own room, she hadn't seen him. She wished she could get him out of her mind because, ridiculous as she knew it was, she was worried about him. She was scared too, of course, but she couldn't help wanting to know how he was coping after being arrested.

She saw Sam every couple of days, either driving her home or taking her to work. He said they were still following a few lines of enquiry in the murders, but everyone was fed up with so many dead ends. He said many of his colleagues still believed Max was the killer, but he was quick to point out they'd found no evidence at all, no murder weapon or blood on clothing. Max had lied and said he was out of London for both of the last murders when in fact he was in a pub in Hammersmith, and the landlord there confirmed it. So there was nothing to warrant charging him with murder. Sam said he didn't think Max was clever enough to cover his tracks so well.

But today Amelia was going to see Miss Briggs, the Guide mistress, with Peanut, and she was hoping a clue to something else would come out of it.

She took great care with her makeup, blending a

concealing cream around her eye, then working foundation over it. By the time she'd finished the bruising didn't show, but she looked like she was wearing too much makeup. It would have to do. A week was long enough to wait, and she wondered if not telling the police about this photograph amounted to 'withholding evidence', which was a criminal offence.

Peanut arrived for her at nine thirty as she'd arranged. 'You look nervous,' he said, as she got into the car.

'I am,' she admitted. 'Not just because I ought to have given the picture to the police, and admitted to Henry Lark that I had it, but also because I intend to tell lies to Miss Briggs, making out I'm writing a background piece on Rosie.'

'In the big scheme of things a few lies hardly matter,' Peanut said, as he started the car. 'The parents of Lucy and Rosie need to see someone punished for their deaths, all the police involved are demoralized, and ordinary people need to feel it's safe to walk around. I'd like to see you skipping off to get the bus again, to know you can go shopping or meet friends for a night out. If we can get a step nearer to that today, I don't care what whoppers you tell.'

'Just don't look at me if I say something you know isn't true or I might blush,' she said. 'But feel free to come in with any questions you think of – we've said you're a senior journalist mentoring me during my training.'

Miss Briggs lived in one of the smaller terraced

houses close to Bedford Park. The front garden was neatly enclosed with a white picket fence that made Amelia think of *Anne of Green Gables*. It was good to see spring bulbs poking up through the soil, and she guessed that in another month the garden would be bright with flowers.

A very slight young woman wearing an overall opened the door. 'Come in,' she said. 'Miss Briggs is expecting you. I'm her cleaner.'

She showed them into a sitting room at the front of the house. Miss Briggs was sitting by the window with a tabby cat on her lap and had perhaps been watching them get out of the car.

'Do come in and sit down. Mrs Calder will bring us coffee in a while.'

'I'm Amelia White,' Amelia said, and walked over to the older woman to shake her hand. 'And this is my mentor Mr Phelps. He has come, as was explained to you, as part of my training.'

Peanut shook hands and they sat down on the two armchairs closest to Miss Briggs.

She didn't look frail – in fact, she looked like she could have been the warrior queen Boadicea. With wide shoulders, a proud stiff back and a remarkably unlined face for a woman who must have been at least seventy, even her gold-rimmed glasses looked light and youthful. But her hands gave away the Parkinson's: they shook as if they were blowing in the wind and she clutched them together, perhaps to hide the insistent tremor.

'I believe my editor told you that I wished to write an article about Rosie Lark, as I did about the other two murdered girls,' Amelia said. 'We hope it might prompt people to remember something they'd seen or heard, and it helps the families to know their girls have not been forgotten.'

'Very laudable, though I hope some of my memories won't hurt her parents' feelings,' Miss Briggs said. She had a voice that matched her appearance, strong with a cut-glass accent. 'I remember Rosie Lark well. When she first joined my Guide company, she was a joy, keen to learn new skills, anxious to get her badges, so helpful. I remember wishing all the girls had the same attitude. But, as I'm sure you know, when girls get to thirteen or fourteen, they often become wilful.'

'Rosie became wilful?' Amelia repeated, sounding surprised. 'I got the impression she was Miss Goody Two Shoes.'

'Her parents were of that opinion too.' Miss Briggs pursed her lips. 'I don't wish to speak ill of her, for obvious reasons, and in her defence, I think she was led into challenging behaviour by another Guide.'

Amelia got the black-and-white photograph out of her bag. 'Was this other Guide one of these girls?' she asked.

Miss Briggs took the photograph right up to her glasses to peer at it. The seconds ticked by and Amelia braced herself to be told she wasn't.

'I apologize for taking so long,' she said eventually.

'I was trying to place where this was and who the other girls are. But I've got it now, at least in part. This picture was taken at Windsor Great Park, in 1957. A world camp to celebrate the hundredth anniversary of Baden Powell's birth. The girls with Rosie weren't in my company, but they came from somewhere close to here, so they stayed with us and we mixed them up with our girls in the tents. The idea was to encourage new friendships. Rosie got embroiled with them, and another girl called Hilary.'

'Do you think the other two girls could have been called Carol and Lucy?' Amelia's heart began to thump with excitement.

'By Jove, yes, that's right! Carol and Lucy. Lucy was a sweet girl, but not the other one. She was a little witch.'

'You don't recognize them as the other two victims of the murderer they call the Creeper, then?' Peanut asked.

Miss Briggs looked at him indignantly. 'Why would I? I don't read the gutter press, or even watch television. If I'd seen pictures of these two as adults, I doubt I would've known them. I only know about Rosie's death through local gossip because she's notorious in Chiswick for being a model. The parents are extremely well known, too.' She paused, suddenly stricken. 'All three of the girls killed?' Her voice was softer now with shock.

Mrs Calder came in with a tray of coffee in a china pot, cups and saucers and some coffee and walnut cake.

She put the tray on a side table and asked Peanut if he would pour it. 'Don't fill Miss Briggs's cup to the top, or she'll spill it,' she whispered to him.

Peanut did his duty, winking at Amelia as he handed the older lady her coffee. 'Cake for you, Miss Briggs?' he asked.

'Oh, yes, please. Mrs Calder always makes lovely cakes, but coffee and walnut is her star turn.'

She drank a little of her coffee, holding the cup very carefully, then ate her cake with relish. 'Mm, scrumptious,' she announced. 'Now back to business. All three girls were killed?'

'Yes, and you're sure the girls in the picture are Rosie, Lucy and Carol?'

'Absolutely. Hilary took the picture – I remember Carol shouting at her to make sure it was a good one. She was often nasty to Hilary.'

'Mr Lark implied that Hilary was a bad influence on Rosie.'

Miss Briggs snorted in derision. 'The other way round, if anything. Hilary was a bit gormless and plain, you see. The three girls used to tease her so I had to step in sometimes to say that wasn't the Girl Guide way. Hilary had moved to Chiswick not long before that summer camp. I seem to remember she was staying with an aunt or a foster mother because of some problem at home. I've no idea what became of her. She came to our Guide meetings for a few weeks before the camp, and I never saw her again.'

'Do you have any contact with the aunt or foster mother?' Amelia asked.

Miss Briggs shook her head. 'She died at least ten years ago. When I gave up as Guide mistress, I lost touch with so many people. Folk can't be bothered with the old, you know. They think we're all feeble-minded because we walk with a stick or get a bit deaf. In my case it's Parkinson's, but there's nothing wrong with my other faculties.'

'I can see that.' Amelia smiled. 'So this teasing, was it nasty?'

'I saw Hilary in tears a couple of times, but then she was the kind to cry at anything, so I didn't take much notice. But that girl Carol was a real piece of work. To my shame, I would say she might have been hurting other girls without any of us adults noticing as she was very crafty. None of them would have told tales either – I think they were too scared of her. I'd say she was responsible for Rosie becoming nasty.'

'Rosie turned nasty?'

'Yes. Nothing drastic, but disappointing in such a previously nice girl. She definitely aped Carol.'

'I don't suppose you've got any idea of which Guide company Carol or Lucy was in?' Peanut asked.

'None at all,' she said. 'I knew they were both in West London, might have been Hammersmith, Acton, anywhere. Back then almost every church had a company attached to it.'

Miss Briggs was silent for a little while. 'Tell me,' she

252

said eventually. 'Do you think the killer picked these three girls for some particular reason?'

'Yes, we do, but until you confirmed you knew all three, we didn't know what the connection was. Can you think of a reason he'd want to kill them?'

'We've come a long way from you wishing to write about Rosie,' she said archly. 'You could have told me the real reason you wanted to speak to me. I'm not gaga yet.'

Amelia blushed. 'I'm sorry, Miss Briggs. I suppose I thought you wouldn't want to talk to me.'

'So you thought you'd soften me up with an article on Rosie? Well, let me tell you, I like straight talking. If you'd come in here, shoved that photograph under my nose and asked who the three girls were, I would have told you. But perhaps your so-called mentor here has taught you that all journalists lie to get a foot in the door.'

'I'm sorry, Miss Briggs. I didn't mean to offend you. You see, I've been convinced there was a common link between the three girls right from the start. But I couldn't find it and the police didn't take me seriously.'

'So where did you get that picture from?' She peered over her glasses, reminding Amelia of her old headmistress, who always put the fear of God into her.

'In Rosie's room.'

'You stole it?'

'Yes.'

To her surprise, Miss Briggs laughed. 'Good for you,

and if it helps solve the murders then God will surely forgive you for theft and telling lies. Now clear off, but let me know when the murderer is caught.'

Once they were outside Miss Briggs's house, Peanut began to laugh. 'She was a fantastic old bird. As sharp as a razor.'

'So sharp we nearly cut our own throats,' Amelia said, as she got into the car. 'What chance have we got of tracking down this Hilary?'

'We don't even attempt it,' he said. 'We go to the police station right now. Show them this photograph and explain there's a link. Then we leave it to them. We can't do any more, Amelia, so take that look off your face.'

'I'll have to own up that I nicked it, I suppose.'

'Yes, but they searched Rosie's room before you went there and didn't find it, so they should applaud your thieving.'

On Saturday Amelia got out of bed listlessly. The whole weekend loomed before her with nothing to do, no one to do it with, and the sun was shining as if spring was on its way. She and Peanut had called in at the police station after visiting Miss Briggs. They had handed over the photograph as proof that there was a link between the girls and told them that it had been taken by a girl called Hilary.

The police sergeant they spoke to didn't seem very impressed – he didn't even ask how Amelia had got it.

As she and Peanut left the station, Amelia said it would probably be shut in a file and would never see the light of day again.

At home later, she looked out of the window and saw her guard was Graham, a boring, bald guy in his late forties. On both occasions he'd driven her to work she was glad when they'd got there because he'd talked about fishing the whole journey. Who on earth was interested in fishing? Apart from other dull men who liked sitting by a river for hours and called it a sport.

So, Graham was not going to be a diversion from boredom. She wanted to go out, to the market, or to a pub, shopping, anything rather than be caged where she was.

She washed and dressed, but only because that made her life seem normal. She put the radio on and danced around the room to 'I'll Never Fall In Love Again' by Bobbie Gentry, but wished it was a more upbeat song, like 'He's No Good' by Betty Everett, when she could roar out the words and feel better for it.

While she was on her third cup of tea of the morning, Graham gave the three-ring signal that he wanted her. By then she thought even a chat about fishing might be better than being alone.

'Hello, Miss White, a friend of yours wanted to see you,' he said, as she opened the door. 'I said I'd ask first.'

Amelia looked past him and saw Kat hovering with a bunch of daffodils in her hand. She looked like a gift from Heaven.

'Come on in, Kat,' she said excitedly. 'I've never been so pleased to see anyone.'

'It's okay, then?' Graham asked.

'Certainly is,' Amelia replied.

Amelia put the daffodils in a vase while she was waiting for the kettle to boil. She thought Kat looked good: she'd had her hair cut shorter with a fringe and it suited her better. She was wearing jeans and a three-quarter length camel coat with a deep brown fur collar.

'Daffs are just the best flowers, coming right when you most need them on dark, chilly days. Thank you. And what a joy to see you. I'm stuck in here, can't go out.'

'Surely you can if you're with someone,' Kat said. 'Max is banged up.'

'Not any more.' Amelia explained that they hadn't been able to find proof for the murders, but they were hoping to get him on other charges.

'How scary for you,' Kat said, in sympathy. 'But he'll have been warned not to come near you, so he won't dare.'

'Well, yes, but we both know that doesn't mean much to some men. My dad used to beat the daylights out of Mum, the police would take him away and he'd be back indoors the next day.'

'So you've lived through things like this before? And history has repeated itself?' Kat pulled a sad face that made Amelia smile.

'More fool me for being so gullible. I'm really ashamed that once again I was taken in by a man. But let's not dwell on that. I hate being stuck in here and I'm desperate to go out, even if just to the shops.'

'Well, get your coat on, girl,' Kat said, with a big grin. 'We could go to the market, maybe get a snack for lunch in the pub. We'll tell your guard dog outside as we leave.'

The market always lifted Amelia's spirits, the crowds, the stallholders' banter, music coming from several different sources, the smell of fruit and flowers, mixed with bacon frying and hamburgers. But even walking down the road felt good, to see the sky properly, not through a car window, to be close to people and hear talking and laughter.

Amelia bought fruit, cheese, bread and some vegetables in the market. Kat bought a china teapot; she said she'd dropped hers a couple of days before.

The rest of the shops in Shepherd's Bush were poor, but to Amelia, having been indoors for so long, they were exciting. Kat laughed at her and said she was nuts.

They had fish and chips in a café, after a couple of halves of cider.

Amelia said she ought to go home then as the police couldn't monitor her when she hadn't told them exactly where she was or when she'd be back.

'Let's go somewhere tomorrow,' Kat suggested. 'If you tell the police in advance they won't need to stay.

We could go to Chislehurst, and maybe the caves. It feels like real countryside there – there's a big pond, too.'

'How do we get there?' Amelia didn't know south of the Thames.

'The tube to Charing Cross, then a train. It's less than half an hour.'

Kat also proposed that they went to the pictures later, but Amelia knew the police wouldn't want her out in the dark. Besides, she felt she'd had enough company for one day, and was happy to go home and watch television.

'I'll come for you at ten thirty tomorrow,' Kat reminded her, as they said goodbye at Amelia's house.

It was only as she watched Kat walk away that she realized Sam was in the police car. She walked up to it and he wound down the window.

'Have you been here all day?' she asked.

He shook his head. 'Graham came back to the nick and said you'd gone out with your friend. I thought I'd come before it got dark. Have you had a nice day?'

'Yes, it was lovely. I've only known Kat for a few months, but she's good company. It was great to be out today, going to the market. I was getting cabin fever. We're going out for the day tomorrow, too. She suggested we went to Chislehurst.'

'It's nice there, not so far from where I grew up. But do make sure you're back before dark, Amelia. Even when someone's with you, it's still dangerous while the Creeper's on the loose.'

'Would you like to come in for a cup of tea, maybe a sandwich or something?' she asked.

'I won't, thank you. I've got a book I want to read, and it's against the rules to be inside. I had a good excuse last time, but not now.'

'Fair enough,' she said, but she was a little disappointed. 'By the way, have any of the police seen Max since he came out of the nick?'

'I don't think so – at least, no one's mentioned it. But a couple of detectives went to Chiswick yesterday to see if they could find out anything about the fourth girl, Hilary. I think they did, but I haven't been told what.'

'I'd better go, it's getting cold,' she said but her real reason was that she felt his conversation was a bit stilted, as if he'd been told off for being too friendly with her.

'Good night,' he said. 'Someone's relieving me at ten but I'll probably be back late afternoon tomorrow for when you come home.'

As she walked up the steps to the house, she wondered if he'd decided she was too much trouble. Perhaps she was.

17

'I feel like I'm going on holiday.' Amelia laughed breathlessly, as they almost fell into the train at Charing Cross station the next morning. They had got to the barrier just as the guard was about to close the gate, but they'd winked at him and wriggled through. Then they had to run to jump onto the train. 'Not that I've ever been on holiday,' she added.

The train was pulling away and it felt like an adventure.

'Never had a holiday?' Kat sounded shocked. 'What — not even when you were a kid?'

'Especially not as a kid. Our family never went anywhere. I'm continuing the tradition. Here I am at twenty-six, still living a few miles from where I was born. I've got the idea that's my destiny.'

Kat laughed. 'Don't be daft. We could go together to Spain or somewhere this summer. But, to be truthful, I haven't had a holiday abroad, only business trips. It's not the same.'

'When I was a hippie chick,' Amelia said, 'we talked endlessly about going to India, Afghanistan and Morocco. I used to believe that one day I'd wake up in one of those places, as if I'd travelled on a magic carpet. We were awfully naive then, weren't we? All daydreams about changing the world, but really doing nothing at all. What about you, Kat, were you changing the world?'

'Hardly,' she said, with a sniff. 'I spent a lot of time and energy on buttering up senior staff at Harrods, who spent their time telling me how fortunate I was to work there. I did go to a couple of those hippie clubs, though – the Middle Earth in Covent Garden was one. I've never seen so many bizarre people in my entire life as I saw there.'

'It was all make-believe really. I was there one night when the police raided it. Once they put the big lights on, everyone looked ordinary. Most were scared, too, as they'd taken LSD and they were afraid they'd be arrested.'

'Did you take drugs?'

'Occasionally,' Amelia admitted. 'I was guilty of wanting to be like everyone else. I liked speed, that was fun, but LSD could be beautiful one minute and terrifying the next. What about you?'

'A few pills, that's all. I wasn't always with people I trusted, and that makes you cautious.'

Amelia put her feet on the seat opposite. 'What about men? Was there anyone special?'

'A big romance when I was seventeen. Joey was a real dish, but he was killed on his brother's motorbike. He crashed into a wall at speed. I spent a long time mourning him, but when I began to recover, I felt I didn't want to get so deeply involved ever again. So then there were short, often passionate romances, which fizzled out quickly. I suppose I'm not the kind of girl men want to marry and keep for ever.'

'You often put yourself down, Kat,' Amelia said. 'Why is that? It worries me.'

Kat looked down at her lap. 'I'm too tall, too plain, maybe a bit odd.'

'You're not odd, you're intriguing. And you should be proud of your height – you're majestic. Models are tall, and they don't worry about it.'

'But they've got slinky lovely bodies. I'm built like a carthorse.'

'You are not,' Amelia said firmly. 'Statuesque is how I'd describe you. I shall work on you, Kat, and make you believe in yourself. I think the new haircut is great. You've got good legs, and you aren't fat. Men may have been put off because you can be a bit intense. Be fun, smiley and excited, like you were yesterday, and all will be well.'

Amelia wished she was brave enough to tell Kat that the coat she normally wore might be expensive cashmere but such a big block of black was overpowering. Today in her camel coat, with her blue jeans and that bright scarf at her neck, she looked good. She remembered that even when they'd first met in summer Kat was wearing all black. She probably had to wear it for work, and maybe she thought it was slimming and sophisticated, but it drained the colour from her face.

However, she needed to be a bit closer to Kat before she started being critical. She'd say nothing more today.

Amelia had always imagined that south of the river was composed of endless housing estates. When the Royal Festival Hall was new, her class at school was taken to see it. She thought it must have been around the same time as the Coronation in 1953. She remembered one teacher saying to another, 'I wonder when they'll clear the bomb site and the slums away. Not much point in having a concert hall on the edge of a wasteland.'

Ever since then whenever she went to the Embankment and looked across the Thames to the South Bank and the Royal Festival Hall, she imagined the wasteland behind it.

As the train went through Bermondsey it was still grim. New Cross and Hither Green didn't look much better either, but then, all at once, they were in an area where the houses had big gardens and there were tree-lined roads and parks.

Chislehurst seemed like the heart of the country as they got off the train. The station had primroses and daffodils planted in tubs, and there were even tiny green buds on the trees as they came out onto the station forecourt.

With the sun shining, feeling quite warm on their faces, and little traffic noise, it seemed hard to believe they were less than half an hour from the centre of London.

'How lovely this is,' Amelia said, as Kat led her up a hill away from the station. There was dainty blossom on trees, birds were singing, and the unpleasantness of the last couple of weeks seemed like something she'd dreamed.

As they walked around the big pond, Kat said she'd lived there when she was small. 'We used to come up here with our fishing nets to catch tiddlers and stickle-backs. We'd put them in a jam jar and take them home, but they were always dead by the next day. We got frog spawn too, and sometimes the tadpoles survived long enough to become little frogs. In the summer we often spent all day up here.'

'Who's we?' Amelia ventured. 'A brother, sister or friend?'

Yesterday, and on the way to Chislehurst, Kat had asked her so many questions: about her family, her work and her involvement in finding the Chiswick Creeper, yet she hadn't volunteered anything about her-self until now.

'My younger sister Angela,' she said.

'Where is she now? Married, got kids?'

'No, she died in a fire,' Kat said. 'With my parents.'

Amelia stopped dead in her tracks, dumbfounded. 'Oh, Kat,' she managed to say. 'I'm so sorry. When was this?'

'Twelve years ago. I managed to get out of a window, but they were trapped. I don't want to spoil our day by talking about anything so dreadful.'

Amelia didn't know how anyone could drop a bomb-shell like that, then carry on as if nothing had been said. But that was just what Kat did. So many times on previous meetings she'd evaded questions, or changed the subject, even when it was something mundane, like people she worked with. Amelia could understand her not wanting to talk about something as tragic as her family being killed. And, indeed, Kat went on to say she knew a little café where they could get some lunch, but it was quite a way further on.

Buttoning her lip so that she didn't ask any more questions was a tall order for Amelia. She had always loved stories, and a house burning down with three people in it, her friend the only survivor, made this a story she had to hear. She had so many questions bub-bling in her head. Kat had said she'd lived here. Where would that have been? She must have been fourteen, maybe a bit younger, as she wasn't sure of Kat's age. How had the fire started and what had happened to Kat afterwards?

But Kat was pointing out primroses on a bank, and the sound of a woodpecker, and then she started to talk about two of the male staff in her bathroom depart-ment at Harrods who had been caught kissing.

'They weren't even discreet about it,' she said, laugh-ing as she told the story. 'They were in one of the show bathrooms. The floor manager who caught them joked that they should've shut the door! Like they have doors in showrooms! Mr Healy, the older of the two, is married, and no one ever suspected he was like that. Mr Simmons, the younger man, is rather camp. He's got lots of boyfriends, but we all like him – he's a real scream.'

'So what's going to happen to them?' Amelia didn't really care: her mind was still on the fire.

'They were both sacked. Awful, really, for Mr Healy – he's been working there since the end of the war. John Simmons will be fine. I was told he went straight to a job in Carnaby Street.'

It was quite a walk to the café, but it was a pretty place with flowers on the tables and snowy white tablecloths. They ordered steak and kidney pudding, the dish of the day.

'I'd like to have a café like this,' Kat said, looking around her gleefully. 'What could be better than feeding people? To feel appreciated.'

'I bet running a café is a lot harder than it looks,' Amelia said. 'Do you like cooking? Are you good at it?'

'Not so good.' Kat grimaced. 'I always like to imagine someone else doing all the boring work. I'd just be arranging the flowers, popping cherries on buns, and buying the pretty china.'

Amelia burst into laughter at that. 'You are funny, Kat! There'd be a whole lot more you had to do than that, the cooking being the main thing.'

'Don't be so practical,' Kat said, with a wide smile. 'There must be something you fancy doing or being that you know you've no real aptitude for.'

'Figure skating and being a ballerina. I can't even stand up on ice.'

They talked for a while about all the things they'd failed at, some silly unimportant things, like doing leapfrog, and it made them giggle helplessly. Amelia even managed to forget her questions about the fire.

The lunch was delicious and very filling, yet they managed apple pie and custard too.

'That long walk back to the station isn't looking so inviting now,' Amelia said, as they divided the bill into two and paid it. 'Ideally I'd like to lie down and snooze.'

'I've got somewhere you can sit down,' Kat said. 'Somewhere I want to show you.'

'Mysterious.' Amelia raised an eyebrow.

'Don't ask any questions till we get there.' Kat chuckled. 'My Magical Mystery Tour.'

They sang the Beatles song as they walked arm in arm away from the café, down a tree-lined lane where the houses were set well back from the road. Amelia thought how great it was to have a girlfriend to go out with. So far it had been the best of days and she liked Kat even more now.

The houses seemed to peter out, but then Kat led her to a narrow muddy lane, overhung with bushes.

'I'm really curious now,' Amelia said, as she swept back branches and brambles to get through. 'I bet you can't get along here in summer.'

'It doesn't go anywhere, except to the place I'm showing you,' Kat said.

Amelia glanced at her friend. She was flushed with excitement. Clearly this place meant a great deal to her.

They went through a rusting iron gate, which had come off its hinges, and just a few yards further on Amelia saw the burned-out house.

It must have been beautiful once, a mellow red-brick Victorian villa with pointed eaves and a portico at the front door. But only the left-hand side of the house was still intact: the right-hand side of the roof was totally gone, along with the ceilings, walls and windows on the upper floor. On the ground floor the windows had been boarded up, but some of the boards had been wrenched off and through the missing and broken panes in the front door Amelia could see the staircase beyond, black like charcoal and on the verge of collapse.

'This was your house?' she asked, tears welling at the thought of such a tragedy.

'Yes – see that window?' Kat pointed to the one on the far left upstairs. 'That was my room. I heard Daddy yelling, "Fire!" and when I opened my bedroom door the whole landing by the stairs was ablaze. I thought he had got Angela out and Mummy. They were on the right side of house. So I closed my door and climbed out of the window.'

She pointed to a downpipe hanging off the wall. 'That's how I got down. But then I realized Mummy, Daddy and Angela must still be inside. I could see the staircase through the glass panels on the front door and no one could get through the flames. I ran to the nearest neighbours and they must've rung the fire brigade. But my memory of all that is hazy. Come with me?'

She took Amelia's hand and led her round the left-hand side of the burned house. There was a narrow pathway made by someone, perhaps Kat forcing her way through, but bramble bushes looked intent on smothering it.

'I came here when I got back from the neighbour, hoping Daddy had got them out the back way.' She led Amelia right down the garden to a large summerhouse at the bottom, flanked by trees. 'I really thought they'd be in here, worrying about me. But they weren't.'

She fished in her bag, drew out a key and opened the door.

It was immediately obvious that Kat was in the habit of coming here. It was clean, only a few cobwebs, and the cushions on the wicker chairs looked new. There was a kind of daybed, a small camping stove and various mugs, plates and a saucepan on a small table.

'I stayed in here that night, watching the flames come out of the roof. I really believed my family were safe somewhere, but they'd forgotten about me. The firemen found me in the morning. I walked out into the garden in my nightie. I was told I was mute, didn't say a word. But all that is like some strange dream. I don't exactly remember any of it.'

'Kat, that's so awful,' Amelia gasped. It was like something out of a horror film, and she didn't know how anyone could continue to live normally after such a terrible trauma.

Kat had sat down on one of the chairs, and Amelia took another. 'I don't really know what to say. It's just too much to take in.'

'It was for me too,' Kat said. 'A real brain overload. I spent some time in a hospital then. I know I didn't want to talk about it. I think it must have baffled the doctors and nurses. But I was just thirteen, and it's hard to process something like that when you're so young.'

'Yet you've been coming back here?'

'This is the first time since November. I've never brought anyone else here. It's kind of sacred.' Kat's voice was cracking with emotion. She was clearly finding it difficult to tell Amelia any more.

'I can understand that. Does someone else own the house now?'

'That's a bit of a puzzle. I'm pretty certain it's legally mine, but my mother's sister, who lives in New Zealand, became my guardian back then as I was underage, of course.' Kat's voice became steadier, almost as if she knew she must tell Amelia the whole story. 'There was talk of sending me out there, but she became ill, or just didn't want to be responsible for me, I don't know which. Anyway, I ended up being fostered. Of course, I couldn't do anything about this house – I couldn't afford a solicitor. Besides, I'd been working and living alone since I was sixteen and I hadn't had any help, advice or even a birthday card from anyone.'

'But you must sort it out now, Kat. Why haven't you? You can't just let it rot away.'

Kat grimaced. 'Apathy, I suppose – and, anyway, how can I get a solicitor to act for me without any money?'

'You chump,' Amelia said affectionately. 'You don't need any money up front. I would imagine the land the house sits on is extremely valuable, and it would be best for the house to be pulled down and rebuilt, but a solicitor will find out if your parents had insurance. It might have been claimed for you already and put in a trust account. I could come with you to a Citizens Advice Bureau to get you some help.'

'Would you?' Kat looked astonished that anyone would help her.

'Of course! It'll take my mind off bloody Max. Think how great it would be if you found you were a real heiress. You could buy a café then.'

'Let's make some coffee,' Kat said. 'I've only got powdered milk, but it's not bad in coffee. In the summer I often come here, sometimes stay a few days. I live on pork pie, apples and biscuits mostly. There's a tap in the garden – I'd thought the water would have been cut off, but it hasn't.'

Kat went off with the little kettle and came back smiling. 'I put a nesting box up near the tap last year and I think some blue tits are in it. Mummy liked feeding the birds and putting up boxes for them. But all of them except this one are gone.'

'A neighbour, I expect. I'm surprised you haven't had squatters in here,' Amelia said.

'Me too, but it's a bit out of the way. And it's hard to get in here once all the bushes start to grow again. I usually come with secateurs. But for now I have to find my matches.'

Kat had slung her bag on the daybed, and Amelia reached over to get it for her. But she only grabbed one handle and the entire contents fell to the floor.

'So sorry.' Amelia jumped up and began to scoop up a packet of tissues, a box of matches, a purse and makeup bag, letters . . . and there beneath them was what looked like a telescopic umbrella in a polka-dotted fabric cover. Amelia grabbed it, but it was far too heavy for an umbrella. There was also a long thin kitchen knife in a plastic sheath. She couldn't resist pulling back the polka-dotted fabric and, to her astonishment, she saw what looked like a piece of heavy pipe.

'What on earth?' she exclaimed.

Kat lunged at her, snatching the two objects, as if they were top secret, and pushed them right under the daybed, her face turning scarlet.

Had Kat laughed and said she'd brought the knife to cut something, and the piece of pipe would be useful, Amelia wouldn't have thought there was anything odd about them being in her friend's bag. But, like a ray of light in a dark place, she knew why the two objects seemed familiar. A length of lead pipe and a long thin kitchen knife were the Creeper's tools.

18

'Get your head out of the clouds, son, and finish that report,' Sergeant Roper said to Sam Hamilton, when he noticed he was staring into space instead of typing.

'Sorry, Sarge,' Sam replied. 'One of those goose-walking-over-my-grave moments. Do you ever get that when someone pops into your head unexpectedly and it feels like a warning?'

'I'll give you a warning in a minute,' the older man growled.

Sam returned to his report as instructed. His sergeant lacked a sense of humour, but perhaps forty years in the job did that to you.

Not that Sam's sudden warning flash was funny: it was a feeling that Amelia was in danger. She'd told him she was going to Chislehurst with Kat. PC Graham Ford had confirmed this, saying no security was needed until late that afternoon. It all sounded fine, but what if this feeling, premonition or whatever it was, meant Max was lurking somewhere, waiting for her?

As the feeling would not go away, and Graham wasn't on the protection rota until later that day, he went up to the canteen, knowing he'd be there.

'This is going to sound a bit odd,' he said, looking

down at his colleague who was eating egg and chips. 'Would you mind calling in to speak to me when Amelia White gets home today? I've been having a bad feeling about her.'

Graham grinned. 'Don't be daft, Sam. She's with her pal, and glad to be out of that flat. I bet she won't be back till late.'

'I thought that's what you'd say.' Sam tried to make it sound as if it was no big deal. 'But do me a favour and ring in anyway.'

'She'll be flattered you care.' Graham laughed. 'I'll tell her when I see her.'

Kat was behaving as if nothing unusual had happened. She lit the gas, put the kettle on, then opened a biscuit tin that held coffee, sugar, and the dried milk.

'These look a bit damp,' she said, 'but I'm sure they'll taste all right.'

Amelia's head was swimming. Was she imagining what she'd just seen? And if she wasn't imagining it, did that mean Kat was a killer? The Creeper?

She looked down and could just see the polka-dotted umbrella cover under the daybed. She certainly hadn't imagined that.

'Why have you got those things in your bag?' she asked, for the second time.

She really hoped Kat was going to give her a good reason, but Amelia couldn't think of one except that she was the Creeper.

Yet it was preposterous to think that. For a start everyone, including the police, assumed it was a man, because murderers mostly were. Yet couldn't a tall woman in trousers, a woolly hat and a long black coat – the long black coat she always wore – pass for a man in the dark? She was strong, too, with broad shoulders. In fact, the more Amelia thought about it, she knew Kat could pass for a man.

Kat had also shown an intense interest in what the police were doing, and it was odd that she had turned up yesterday with flowers, knowing that Max was no longer there.

Had she brought Amelia here to kill her? Or had that been the plan and she'd changed her mind?

'Do I need to repeat my question again, Kat?' Amelia said. She was still sitting, perched on the edge of the chair as if ready to flee. 'Please answer me.'

She didn't think Kat had brought her here intending to kill her. After all, it would be the first place the police would look as she'd told Sam she was going to Chislehurst with Kat.

But was Kat even her real name? She suddenly realized she actually knew very little about the girl. Questions never answered, subjects changed. That hadn't seemed important until now, but was this place her old home? Or just some burned-out house she'd found, then made up the story about her family dying in it? Only someone mad or very disturbed would come up with such a story, but surviving an ordeal like that could surely send you mad.

A cold shudder went down Amelia's spine. She didn't feel it was a lie, just as she really didn't think Kat wanted to kill her. But she would have to if she really was the Creeper. Amelia knew too much.

So what was she to do? She could make a run for it, but Kat, with her long legs, could almost certainly outrun her. Besides, attempting to flee would make Kat feel threatened and angry, which could be extremely dangerous.

Kat turned away from fiddling with the coffee-making things to look at Amelia, her face cold and unreadable. 'If you must know, I picked up the pipe in the front garden of my house. I thought it would double as a hammer if I couldn't get the door open here. It does tend to stick. As for the knife, well, I haven't got one here and I often need one, to cut up a pie or peel fruit.'

That was plausible, and had she said it straight off, and not snatched up the items when they fell out of her bag, it might have been believable.

'Such a long knife?'

Kat's lip curled, almost like a dog about to turn savage. Or was that Amelia imagining things?

'I picked that one as it had the plastic cover, so I wouldn't cut myself on it. Just as I put the bit of pipe in a bag because it was rusty. Why do you find me having these things sinister? What's so odd about them being in my bag?'

'You know very well why I think it's sinister,' Amelia

said quietly. Her voice was shaking but she tried to control it. 'Tell me, should I make a run for it?'

'I don't know what you mean.'

Despite what she'd said, Amelia knew she was on the right track. Two red spots of colour had come up on Kat's cheeks, and she couldn't look her in the eye.

'You do know what I mean, Kat. I realize from what you've already told me today that you've had a hard, lonely life. I think you met up with Lucy, Carol and Rosie many years ago and they did something awful to you. So you took your revenge.'

'No! I don't know them, and I could never kill anyone.'

Her denial did not ring true. Her voice was strangled, as if she'd had a job to get the words out, and she was hanging her head. Wouldn't an innocent person shout in anger at being accused of something so terrible?

Amelia held her nerve. 'Tell me the whole story, Kat. You'll feel better if you do. I don't mind if we stay here all night. I want to help you.'

Kat took a step nearer Amelia. She looked scary, towering over her, but she was determined not to be intimidated, so she leaned back in her chair as if she was relaxing.

'You're being utterly ridiculous,' Kat said, but she still wasn't making eye contact. 'You've got far too much imagination and no common sense. And you've got those murders on the brain. How do you think someone like me could kill three girls and get away with it?'

'Because those three girls did something horrible to you and you were hell bent on revenge. But you're also clever and I suspect you didn't much care if you got caught because there's nothing but anger towards those girls inside you.'

The truth was written on Kat's face, almost delight that her pain was recognized, and pride that she'd been clever. But an expression on someone's face wasn't proof.

'When my family died in the fire, I saw some of the top psychiatrists in the country, but they were unable to find out why I couldn't or wouldn't speak,' she said, her voice silky. She thought she had the upper hand. 'What makes you, a little gofer in the newspaper office, think you can work out what's in my head? And have the cheek to pin something like this on me?'

'Sit down, Kat. It's giving me a crick in my neck looking up at you,' Amelia said calmly. To her surprise, Kat obeyed. 'That's better! I wouldn't be so crass as to imagine I could fully understand how terrible it was for you to lose your family in that way. But I do understand the feeling you must have had afterwards, of no one caring, of being totally alone, even though there were people around you.' She paused. She'd been told that people don't take in what you're saying unless you break it up, and speak slowly.

'My life was all disappointments,' she went on eventually. 'A bully of a father, a useless mother, awful living conditions. I was moved into my room in Godolphin

Road by social workers after I'd been savagely beaten and taken to hospital. They didn't care whether I turned to drink or drugs, they just stuck me there. And it became my refuge from the world.

'But I wasn't full of hatred for anyone. Maybe if I had been, I could've done what you've done.'

'My God, you think you're so superior, don't you?'

'No, Kat, I don't. The truth is, I'm a mass of insecurities. I expect that's why Max turned on me, and all the other men I've met soon lost interest. I'm like you, Kat. I haven't got any real friends either. I'm a loner. That's why it was so lovely being with you. If it hadn't been for those things falling out of your bag, it would never have occurred to me that you were the killer. So, were you, or are you, planning to kill me too, Kat?'

Different expressions flew across Kat's face. Indecision, fear – and cunning. Maybe she was aware she felt no hatred towards Amelia, which would have made it easier to stick the knife into her, yet at the same time she knew she must kill her, or she would be caught and tried for murder.

'Let's have that coffee.' Amelia got up and walked over to the camping stove. She was very scared, but she forced herself to appear calm because that was the only way she'd perhaps get out of there alive.

The kettle was close to boiling now. Kat had sat down on one of the ordinary chairs, and the pipe and knife were under the daybed. If she could make the coffee and sit down on it, she could snatch up the knife when Kat was distracted.

'How many sugars?' she asked, as she spooned in the coffee. Kat was right: it was a bit damp.

'Two sugars, but three of the dried milk. Of course I didn't plan to kill you, Amelia. I like you. But you've spoiled everything now.'

Amelia glanced over her shoulder. Kat was picking nervously at her nails. She didn't look like a killer, just a girl with a problem. 'I can imagine how difficult it is for you.' Amelia stirred the coffee noisily. 'Let's just have our coffee and you tell me about those girls and what they did to you. Where did you meet them?'

She handed Kat hers, and sat down on the daybed. She turned her right foot onto its side and felt cautiously for the knife. She found it. Now, bit by bit, she must nudge it out.

'I knew Rosie Lark first,' Kat said, astounding Amelia that she was going to admit to knowing them. 'I was fostered by some people in Chiswick and they got me to join the Guides. Rosie was kind then – she even invited me to tea once. She went to a private school, so I didn't see her much, except at Guides. But then we went to the World Camp, at Windsor, and that's where I met Lucy Whelan and Carol Meadows.'

In a flash Amelia realized Kat was the fourth girl, the one they'd called Hairy Hilary.

She was suddenly saddened that she was right about Kat. She didn't want to be: she had grown to like her.

Coming here and sensing what her life with her family had been like before the fire, she could understand that such a trauma in adolescence was likely to cause permanent mental damage.

But was it bad enough to kill? And how could someone so unbalanced plan those killings? Amelia could understand someone killing an old adversary in the heat of the moment. But all that plotting! And she didn't know how unpredictable Kat was – she could lash out at Amelia at any moment.

All she could do was try to stay on an even keel, to choose her words carefully too. 'So how did you feel about them? When you first met, I mean.'

'Those three other girls and I were all put in one big bell tent. I think the idea was to mix up the different groups of Guides to make us all friendly to one another. I knew Carol was going to be trouble straight off. She pushed a black girl out of the tent and told her to go somewhere else because she smelt.

'Lucy didn't like that any more than I did, but maybe she was afraid of Carol picking on her because she said nothing and started sucking up to Rosie, admiring all her badges. I think she already knew Rosie's father was rich and they had a big house because she lived quite close to both of us.'

'Did the black girl smell bad?' Amelia asked. The question was only to keep Kat talking. She was still trying to get the knife to where she could reach it easily.

'No, not at all. Carol was just incredibly nasty. I

saw later that she was cruel to any of the Guides who came from abroad. But the reason she turned on me was because I tried to stop her hurting that girl. I said she should be ashamed of herself, that Girl Guides were supposed to be kind to one another, regardless of colour or creed.'

'That was brave of you, Kat. What did she do to you?'

'She saw I had hair on my back when we were getting changed and she told everyone and called me names.'

So Amelia had been right in thinking Kat was Hilary. 'How did Rosie and Lucy get involved?'

'Carol lured them both into her nastiness. I can only suppose they went along with it because they were afraid Carol would turn on them if they didn't. But what they did the next day haunts me now. Carol sat astride me in the tent and got Rosie to hold my arms down and Lucy my feet. Then she smeared Immac hair-removing cream in circles on my head. I thought that was bad enough, but then she pulled all my clothes off and set fire to my pubic hair. She kept calling me Hairy Hilary, and laughed at me as I was pleading for her to stop. She burned my thighs and stomach along with the hair. I started to scream, so she gagged me.

'When she finally got bored with hurting me, she pushed me out of the tent stark naked. There were hundreds of people about. I wanted to die. I went back in the tent to try to get my clothes, but she'd taken them away somewhere.'

'Didn't the Guide mistresses do something?'

'One found a nightdress to cover me up, but when they rinsed off my hair, there were all these big bald spots. I looked so terrible I wanted to die. I was afraid to say who had done it because she said she'd do something worse next time.'

'And Lucy and Rosie didn't try to help you?'

'They were almost as bad as Carol. But it didn't end there. That whole week they found ways to humiliate me. I had to keep my Guide beret on all the time to hide my hair. They'd trip me up, throw stones at me. I got in my sleeping bag one night and they'd put a soiled sanitary towel in it. By the time the week ended I was nearly a basket case.'

'Why didn't you tell Miss Briggs? I've met her. I know she must've seemed a bit fierce, but she struck me as a fair person, and I don't think she would've let Carol get away with that.'

'I was too scared of Carol to do anything. She said if I started telling tales she'd get me. I believed her too.'

'But it ended when you got home?'

'No, it got even worse. It was the school holidays. She'd be hanging around close to where I lived in Chiswick, and she'd follow me, taunting me with what she was going to do next. The other two were around most days, too, and bullying me was their favourite sport. You wouldn't believe the things they did! Then one day they seemed to be nice, and they had a bag of doughnuts. They gave me one, but when I bit into it, there was dog shit in it! Can you imagine anyone being so completely evil that they'd do something as repulsive as that? I was sick, vomiting right there in the street, and they just laughed. I never really got over that. I could taste it whatever I ate.'

Amelia was beginning to think the three girls deserved punishment, not to die, of course, but something severe. Especially Carol. Having been on the end of bullying herself, albeit nowhere near as bad, she knew the complex it gave a child. But her priority had to be to get away from here, as soon as possible.

The knife was between her feet now, and unless Kat got up, she wouldn't see it. But Amelia knew that to get away she had to be prepared to use that knife to defend herself. If she faltered, Kat would kill her.

'So what made you decide to kill them?' she asked.

'I didn't say I killed them.'

That threw Amelia. It wasn't so much the words, but the way she delivered them: strong and indignant, not snivelling and hoping to put the blame on someone else.

'But you did, Kat. And you hit me with that bit of pipe. But that was just to frighten me, wasn't it? So I'd lose interest and move on to something else.'

'Like I said before, you've got too much imagination. I told the social workers I wasn't happy in Chiswick, and they said they'd find new foster parents for me. But it was out of the frying pan into the fire. The Coles were cold people. They fostered me for the money, not out of compassion or love. But they fed and clothed me well, saw I got to school and did my homework. Like I was a dog in a kennel when the owners go on holiday. But never a stroke, a pat on the head. Just business.

'Then I went on to the Hardys in Kentish Town. Pop Hardy, as he made me call him, kept putting his hand up my skirt, Mrs Hardy slapped my face when I told her. They drank a lot, and I never felt safe in that house. By then I wanted to kill myself. There was no light, no happiness at all in my life. I was an outsider in the new school I'd been sent to – no one wanted to know me. The social worker said I'd got to grow up and stop complaining. I took an overdose of aspirin but Mrs Hardy found me and called an ambulance.'

'Oh, Kat, that's awful.' She could completely sympathize with that feeling. She'd often thought of taking an overdose herself. 'Did you have to go back with the Hardys?'

'Yes, but they virtually ignored me from then on, and as soon as I was sixteen, I was transferred to a girls' hostel in Archway. I'd been accepted to work in Harrods then, and for a short while I thought my life would improve. I suppose it did, given that I wasn't being bullied any more, just pushed around at work. But it was only the other rejects who ever talked to me in the canteen. The girls in fashion and beauty were all convinced they were goddesses.'

'But then you moved to Godolphin Road?' Amelia saw that Kat had turned her head away. She picked up the knife and slid it up her left sleeve. 'What a shame we didn't meet back then. We might have been good for one another.'

Kat turned towards her, tears running down her cheeks. 'I used to see you all the time. You looked so pretty in your cheesecloth smocks. You went out one night in a brown velvet kaftan – it had gold stars appliquéd on it, and you had a gold band around your forehead. You didn't notice me, but I was trying to pluck up courage to tell you how lovely you looked.'

It was strange to discover Kat had been watching her for years, scary strange too, like she was under a microscope. She thought it was just as well she'd been genuinely friendly to her when they'd met in the launderette, or she might have become one of her victims.

'I would've appreciated that,' she forced herself to say. 'I never believed I looked right. That dress was ruined – I caught it on a metal fence and the tear was too bad to mend.' She looked out onto the garden – she could see it was nearly dusk. 'Let's go home now, Kat. It'll be dark soon, and it's been a long day.'

'You don't really think we can go home as if nothing's been said today, do you?' Kat asked. She sounded so forlorn that Amelia almost felt like cuddling her, like she would a sad child.

'If you didn't kill the three girls, but knew them all, why not just come with me and we'll go to the police so you can tell them that, too?'

Kat's head came up sharply. 'I can't do that! Are you mad?'

'You know I'm not. I just want you to do the right thing. You can't pretend any more, Kat. If I don't get home soon the police will start looking for me, and as they know I'm with you in Chislehurst, it won't take them long to find this place. If I come with you to the police I can speak up for you. I'm used to talking to people in my job. I'll be able to convince them that terrible things were done to you in the past. I can even embellish it – I'm good at that.'

Amelia knew she was waffling. Nothing she could say would convince Kat to give herself up: she was like a wounded animal that would fight till the last.

'You mean well, I know that,' Kat said. 'Earlier you said something right – that if we'd met years ago it might all have been different.'

Amelia stood up, picking up her shoulder bag and putting it over her head so the strap crossed her chest. 'Whether you go to the police or not is up to you. I'm going home,' she said, even though she was shaking with fear.

Kat stood up, too, and her expression was terrifying: her eyes were wild and her nostrils flaring. Amelia knew it was make-or-break time.

She began to move towards the door.

'Stay here,' Kat said, her voice low and threatening. 'I don't want to hurt you, but I'll have to if you try to go.'

Amelia had let the knife slide a little down her sleeve so she could grab the handle with her right hand. She quickly pulled it the rest of the way out, snatched the plastic sheath off and brandished it. 'Okay, Kat. You've got a choice between letting me go in peace, or me sticking this into you,' she hissed, holding the knife in front of her. 'I don't want to hurt you, but I will if you come near me.'

'You'll never use that knife. You haven't got it in you,' Kat taunted her, moving closer.

Amelia pulled the door open with her left hand. 'Just try me.'

Kat sprang forward, attempting to knock the knife out of Amelia's hand. But Amelia was holding it tightly and she made a warning slash, catching Kat across her knuckles and drawing blood.

'I told you I would do it,' Amelia roared at her, as she walked out of the door. 'Now back off or next time it will be serious.'

It was dusk now, and Amelia was forced to walk backwards for fear of Kat coming up behind her. She'd noticed earlier in the day that although Kat was so tall and a little ungainly she moved silently and quickly. It seemed the Creeper had been an apt nickname.

But walking backwards in an overgrown garden was not easy. She didn't know if there were obstacles hidden in the grass and weeds, so she kept turning her head to check. Kat was still standing at the doorway of the summerhouse, but Amelia didn't think for one moment she was going to stay there.

Once at the side of the house and out of Kat's line of vision, the path was a little clearer, so Amelia made a run for it, pushing her way desperately through the bushes that were almost blocking the path to the lane. She was listening for Kat coming after her, but she couldn't hear anything.

Reaching the lane, she paused just for a second to listen again, but there was nothing, so she broke into a trot as she went up the hill towards Chislehurst Common.

She remembered a house about fifty yards or so from the lane leading to Kat's old family home. She would run in there and ask them to phone the police.

But suddenly Kat was on the lane in front of her, nearly giving Amelia a heart attack. She had no coat on, just her jeans and a cream sweater.

'You aren't much good at this, are you?' she said scornfully. 'I went through the bushes and over the neighbour's fence to head you off. They aren't in so there's no point in screaming. Just give me the knife.'

It was fortunate Amelia had stuck it into the side of her bag, so she had both hands free, but at Kat's words she snatched it up again and brandished it as she continued to walk up the hill, passing Kat.

Terror made Amelia bolder. She knew she could use the knife if it was a choice between her life and Kat's.

'There's only one way this might get better for you,' she shouted, hoping against hope that Kat's neighbour might be in and had come into the garden to see what the noise was. 'You let me call the police and you tell them your side of the story. If you won't do that, then

Heaven help you because I will stab you if you come near me.'

'You turncoat,' Kat shouted back at her. 'All day you've been my friend. You said you liked me, but it was all lies, wasn't it? You want to see me behind bars so you can write for your paper how you identified and captured the Creeper. Shall I tell you something else? Remember how I went to your flat when you were out and brought you some flowers? Well, I had sex with your precious Max in your bed. How do you like that?'

'So what?' Amelia replied, even though she was shaken by what Kat had said. 'He was a liar and a no-hoper like you.'

Kat rushed at her then, but Amelia stood her ground, holding the knife firmly, waiting for the other girl to try and grab her. As Kat reached out for her shoulders, Amelia thrust the knife into her.

Kat's eyes widened with shock. She took a step back looking down at the knife. It had gone in just above the waist of her jeans, only the hilt sticking out and her cream sweater was already turning red with blood.

Amelia might have said she'd stab Kat, but the reality of it made her want to be sick. 'Don't try to pull it out, you'll bleed to death,' she said instinctively, something she'd picked up from the TV. 'I'll run to get an ambulance.'

As shaken and sick as she felt, Amelia ran like the wind to the top of the hill. She'd remembered seeing a phone box just around the corner.

She dialled 999 and blurted out breathlessly that her friend had been stabbed, and told the operator where she was. She didn't linger to give names or any details – there was too much to explain. Besides, she was fairly certain a stabbing in Chislehurst was an extremely rare event and that the ambulance would be there within minutes.

She heard the ambulance bell in the distance almost as soon as she came out of the phone box. Still out of breath from her run up the hill she walked back down the road.

But as she turned the slight bend, where the nearest house was, she couldn't see Kat.

She broke into a run again, thinking she had collapsed and fallen into bushes.

But Kat was not there, just a pool of blood on the road at the spot where Amelia had stabbed her.

19

'You'd better come with us, Miss.'

Amelia looked at the two policemen's faces and saw that they believed her to be either a fantasist or on drugs as there was no girl with a knife sticking out of her. There was the blood on the road, but they seemed not to be taking any notice of that.

She was so overwrought, not just by what she'd done but that Kat was gone, that her story didn't even make sense to her.

The ambulance, which had come so speedily, left when the police, who had followed very soon after in two cars, had searched and found no one injured. They were local men who knew the area, and while two of them stayed with Amelia, listening to her tearful and somewhat garbled story, two more men checked the burned-out house and its grounds. Now those men were knocking on doors and asking questions. It was pitch dark and very cold.

The tall, lanky policeman with a pockmarked face had put his hand on her shoulder. Not in a reassuring way but as if he thought she was going to make a run for it.

'Of course I'll come with you,' she said. 'She'll have

gone somewhere to get out of the cold and have a hot drink. Will you ring the police at Shepherd's Bush and speak to them? The girl I stabbed is called Kat Somerset, and I only did it because she was going to kill me. She's the one they've been calling the Chiswick Creeper. She's killed three girls already.'

'And you say the knife was still in her stomach?'

His tone told her he didn't believe a word she'd said.

'Well, it was when I ran to find a phone. There'll be a blood trail, though I suppose you can't see that in the dark. You need to find her quickly.'

At the local police station Amelia was ushered into a small interview room and left there for a good half-hour before another much older policeman came in with a young woman officer.

'I'm Detective Inspector Welsh,' he said. 'This is WPC Mortimer. I understand you are alleging that the girl you were with and stabbed is none other than the Chiswick Creeper. Is that right?'

'I'm not alleging,' she replied indignantly. 'It's a fact. I know everyone's been thinking it's a man, but it's not, it's Kat. I've been under police protection for some time now because I was attacked, too. Kat lives in the same road as me, but I never suspected her. She was a fairly new friend, and I came out to Chislehurst with her today for a change of scene. Everything was quite normal at first. We had lunch and then she took me to show me where she used to live. We were in the summerhouse at the burned-out house when her bag dropped off a chair and a long thin kitchen knife and a bag with a lead pipe tumbled out. Suddenly it all fell into place and I knew she was the killer. She even told me all about the three girls.' She paused to take a deep breath. She might be in serious trouble herself.

If Kat was dead, would she be charged with murder?

'I only stabbed her because I was afraid she'd kill me. It was self-defence.'

There was a heavy silence. Neither the policeman nor the WPC said a word. That was more disconcerting than if they'd accused her of lying or taking drugs.

'Please ring Shepherd's Bush police station and tell them you've got me here. Sam Hamilton is one of the officers who's been protecting me and Sergeant Roper knows me well too.'

Welsh looked at her thoughtfully. He appeared to be in his mid-fifties, with a craggy, lived-in sort of face, tired brown eyes and sparse, sandy hair. 'Why come to Chislehurst?'

'I told you, she said she used to live here and it was a nice place. So it was, until she turned on me,' Amelia said sharply. 'She told me that burned-out house was her family home and her parents and sister died in the fire there. Is that true?'

He didn't answer for a moment, as if weighing up whether she was speaking the truth. 'The people who own that house bought it, then went abroad with their business. While they were away some squatters got in there and started the fire. The couple who own it have no children and were going to start rebuilding it shortly. So this Kat, what's her surname?'

'Somerset. She works at Harrods, and lives just along the road from me, but I think she was called Hilary and changed her name later. But all that could be verified by the Shepherd's Bush police.'

'Very well, Miss White. I'll look into this further and come back to you,' he said, getting up and moving towards the door. The WPC followed him, but looked back at Amelia as she got to the door. 'I'll get someone to bring you some tea,' she said.

Amelia kept glancing at the clock in the interview room. It was a quarter past eleven now, and she wondered how she'd get home if they didn't let her go soon. She was alone. The WPC had brought tea and stayed for a few minutes, but DI Welsh hadn't come back. She wondered why it would take so long to verify her story with the police in Shepherd's Bush.

She was only a whisker away from bursting into tears. She didn't think she'd ever felt so alone. When she'd told Kat they were alike, both lonely and friendless, she hadn't meant it: it had been more a gambit to get Kat to talk about herself. But now she saw it was true. She didn't have anyone. By day she could have called Jack at the newspaper, but he was only her employer, not a real friend. For a while Max had filled the big hole in her life, but the love he promised had been a mirage. Was it true that he had had sex with Kat? He had acted a bit strangely about her coming round. Was that because he was afraid Kat would tell her?

Not that it mattered either way. She would rather be alone than with a bully.

She was worried about Kat, though. Where was she? How could she have run away with that knife still in her? Or had she found somewhere to hide and died of her wound? Had she killed her?

Why were the police keeping her here? Would they take her off to Holloway Prison tonight if they thought she'd killed Kat?

Kat was hiding under a bush on Chislehurst Common. She had pulled the knife out of her stomach and the amount of blood that came out with it had terrified her. She was in pain, icy cold and lightheaded, which she assumed was due to the loss of blood.

Amelia had called the police, of course: Kat had heard the sirens as she went further down the lane to another turning, which led her back to the common. She had wanted to go to the summerhouse and get her coat, but she was afraid she would be caught there. If she didn't get that coat, though, she would freeze to death, and when daylight came the blood on her jumper would immediately give her away.

Would the police have mounted a guard on the summerhouse?

She didn't know the answer to that, but as she needed

to lie down and to get her coat and handbag with her money in it, she had no choice but to chance it.

The pain when she crawled out from under the bush was excruciating, and she could feel the warmth of fresh blood coming from the wound. But she managed to get up and, pressing her hand against the cut, began the walk back to the summerhouse.

By the time she reached the overgrown path to the house she was staggering and knew she was close to collapse. It was so dark she had to grope her way along the path, brambles snatching at her and swinging into her face. She nearly fell several times as she made her way to the back garden and had to stop frequently to lean against the house. But finally she made it to the summerhouse, lay down on the daybed and pulled her coat and a blanket over her.

Every other time she'd come here it had been her sanctuary, a quiet place where she could escape real life. She would stay for a weekend and go home refreshed.

It didn't feel like a sanctuary now, more like a prison, because she knew she couldn't go anywhere else. By morning the police would be here looking for her.

She'd never been one for regrets, but this time she regretted bringing Amelia here. And for telling her all those lies.

Her father had always said, 'You can lock up from a thief, but you can't lock up from a liar.' He'd warned that lying would get her into serious trouble.

She had never lived in the burned-out house. Her

parents and sister hadn't died in a fire. She hadn't even lived in Chislehurst. She didn't work for Harrods but at a newspaper shop in Acton.

Sometimes she could barely recall the truth because she'd grown so used to trotting out fiction. The truth was that she was Hilary Wentworth, and had grown up in Ealing as the middle one of five children. They were a normal family, hard-up because there were so many of them. Her father was a fitter for the Gas Board, while her mother stayed at home and kept house.

She was sent to Child Guidance when she was twelve because of her lies, but she even lied her way through that. She said her father interfered with her, and her mother knew but ignored it. That was the real reason she had been sent to foster parents in Chiswick: when her parents were investigated, they were so horrified by her lies that they said she had to be taken away for fear of corrupting her younger siblings.

She really did join the Girl Guides and went to the World Camp where she met the three girls, and what she'd told Amelia about what they'd done to her was true. But what she had kept to herself was that she'd told the other girls some whopping lies: she'd stayed at Windsor Castle often because her mother was a lady-in-waiting to the Queen. The Guide mistress had laughed when Rosie asked if this was true. It was common knowledge, she said, that Hilary lied as easily as she breathed.

That was another reason they had for attacking her.

When she got home to her foster parents, she told them what Carol, Rosie and Lucy had done to her, but she wasn't believed. They thought she'd put the Immac cream on her hair to gain sympathy. As a result, by the end of the summer and more stories of bullying, they had lost patience and asked for her to be placed in another foster home.

She had always wanted to work at Harrods, but they turned her down at the interview. She had changed her name to Katherine Somerset when she moved into the bedsitter in Godolphin Road.

Hate continued to burn inside her, not for her parents and siblings, who didn't want to see her again, or for the foster parents who had given up on her. But for the three girls who had humiliated her at the Guide camp. She plotted and schemed, watching them when she could, learning about their lives and families. She knew she would never rest until she got her revenge.

At first, she just wanted to find a way of publicly humiliating each one, but that proved difficult because she would need to show her hand. Then the idea to kill them came to her and she was filled with excitement, which made her lonely life easier to bear. It was thrilling monitoring their movements – the friends they visited, the men in their lives, their workplaces, even the stores they shopped in. She knew it all and loved lying in wait for them, never knowing if this would be the perfect opportunity for her to pounce. It made her feel important, like one of those women who worked for the French Resistance and blew up munitions' trains.

Nothing in her life came close to the thrill of those glorious decisive moments when she knew this was the instant she'd waited for. She experienced a rush of pure joy at seeing each of those girls fall to the ground when she hit them with the pipe. She rolled them over to look at their faces and said their names. What a buzz it was to see the recognition and terror in their eyes. Then she thrust the knife into them.

She had loved to read in the press about the Chiswick Creeper. Journalists said the police were baffled and advised young women not to walk alone at night. There were reports of sightings of this exceptionally dangerous man as far afield as Surrey and Buckinghamshire. To know she was causing such terror and mayhem was far more rewarding than any lie she'd ever told. She even had visions of her fame lasting for ever, like Jack the Ripper's.

Yet now as she lay shivering and in agony, feeling her strength slowly ebb away, she hoped she would die: the prospect of prison terrified her.

WPC Mortimer came into the interview room around midnight. 'Someone from Shepherd's Bush police station has arrived to take you home,' she said. 'This won't be the end of it for you, I'm afraid. We have to find Miss Somerset, hopefully still alive and able to tell us her side of the story.'

Amelia felt sick with anxiety. Kat had told so many lies: how many more would she tell when she was found?

Her fears abated a little when she reached the reception area to find Sam waiting for her. 'By all accounts you've had an exciting day,' he said, as he led her to the car. 'This afternoon I had a weird feeling something was wrong. I asked Graham, who was on duty at your house, to ring me and let me know you were back. When he didn't, I was really worried.'

As they drove back to Shepherd's Bush Amelia told him exactly what had happened. He listened without interrupting, and when she'd finished, he reached over and took her hand to squeeze it. 'What a nightmare. Let's hope they find her in the morning, and she confesses. My DI has arranged a search warrant for her room. We might find something useful there. Worst-case scenario is that she's dead but you can claim self-defence. Hopefully she had never cleaned that lead pipe properly and the blood of her victims will still be on it.'

'I'm scared she's dead,' Amelia said, and just the thought of what that meant made her burst into tears. She didn't say she was afraid that if Kat was still alive she'd come and kill her.

'Please don't cry, at least not until we get to your place and I can hug you,' he said. 'If it'll make you feel any better, the DI believed you totally. Of course I do, but you already knew that.'

'I just can't believe it's come to this,' she sobbed. 'I

wish I'd never found Lucy's body – I would never have met Max then and Kat would've been just a girl living up the street that I said hello to.'

'We all have times in our lives when we wish we could rewind to before some unpleasant incident and take a different turning without losing our temper, hurting someone or just being an idiot. I've had loads of those.'

'But when I look back on the nasty things that happened, I can see I took the only road there was. I had to report Lucy's body. When I interviewed the families of the dead girls it was with the intention of setting the record straight. If you remember, the gutter press implied Lucy worked in a strip club. I suppose I did get carried away with seeing myself as a private eye. But now I know that all three were cruel to Kat so maybe they had it coming to them.'

'You don't believe that. When they bullied Kat they were all just kids,' Sam said, smiling at her. 'You set out with the highest of intentions, and that will come out if you end up in court. But for now you've got to hold your nerve, tell the truth, and let's hope Kat survives.'

They pulled up in front of Amelia's house. She looked up at the dark windows of her room and shuddered.

'I'll come up with you,' Sam said, clearly seeing how upset and nervous she was. 'We'll put the fire and lights on, draw the curtains and then you must go to bed. Everything will look better in the morning.'

He took her keys and went ahead up the stairs to put on the lights. She stood in the doorway watching him light the gas fire and draw the curtains. Her room soon looked as cosy as it always did. But she was still scared.

'Come on now,' he said gently. 'Let me take your coat. Shall I make you a drink? Hot milk or cocoa?'

As he came close to take her coat she leaned into his chest and immediately his arms went around her. 'I'm scared,' she admitted. 'This room was once a haven, but it doesn't seem like that any more.'

'Would you like me to stay with you? I know I'm on duty, but what the hell! Sleep in the chair, I mean. Just so you feel safe.'

She looked up at him and saw concern in his blue eyes. 'I couldn't ask you to do that. I'll be fine,' she said, though she wished he would stay.

He drew her closer to him and she lifted her face to his. All at once he was kissing her and suddenly her room felt safe, like home again.

'We shouldn't be doing this,' he murmured, against her neck, 'but I can't help myself.'

'Me too,' she whispered back. 'But under the circumstances we must stop. Go home, Sam. I want you, but for your job's sake we have to wait until I'm in the clear.'

'Are you always so sensible and controlled?' he said, moving back a few inches so he could see her face, yet still holding her arms.

'I don't know. I've never been in a situation like this before,' she admitted. Looking at his face made her feel weak at the knees. It wasn't just his lovely eyes or his blond hair, it was his kindness, his interest in her, and the full mouth that was designed to be kissed. She wanted him more than any man she'd ever met. 'Just go now, Sam. This can wait until the time is right.'

20

Amelia peeped through the crack in the curtains as she heard a car draw up outside. It was two a.m. and, as she had expected, the police guard's shift had ended and this was his replacement.

She hadn't been able to fall asleep: the events of the day were too disturbing. Regardless of what Kat had done, it was terrible to think of her lying somewhere in pain and the freezing cold. The kiss from Sam was disturbing too, though in a completely different way. Her head was telling her she shouldn't get involved with another man until all the complications in her life had been resolved, but her heart was saying, 'I want you now.'

She watched Sam get out of his patrol car to speak to another officer. She didn't recognize him, but he had dark hair and looked young. Sam's blond hair shone like a beacon under the streetlamp and, once again, she felt a fluttering sensation inside her.

She hadn't thought to ask if she could go to work today, or if she'd be expected to go back to the police station for more questioning. She so much wanted to go into the office and tell Jack what had happened. Gruff and insensitive as he often was, and hungry for a story, he had a knack of putting things into perspective.

Sam glanced up at her window before he got into his car. She wanted to pull back the curtain and blow him a kiss, but the other officer might have seen.

She heated some milk on the stove and took it back to bed with her. Even if she couldn't fall asleep, she could think about Sam and perhaps that would block thoughts of Kat.

Jack literally pounced on Amelia as she came through the office door. 'My God, Amelia, you can't be left alone for a minute without getting into mischief.'

'Sorry!' She frowned at him. 'What mischief?'

He brandished a copy of the *Daily Mirror* and read the front page. 'A young woman believed to be a journalist was questioned last night in connection with the Chiswick Creeper,' he barked. 'It's obviously you, even if they don't give your name.'

'I didn't think you'd have heard about that yet,' she said. 'Why call it mischief? It was a nightmare. And are you going to stand there yelling at me, or can we sit down with a cup of coffee and I'll tell you what really happened?'

'You're getting a bit uppity for someone who sells ad space,' he slung back at her, 'but, yes, we can sit down.'

'It might be a sensible plan for me to tell everyone what happened so they all get the true picture,' Amelia said, looking around the office at the eager faces, whose owners were clearly burning to know the whole story.

'A good plan,' Jack said. 'Go and make the coffee for everyone.'

If Amelia hadn't been all cried out, she might have burst into tears. She'd expected he'd be kind and supportive, but instead he'd reverted to his bullying self.

Five minutes later everyone had pulled their chairs up to the front of the office. Amelia handed out the coffees, then related what had happened. There was a gasp from everyone when she told them about the knife and the pipe falling out of Kat's bag, but a far louder one at the bit where she had stabbed Kat.

'You need to understand I never suspected her before I found the knife and the pipe,' she said. 'We went to the market together on Saturday and it was lovely to be out and about again. When she suggested Chislehurst the following day, I was all for it. She was good company. It still seems unbelievable that everything could change in an instant and that I left her in the lane with a knife sticking out of her stomach.' She pointed to the position of the knife on herself. 'But I had to do it, or she would've stabbed me. When I got back from calling the ambulance, she was gone. Unless the police have found her since it got light this morning, she's still out there somewhere, or dead.'

'Bloody hell!' Jack exclaimed. 'That's the kind of story I dream of having on my front page.'

Jack was so predictable, she almost laughed. 'Never mind front-page stories. I think you should contact your friend at the police station and see if they've found her yet. If they have and she's dead, they're likely to come and arrest me,' she reminded him.

She was pretty certain Sam would've rung her or come to the office if they had found Kat, but she wanted to get back at Jack.

She hadn't noticed that Peanut was in the room. It was only when he got up to walk towards her that she saw him, and the concern on his face brought tears to her eyes.

'You're responsible for this.' He looked scathingly at Jack. 'You should never have encouraged Amelia to dig into this. Right from the start I had a bad feeling about it, and now our Amelia might be in extremely hot water.'

'Our Amelia' made her tears flow faster.

Peanut put his arms around her and addressed the room. 'None of you are to tell anyone anything about Amelia,' he warned them. 'As you know, every news-hound in town will come sniffing around. But not a word. With luck, Kat will survive, and after her trial, with Amelia's permission, we can have a field day. But for now all mouths to remain buttoned.' He looked pointedly at Jack who made a gesture of surrender with his hands.

'Peanut's right,' Jack said. 'I'm not proud of myself for pushing Amelia into the front line, but now we must protect her. I'd better get down the nick and see if I can find out anything.'

Although she was overcome with this show of

solidarity for her, Amelia went to her desk and picked up the latest list of potential advertisers. She needed to get back to work and bring some normality into her life.

Behind her she heard the scraping of chairs on the floor as, one by one, everyone returned to their desks. No doubt before long they'd have questions to ask, but if they saw her working perhaps they would wait at least for tea breaks.

She was just checking through the businesses, deciding which ones were likely prospects to be talked into advertising with the paper again, when Peanut slunk up behind her. 'I've been very worried about you, and it seems with justification. Promise me when this lot is all sorted you'll never become so involved again.'

She patted his cheek affectionately. 'I promise, and it's lovely to hear you care enough to worry. I'm just hoping we hear Kat is alive and on her way to hospital.'

'And what are you going to do about that thug of a boyfriend?' His expression was now one of a concerned father.

'I won't be seeing him again. It's over.'

He smiled then. 'I'm glad to hear that. Any man who hits a woman is a bully and a coward. You deserve far better.'

'Thank you, Peanut. I'll work on that one. Now I'd better get on.'

*

Jack came back with the news that Kat hadn't been found. His police source said they had found a trail of blood to and from the summerhouse, so assumed she'd spent last night there and left in the morning. The lack of a fresh blood trail suggested she'd managed to dress the wound before moving on. They had found the lead pipe, though, and Forensics had it now for testing.

That Kat was fit enough to move on meant the police weren't thinking of charging Amelia with anything for the time being. Meanwhile they had searched Kat's room and found a series of notebooks that documented how she had kept watch on each of the dead girls. She was in the habit of following them from their homes onto tubes or buses; she had kept car registration numbers of people who picked them up; she had lists of which shops they used, when they went to launderettes, pubs and restaurants. She had even taken photographs of the girls and any men or friends she'd seen them with. More chilling still was that she had befriended Carol's mother and had been invited into her house. The police wondered if that visit had tipped the poor woman over the edge into committing suicide.

Jack related all that to anyone within hearing distance. He must feel tortured, Amelia thought, to have so much meaty information he was unable to put into print until Kat either died or came to trial.

When he'd finished, he beckoned Amelia into his office to tell her something more.

'I don't want them out there to know this,' he said,

waving his hand at the other staff in the adjoining office, 'but the police found what amounts to a dossier on you, sweetheart.'

Amelia gasped and Jack patted her shoulder to reassure her.

'She didn't intend you to be another victim, but she clearly had some sort of obsession with you, from some time before you got to know her. There were descriptions of outfits you wore on certain days – she even followed you, maybe hoping to engage you in conversation. The police are finding it hard to believe she managed to hold down her job at the newsagent's because she was so busy keeping tabs on people. But her employer said she was always phoning in sick, and he'd suspected her of stealing from him, but couldn't prove it. She had told him as many lies as she did everyone else.'

Amelia realized that her life as she knew it had to be put on hold until Kat was found. She was still scared the woman would come for her, and meanwhile she was under a spotlight.

Jack said he had been told the police were going to have a telephone installed in her room for her safety – it would save them the expense and manpower of a police guard.

That evening, when Sam arrived to drive her home, she told him how she felt. 'If I can't have you just outside the house I'd like to go away, somewhere quiet and pretty, perhaps by the sea, where no one knows me, and I can just lie around and read books or go for long walks. I'm sick of being questioned, asking questions, and people looking at me.'

'I could look at you all day,' he said, grinning at her.

Amelia laughed. 'I wouldn't mind that.'

'I'd like to be in that quiet pretty place too,' he said. 'But most of all I'd like this business to be over so I can take you out, walk down the street holding your hand and say you're my girl.'

Amelia thought that was the nicest thing any man had ever said to her. 'I'd like that too. Tell the other chaps down at the nick to find Kat as we have things to do.'

'Tomorrow they're going to put the phone in for you,' Sam said. 'At least we can talk to each other then. Mind you, it's not just talking I want to do.'

Amelia giggled. She'd had the same thought.

Sam was in civvies that evening and in an unmarked car, so Amelia asked him if he could take her to the launderette. She hadn't been able to get any washing done since her protection order had been issued and she was desperate for clean clothing.

The launderette was quiet for once, only four people using it. 'Well, this is a fun date,' Sam whispered to her, as she began putting her clothes into a machine. 'I'd considered a posh restaurant or the pictures!'

Amelia laughed. 'Time for that in a few weeks. Funny to think I met Kat here. She seemed so nice, such good company, though now I know almost everything she told me was a lie.'

'Did you tell her stuff about you and your background?'

'No, I don't think so. I was too interested in her telling me about buying trips to Rome and the men she was wined and dined by. I suppose I envied her. Do you think that might have been why she told those stories? So people would look up to her and envy her?'

'Maybe. Her real life story hasn't got much glamour, has it?'

'Nor has mine, but it hasn't made me invent a new one.'

'You don't say much about it. Why is that?'

She shrugged. 'It's not a happy story, Sam. Five kids, drunken bully of a father and a weak messed-up mother. You wouldn't want to meet them, that's for certain.'

'How long is it since you had any contact?' he asked.

'At least seven years,' she said. 'I hear from Michael, my oldest brother – he broke away and is a doctor in Suffolk – but the rest are just awful, and I don't want to be involved.'

'I did a short course on family counselling a while back. I was told that people who have become estranged from their families can often benefit by going back. The idea behind it is that sometimes they demonize their families, and often find explanations by going back to take another look. They didn't suggest it was a cure-all, or that miraculously you'd find you were completely wrong about your family, but many people find new understanding and clarity.'

317

Amelia shook her head. 'I saw them clearly enough the first time, thank you. My idea of Heaven would be to discover I didn't even belong to that family.'

He pulled a sad face. 'Okay, your choice. Just passing on a bit of information.'

'What about your family?'

'Boringly normal,' he said. 'Well, perhaps not boring. My dad runs a pub in Staines called the Waterman. My mum died several years ago from cervical cancer.'

'Oh, no, how sad.'

'Yes, it was awful, but Dad pulled us all through. My brother Tom is a stockbroker in the City, and sister Ellen is a nurse – she's getting married soon. Dad has married again. Susie is ten years younger than him and she's given him a new lease of life. They're very happy and we all like her very much. That's about it.'

'Sounds a good life to me, except for your mum dying,' Amelia said.

'I've got nothing to complain about, except that perhaps I'd like my future to be a bit more exciting.'

'I'd like a home with my own bathroom and to get a book published,' she said. 'I'll gladly forgo excitement.'

'I imagined you writing a book when I first met you,' he said, 'probably only because you're a journalist and the two things seem to go together. Soon you'll have a complete story to write. It'll be brilliant, too, as you have all the inside information.'

Amelia got up to take the washing out of the machine and transfer it to a dryer. 'Maybe. That was the idea when I first started poking my nose into each victim's life. But it's disappointing to find that in reality there are no true heroes or villains, just flawed, troubled people who can be nasty, mean, and all the other bad stuff, with just a veneer of decency hiding it.'

'An extremely cynical view,' Sam raised one eyebrow. 'But I suppose if you just mean the people you've met through this, maybe you're right. But I wouldn't agree about the whole of humanity.'

'No, you wouldn't. You're one of the good guys,' she said, with a smile, as she folded her bed linen.

Sam carried the big bag of clean washing up to her room, but after a quick cup of tea he said he had to go back outside. 'I wouldn't put it past Sarge to turn up, wanting to make sure I'm at my post,' he said.

'Kat's not going to come here, is she?'

'You never know. She's unhinged, Amelia. People like that don't always think of the consequences. And then there's Max. What if he comes back? We've been watching out for him, and he hasn't been spotted, but he's still got a lot of gear in his room. I can't see him abandoning that. But I'll be happier when the phone is put in.'

He kissed her again before leaving. 'Our time will come soon,' he said at the door. 'And it will be all the sweeter for waiting.'

'That sounds like something a vicar would say,' she said, and pouted. 'Good night, Sam. I'm so glad you are keeping me on the straight and narrow.'

*

319

The days seemed to crawl by, with still no news of Kat. Amelia was told there was dried blood on the pipe from Kat's bag, but they could only tell it was human, nothing else. The telephone was installed in Amelia's room, but although it was comforting to know she could summon help if necessary, it made her feel more alone, because no one other than Sam ever rang her, and she knew few people with a phone.

At work everyone was waiting for news that Kat had been found and arrested. Pictures of her had been circulated and Sam said that every place mentioned in the notebooks in her room had been thoroughly checked. What more could anyone do?

Mr and Mrs Lark and the Whelans kept demanding that their daughters' murderer must be found and tried. There were even theories that the young woman the police believed was responsible was an invention to keep the heat off their investigation. Meanwhile the real murderer was roaming the country, free to kill someone else.

Mabel Livingstone, the model friend of Rosie Lark, was featured in a full-spread article in *She* magazine. She claimed that the real killer was someone high up in government, a man her friend had had an affair with, and that he was so important the police wouldn't call him in for questioning.

Amelia telephoned her one evening and found Mabel half cut. She said that people kept badgering her about

Rosie, and her agent had told her that her friend was seeing a government official.

Amelia gathered from the drunken ramblings that Mabel had been persuaded to enlarge on this story for the press.

'Don't you think you're betraying your friend by spreading false stories?' Amelia asked. 'I know for certain Rosie was killed by a woman, someone she and the other two victims had been cruel to years ago. Rosie might well have been seeing a government official, but he certainly didn't kill her. If this man is married with children, you're going to wreck his life and his marriage. That isn't right.'

'Married men shouldn't get involved with other women,' Mabel slurred. 'It serves them right if they get found out.'

'It is a two-way thing,' Amelia reminded her. 'And don't tell me girls don't know if a man is married or not. I've always sensed it, and I bet you have too.'

'Don't be such a prig, Amelia,' Mabel said. 'I like married men. They buy me lovely presents, take me to super places and they're usually great lovers. But the best thing is that you can get rid of them easily when you're bored with them.'

Amelia had to laugh. She could hear the truth in what Mabel had said. 'I just hope you don't get your fingers burned one day then,' she said. 'That's the other side of married men — they rarely leave their wives.'

'You're right there,' Mabel agreed. 'You know, you and I ought to go out together sometime. I like you, even if you do seem to be on the side of the angels.'

'I like you too,' Amelia responded. 'But behave and don't get any innocent men into trouble.'

Mabel gave a throaty laugh. 'The only innocent man I know is my father. Can I take your phone number? When I'm sober, I'll ring to arrange to go out.'

As Amelia put down the receiver it occurred to her that Mabel was probably as lonely as she was. Being beautiful and a successful model didn't necessarily guarantee a perfect life.

Kat jumped back into her mind, as she seemed to do constantly. Whatever she'd done, Amelia couldn't help but worry that she was holed up somewhere, alone, frightened and in pain. How could she try to find her? Was there something Kat had told her that was a clue?

21

A soft noise at her door woke Amelia. She rubbed her eyes and reached out to turn on the bedside lamp, thinking it was Sam creeping in to see her.

To her shock it wasn't Sam but Max, unshaven, dirty and wild-eyed.

'What are you doing here?' she said, a ball of fear knotting in her stomach.

'I've come to see you, of course,' he said, moving to sit down on her bed.

She knew the police had changed the locks, so he must have forced them.

'Forcing doors in the middle of the night? Did you really think I'd want to see you after all this time? Get out now!'

'Now, now, Mimi, you said you loved me. Does love vanish at the first hurdle?'

Amelia sat bolt upright. 'You hit me, you lied to me about everything. Do you really think I could love you after that? Now get out or I'll ring the police.'

She reached out for the telephone receiver, but he snatched it from her. 'You got me arrested and my room searched! There's been a police guard outside, and I knew they were waiting for me to come back to pin something else on me.'

'I didn't get you arrested. It was your own stupidity that prompted that. Now go or I'll scream and alert the other tenants.'

He sneered at her. 'Whatever happened to the pathetic, lonely girl who was so grateful for any company or attention she'd do anything to please?'

'I've never been pathetic,' she snapped. 'But you are because you told me a pack of lies about your family, your work, everything. Why, Max? And that isn't even your real name, is it? Fuck off, Brian, or you'll live to regret coming in here.'

He lunged at her, grabbing her by the throat with both hands. 'You don't tell me what to do. I want food, money, and if I decide I want sex, I'll just take that too.'

She tried to scream but he was holding her throat too tightly. All she could do was thrash her legs about and try to get his hands off her throat.

'I always wondered what it would be like to strangle someone,' he said, with a wolfish grin. She noticed his teeth hadn't been cleaned for weeks and his breath smelt sour. 'Was it you who got my landlord to change the locks on my room too? What right did you have to do that?'

Amelia was terrified. The lock-changing on his room had had nothing to do with her. She had always half expected him to come back here at some time, but imagined he'd be on his best behaviour, penitent for hurting her, asking if they could start again. Not this.

'I – I – I –' She tried to speak but he was still holding her neck too tightly. She waved her hands at him, hoping he'd loosen his grip.

'Yes? You want to say something?'

She tried to nod.

'Okay, but one hint of a scream and I'll finish you off,' he said, and loosened his grip enough for her to speak.

'Let me up and I'll get you money and food,' she said.

'I can tie you up and gag you and get it all by myself,' he said. 'And there's sod all you can do about it.'

To demonstrate this he reached over to the chair near her bed where she'd left a silky scarf. He pulled it towards him, punched her cheek, then shoved the scarf into her mouth.

'There.' He grinned down at her again as he pushed it further and further into her mouth until she began to retch. 'That should shut you up.'

He turned away from her to pull the belt from her dressing-gown. In that moment, Amelia reached for the telephone receiver. There was no time to call 999 but if she left it off the hook, tucked under the edge of the bed, there was a slim chance Sam might try to ring and guess she was in trouble when the line was permanently engaged.

Max didn't appear to notice what she had done: he was too busy testing the strength of her dressing-gown belt. Then when she expected him to grab her hands, he pulled her to her feet. 'I want a rest on the bed, so you can sit on a chair and watch me.'

He put the belt around her waist, and secured her to one of the dining chairs, the knot at her back. Next, he opened her wardrobe and pulled out two leather belts. He wound one in a figure of eight to hold her feet to the legs of the chair, then yanked her arms around to the back of it and pulled the second tightly around her wrists. He had made a first-class job of attaching her to the chair. When she tried to move there was less than an inch of play on her feet and wrists.

Standing back and looking at her, he grinned again. 'Got you just where I want you now. I'll get myself some food, find your savings and have a snooze. I do hope one of those coppers who've been guarding you comes around at some time during the day. Won't be nice for you sitting in piss and shit.'

He laughed at that, and she wondered how she could ever have believed he was the man of her dreams.

She was beyond crying or panicking. Her face was throbbing from the punch, and she was aware that the scarf in her mouth could easily get sucked further down her throat and suffocate her, just through breathing.

She watched as he threw bacon into her frying pan and tipped a tin of beans into a saucepan. He kept up a running commentary of what he was doing, breaking off every now and then to tell her what a pathetic bitch she was.

'I fucked that mate of yours,' he said gleefully. 'It was the day she called with flowers for you. God, I wish I hadn't bothered, never saw such a hairy snatch – it was halfway to her knees. Turned my stomach. But, hell, was she grateful! Must've been the first fuck she'd had in years. I heard she's the one who killed those three birds. Bloody hell, what a turn-up! You don't half get mixed up with some weird people!'

Amelia could only think he was the weirdest of the lot, and indeed wondered if he was on some drug – he seemed like a different person. She also wondered where he'd been holed up all this time. As he knew she was being guarded he must have been close by all along and had come tonight because the patrol car was no longer there.

So Kat had been speaking the truth about having sex with him. That disgusted her rather than hurt, and it only made him more loathsome. He was frying eggs now, and he had the gas so high they would burn.

He finished cooking, took off his windcheater and sat down on the bed to eat. Although the bedside light wasn't very bright, she could see how dirty the collar of his shirt was. The blue V-necked sweater was filthy too. It looked like he hadn't changed his clothes for days, just as he didn't appear to have eaten much either. Wherever he had been these last few weeks, she assumed there was no real bathroom or kitchen. Could he have been squatting in the empty property six doors along?

The way he was eating made her stomach churn. He

327

had made a sandwich with a fried egg and some of the bacon and was shoving it into his mouth, taking huge bites. She remembered her father used to eat like that, particularly when he'd been drinking.

He dumped his plate on the table when he'd finished, muttering something about getting his head down. Then, to her disgust, he peed noisily into her sink, looking round at her to see her reaction.

'Just being thoughtful to the other tenants,' he said. 'Don't want to wake anyone by flushing the toilet.'

Finally he took off his shoes, filling the room with the smell of sweaty feet, and got into her bed. Within a few minutes he was asleep.

It was like being trapped in a cage with a sleeping wild animal, Amelia thought. Safe enough while he slept but he'd be dangerous when he woke. She was extremely uncomfortable too. The dining chairs had hard seats and straight backs, and he'd tied her so securely that she couldn't ease the strain on her body. He hadn't lit the fire, and in only her nightdress and with bare feet she was cold. At least while Max had been awake and walking round her room, she could anticipate his next move, but now she had no such distractions all she could think of was what he might do to her when he woke.

It was unlikely anyone would come to her aid. When the policeman had brought her home earlier, he'd said her protection had ended now that the phone had been installed. One of the other tenants might notice the front door downstairs had been forced, but even if they tried to check on her, she couldn't make them hear her.

Much later Amelia heard the milkman doing his rounds. Soon after, the sun came up. The flimsy curtains let light filter through them, illuminating all the mess Max had made while he was cooking, and indeed how filthy he looked as he slept on.

She wondered if Jack would phone to see where she was when she didn't come in at nine. Had she even given him the number here?

Sam was her best bet. If he was doing nothing this morning, or at least close by, he might call round to take her to work. *Please do that, Sam,* she willed him. *I really need you.*

At eight she heard Mike in the room next door speak to Barbara who lived on the top floor. From their voices she guessed Barbara was just going into the bathroom at the back of the house.

'Looks like someone forced the lock on the front door last night,' Mike said. 'I nipped out to get some milk earlier and noticed it because the door was open. But I didn't hear anything, did you?'

'You don't think it's anything to do with Amelia, do you?' Barbara asked. 'The policeman told me yesterday they wouldn't be outside any more because they'd put a phone in her room.'

'Let's bang on her door to check,' Mike said.

Amelia tried to rock her chair to make a noise, but with a carpet underneath there was no sound. Mike rapped twice, and although Amelia tried to make noises to alert him, all that came out were little grunts. She heard him tell Barbara he thought she must have gone to work already.

'She'll be ringing the police about the door, I expect,' Mike added. 'Maybe they'll send someone round to fix it.'

Amelia was watching her clock all the time now, and she was dying to go to the toilet, so she became increasingly uncomfortable. At nine she tried willing Jack to be concerned that she hadn't come in. *Phone the police.*

Ten o'clock came, then eleven, and still Max slept on. Her bladder felt like a huge inflated balloon now, as if at any minute it would burst. Why wasn't Jack concerned she hadn't come in? Surely someone in the office would find her absence suspicious.

A car drew up outside. She silently willed it to be Sam or another policeman. She heard footsteps on the stairs and found she was holding her breath: her whole being begging it to be a rescuer. The footsteps stopped outside her door. She grunted and rocked the chair.

Suddenly the door opened and Peanut peered in.

With the curtains still drawn the light wasn't great but he saw her straight away and gasped. She fluttered her eyes and rolled them towards the bed to warn him she wasn't alone. He cottoned on immediately and without saying a word came right into the room and saw Max.

'Bastard,' he murmured. He went to the sink and

picked up the saucepan in which Max had heated his beans.

Amelia held her breath as Peanut advanced on the sleeping man, the saucepan held out in front of him, ready to be used as a weapon. He was fit and strong, but a lot older than Max, and the last thing she wanted was for him to be hurt.

Peanut paused by the bed, bracing himself. Then, lifting the saucepan high, he brought it down with force, whacking Max's head.

Not satisfied with that, he hauled the stunned man up with his left hand and punched him in the face with his right fist. He hit him so hard Amelia thought she heard a bone crack. He dropped him back on the bed.

'He's out now, but he'll survive. Let me get those belts off you and tie him up,' Peanut said breathlessly.

He had them both off within seconds and returned to the bed to roll Max over and secure his hands, then rolled him back and did the same to his feet.

Amelia, meanwhile, managed to untie the dressing-gown belt and pull the scarf from her mouth. 'You are my hero,' she said. 'But I must rush to the bathroom.'

When she got back, Peanut was standing over Max, who was clearly coming to, his eyes opening and rolling round. Amelia snatched up her dressing-gown and put it on.

'Where's your phone?' Peanut asked.

Amelia pulled it from beneath the bed. 'I managed

to knock it off the hook last night but didn't have time to ring the police.'

'Ring the number they gave you now,' he said. 'I'll watch him.'

'Who hit me?' Max sounded groggy. 'I can't move.'

'You're lucky to be still alive,' Peanut hissed at him. 'What sort of low creature does that to a woman? I hope they lock you up and throw away the key.'

'You don't know what she's like,' Max said, his voice plaintive now. 'She makes out she's sweet and kind, but she's a stupid treacherous bitch.'

'I know what she's like and I can tell you she's far too good for you. Now shut up or I'll knock all your teeth out.'

Amelia put the phone down after reporting what had happened. 'Thank heavens you came,' she said. 'I was beyond desperate.'

'I didn't get in till half eleven and as soon as I saw you weren't there, and they said you hadn't phoned, I came straight over. When I saw the front door had been forced, I thought Kat had broken in and killed you. But I couldn't bring myself to run to the phone box without checking your room first. Thank God I did.'

'You were amazing.' Amelia put her arms round him and kissed his cheek.

'So you're having it off with him now, are you?' Max said.

'Not all relationships are about sex, you dirty-minded ignoramus,' Peanut retorted. 'I'm honoured to be Amelia's friend, and she's a wonderful girl. You'll be in prison for so long you'll probably lose your hair, your wits and any looks you had. No woman will ever want you again.'

Amelia giggled. She just hoped the police had enough evidence to charge Max and that he would go down for a few years.

The police arrived twenty minutes later in two cars. One of the men had been on her protection for a couple of nights, but she didn't know the others. Two untied Max, put handcuffs on him and led him away, leaving the other two to take statements from Amelia and then Peanut.

After giving hers, Amelia got up with the intention of clearing the mess Max had left and to make them all tea. But she had only just put the kettle on when she felt very strange.

The next thing she knew she was on the floor and Peanut was leaning over her.

'You fainted,' he said. 'I think it was the shock.' He helped her up and into a chair and gave her a drink of water. 'You must come home with me when the police have finished. My wife will look after you.'

Amelia knew what was wrong: Max had violated her room. Breaking in, being in her bed when he was filthy, peeing in her sink. She didn't think she could ever touch the sink again; in fact, she didn't want to live there any longer. But she didn't think the men would understand that, so she kept quiet.

It had been just after two in the morning when Max broke in. Peanut had arrived to rescue her at twelve. Ten hours of being strapped to that hideously uncomfortable chair, fearing she would have to remain there for days. She was never going to forget that.

Peanut poured bleach into the sink and scrubbed it. Then he washed the cups and plates under the running tap. The policeman who made the tea asked if she would like him to strip the bed. Perhaps the men did understand.

She couldn't answer, she was too choked up, but Peanut agreed that would be a good thing and they would take the bedding to his house to wash it. The other policeman said he would get a locksmith to sort out both damaged locks.

'We know how traumatic this has been for you,' the older of the two policemen said. 'You must feel like you've been persecuted for finding the murdered girl as all these things have stemmed from that. But it's ending now. We have Brian Caulderhill – or Max, as you know him – in custody, Kat will be found very soon, and we have you to thank for solving the Chiswick Creeper murders. However, we recommend you give up sleuthing now.'

Amelia managed a tearful smile.

Late in the afternoon at Peanut's home, a pretty white-painted Georgian villa in Barnes, Amelia dozed in an armchair placed by French windows overlooking the garden. She had thrown some clothes and other essentials into a suitcase before leaving Godolphin Road, but she'd been uncertain about going home with Peanut in case his wife didn't like the idea.

She needn't have worried: Mavis was one of those earth-mother women who, Amelia instinctively knew, had been comforting and patching up people's lives for most of hers. She was probably in her mid-forties, wore a loose kaftan-style dress in wild colours, and her curly hair was henna red. She called her husband Pea, which he laughingly pointed out was not just short for Peanut, the nickname he'd had his whole life, but for Peter, his real name.

'When we first met she did her absolute best to block the nickname,' he told Amelia, as they had a cup of tea. 'She said it was cruel and nasty. But I was a tough professional footballer then and we all had nicknames. I quite liked hearing the fans in the stadium chanting mine. So Pea was her compromise, hoping one day everyone would use it. My oldest son called me Peaddy when he was little, instead of Daddy.'

Peanut went back to work, and Mavis put some ice in a tea-towel and held it to Amelia's swollen cheek.

'Pea's very fond of you. We've got two boys, both at university now, but he would've liked a girl. As I would, too, but we can't have everything we want, can we?'

She showed Amelia to one of the boys' bedrooms and said she must make herself at home. 'Neither Pea nor I think you should go back to that room of yours.

Maybe we can find you somewhere else once you feel better.'

'I'm all right really,' Amelia said, 'but I agree. I don't want to live there any more. It's so kind of you both to put me up.'

'I like to think that if either of my boys got into difficulties while they were away from home someone would help them. Though for now all they want when they come here during the holidays is feeding, their washing done and money. Then they disappear to see their friends.'

'They'll grow out of that,' Amelia assured her. 'One day they'll be bringing a special girlfriend home, and suddenly your family will have expanded.'

Mavis ran her a bath, saying clean clothes would make her feel better. Amelia intended to tell her later how good it was to be in a warm, pretty bathroom, and to know that tonight she'd sleep soundly, protected and soothed by unexpected kindness.

That evening, after a delicious spaghetti bolognese, Mavis asked her a little about her family.

' "Dysfunctional", I think they call such families,' Amelia said lightly. Joking about them was the only way she could deal with it.

To her surprise, Mavis put her arms around her and drew her to her chest. 'You don't have to cover your embarrassment about them with jokes. It's better just to tell the truth. But maybe it's time to go back and face them too. You've learned so much recently about human nature. Go back and see if they have some redeeming features.'

'That's funny. Sam, one of the policemen, said I ought to do that.'

'Is he the one who's sweet on you?'

Amelia blushed, guessing Peanut had made the observation. She wasn't used to people who spoke out without any filter. 'I suppose he is.'

'Sounds to me like he's the right sort. You know, Amelia, I can't help thinking that what you really need right now is a love affair. And Sam sounds like a kind, good man.'

22

It was heaven staying with Peanut and Mavis. It was a lovely area to be in, so close to the Thames, and Peanut took her to work, then brought her home afterwards. Her meals were cooked, washing done and, best of all, she felt completely secure.

Amelia remembered how she'd once been scared to move out of that room in Godolphin Road. It had been her safe place. She'd arranged and decorated it with love, and until now she couldn't really imagine living anywhere else. But now she could see it had become almost a fortress, a place that kept her from the real world, somewhere that stifled her. She didn't want to see it again.

Peanut had asked someone he knew to pack up her belongings and bring them to Barnes to store in his garage. Amelia had telephoned her landlord to give her notice.

Each evening they studied the 'flats and rooms to let' section of the paper, but while Amelia's face was still so bruised, she hadn't gone to view any rooms for fear of frightening the landlords. But Peanut and Mavis weren't anxious for her to go and they showed her the kind of parental affection she'd always longed for.

On a Friday, more than two weeks after her ordeal with Max, Amelia received a letter addressed to her at the newspaper. There was nothing unusual about that: when she had published her first article, about Lucy Whelan, she'd had stacks of letters. Jack called them her fan mail. Since then each time she had written an article there had been more mail, but never the amount of that first time. Lately as she hadn't been writing articles, the trickle had almost dried up.

She'd taken a cup of tea out onto the fire escape at the back of the office as the spring sunshine was glorious and tucked the letter into her jacket pocket to read it out there. When she opened it, she nearly dropped her tea. It was from Kat.

She didn't know why she didn't rush back into the office and announce it but, as she told herself later, she'd always tended to be a bit secretive.

There was no address at the top. It was written on a piece of paper torn out of a notebook, and somehow she sensed pain and desperation before she'd read one word.

Dear Amelia,

I know I don't have the right to ask for your help, but you are the only person I've ever known who has a heart big enough to overlook what I've done and come to see me. I know I haven't got much longer to live. My wound is badly infected, and it is taking all my strength to sit up and write this, and somehow, I need to get outside to post it to you today too. Before the infection I wrote down everything about how I killed the three girls, and how I'd been stealing money from the paper shop, shoplifting, and other things I did. I want to make a clean breast of it all. Thankfully, I even bought a stamp, with the intention of writing to you, but I was ashamed and didn't.

But now, more than anything, I want to see you before I die. To ask for your forgiveness, and to tell you what it meant to me that you did talk to me, when no one else would. That weekend with you, even if it all went wrong at the end, was the happiest time I'd ever had.

I'm in a shed on an overgrown allotment that nobody cares for. You told me you grew up in White City so you might know it. Addison Road, right at the bottom, the gate is locked but the fence is broken.

After you've been you can call an ambulance and the police. I know you must. But please come to me first. Once they've got me, they won't let me see you, and I know I haven't got long. No tricks from me, I've got no knife, no pipe to hit you. Just me in a filthy mess and needing to see the only person who ever saw me as their friend.

Love, Kat

Amelia's eyes welled. She did know Addison Road, and back when she was six or seven, she'd used to wriggle through the fence onto those allotments. They were looked after then. She'd eat raspberries and gooseberries and marvel at the neat rows of carrots and the runner beans climbing up a wigwam of poles. An unexploded bomb was found there. They blew it up, but rumour had it that the ground was poisoned, so the council closed the allotments for good.

She had gone back there several times the first summer after it was closed, always with a couple of friends. They made a camp in a shed there and they often lit a bonfire too. But the following year it had become so overgrown with brambles it was no fun any more.

When she was twelve, she went back there for the last time. The brambles were so thick that she couldn't get in and it reminded her of the story of Sleeping Beauty. She liked to imagine there was a house with a sleeping princess in the centre of it.

It was that memory which made Amelia feel she must go there. If Kat had been anywhere else, she would probably have handed the letter to the police and let them deal with her. But imagining her in the shed she'd once played in, dying from an infected wound with perhaps no food or water, needing forgiveness and someone to hand her confession to, that was too distressing to ignore.

It wasn't sensible to go alone. In fact, it was completely hare-brained: she knew what a liar Kat was. But what would Kat gain by trying to lure her there? A hostage, she supposed, but that would only work if Kat had a gun or other weapon to threaten to kill her, and the police were standing by, ready to negotiate terms. Somehow, she didn't think Kat wanted to harm her.

She decided to go at lunchtime – it was always less hectic on Friday afternoons as the paper went on sale on Friday morning. If she came back with a ripping story Jack wouldn't be angry she'd taken a long lunch hour. As for Peanut, he always had Friday afternoons off as he attended sporting events on Saturdays, which he'd be writing up, so he wouldn't be suspicious.

As a precaution in case something nasty did befall her she decided to write a letter to Jack, telling him where she was and why and leave it on her typewriter. He always had a long boozy lunch on Friday and was rarely back before four. By which time she would be back too.

'I'm going up to Oxford Street to get new shoes,' Amelia said to Stephanie, the girl who sat at the next desk. 'Cover for me if I'm a bit late back – you know what it's like when you get to the shops.'

'Will do.' Stephanie grinned. 'But don't get so carried away you forget to have some lunch too.'

Amelia assured her she wouldn't.

It was lovely to feel the sun on her face – the winter seemed to have lasted so long. The joy of sunshine and a glimpse of summer on its way appeared to be affecting everyone. People were smiling, and most had abandoned their coats as she had. So instead of feeling nervous about seeing Kat, she was happy to be outside, and even to be going back to a childhood haunt.

Once on the tube she was at White City in just a few minutes. As she had remembered, it was about

343

a ten-minute walk from the tube to Addison Road. Everywhere looked smarter than it had when she was a child: neater gardens, not so much rubbish and a great many new houses to replace the old prefabs that she remembered from her childhood.

While walking she considered Sam and Mavis's suggestion that she should go home to lay some ghosts to rest. Perhaps it was only because she was so close to her old home, but for the first time she thought they might be right, and it would be good for her. But not today: she had to see Kat first.

She saw the pillar box where Kat must have posted the letter. It was right at the end of the road, by the old allotments. As she got closer the brambles didn't look as impenetrable as they had at her last visit. On the other side of the broken fence there was a narrow but obvious way through. She looked around her before going in, just to check no one was watching. The road was deserted, so she ducked down and went through the broken fence, remaining stooped to cross the thicket of brambles.

At first it didn't appear to be the same place. No clear paths or patches for vegetables, as it was all overgrown. In a few weeks' time, when the leaves appeared on the brambles and other bushes, and weeds began to sprout, she doubted there would be any soil or paths visible. But the hut was exactly as it had been on her last visit. The door had been painted bright blue back then, but now it was faded and weather-worn. Yet it still looked a

344

sturdy little building and equally sturdy was the bench outside it.

She went to the door and pushed it open. The first thing she noticed was an unpleasant smell. 'Kat,' she called, as it was dark inside after the bright sunshine.

'Is that really you, Amelia?' a thin, wavering voice replied. 'Push the door wide open so you can see.'

Amelia was so shocked by Kat's appearance she couldn't speak. She was lying on the floor on what looked like an old mattress and a pile of army-style grey blankets. Her face was just skin and bone, like an old woman's. The smell was coming from her, almost certainly her wound, which had to be badly infected. She was wearing men's trousers, and a thick grey sweater, which was blood-stained.

'I was afraid you wouldn't come,' she said weakly. 'I'd resigned myself to dying here alone.'

Amelia had never seen anyone close to death, but she instinctively knew this was what she was seeing now. With no regard to the dirty floor or the smell, she sank onto her knees and took Kat's hands. They were just bone, the skin covering them like flimsy paper. 'When did you last eat?' she asked.

'I can't remember. The days and nights have all blurred into one. The hardest thing was going out to post that letter to you. But now you must collect up that notebook.' She pointed to it by a Primus stove. 'That's my confession. Give it to the police, and please call an ambulance for me now.'

'I will.' Amelia began to cry. She couldn't believe any human being could let herself get into the state Kat was in rather than give herself up. She looked skeletal. 'I'm sorry I stabbed you, but I thought you were going to hurt me.'

'I would've done,' Kat admitted, putting her hand onto her wound. 'I'm not right in the head, Amelia, I never was. Since my wound got bad and I couldn't get up and move around, I saw that for myself. But I'm asking for your forgiveness because, until that moment when I felt cornered, I never intended to hurt you. I used to watch you long before I met you in the launder-ette. Long before I took my revenge on those girls too. I thought you looked terribly sad, and I didn't under-stand why because you're so pretty. You're clever too, and so truly kind.'

'Where have you been all this time since Chislehurst? How did you know about this place?'

'I was fostered by some people near here. I made my way to this shed the day after I last saw you. I knew the police would keep going back to the summerhouse.'

'Strange, really – we could've met all those years ago when we were children because I came in here too. I'm going to call for the ambulance now, Kat,' Amelia said, wiping away her tears with the back of her hand. 'I may have to wait out in the road so I can direct them into here. But I won't go away. I'll come with you to the hospital.'

With that, Amelia picked up the notebook and

backed out of the hut, still looking at Kat on the make-shift bed. She didn't think she'd ever felt such sympathy for anyone before. Maybe she should be more on the side of the three women Kat had killed, but they had been loved and privileged: Kat had never had that.

It seemed an awfully long wait between rushing down Addison Road to the phone box, calling the ambulance and the police, then waiting for them to arrive. In fact it was less than ten minutes before she heard the siren. She didn't tell the men anything other than that a woman was gravely ill and injured on the allotments and gave her own name. To say more would only cause complications.

The ambulance arrived first, and as the men jumped out, she said her piece and wriggled through the fence and bushes, only looking back to check they were following.

'Kat, the ambulance is here now,' she said, at the door of the hut.

She thought Kat had lost consciousness as her eyes were closed but she opened them at Amelia's voice.

'Oh, my goodness,' Amelia heard one of the men murmur as he saw Kat. 'How long has she been here?'

'I don't know,' Amelia said truthfully. 'I got a letter today to say she was here, and I came. She has a stab wound in her side, which must be badly infected.'

Amelia stood back and let them look at Kat. As they pulled up the blood-stained shirt beneath her sweater and peeled back a soggy dressing, the smell was so bad that she had to cover her nose and look away.

'Okay. We'll have to open that gate to get a stretcher for you. Just hold on. We won't be two ticks,' the older ambulance man assured Kat.

When the police arrived, Amelia went outside to fill them in about Kat, and her own involvement. The more senior officer, a sergeant, appeared to be the most knowledgeable about the case. He told his two colleagues that Kat was what had been known as the Chiswick Creeper.

'Clearly no danger to anyone now,' he said, as he stood at the shed door looking in.

'May I go to the hospital with her?' Amelia asked. 'I don't think she's got long, and nobody should be alone at such a time.' She handed him the notebook. 'She told me in the letter she sent me that this was her confession.'

'Why didn't you ring the police when you got the letter?' he asked, his face frosty.

'Because of the tone of it,' she said. 'Because this is a place I came to as a child. Because it was me who stabbed her, if you remember.'

'Are you sure it wasn't because you wanted the final scoop on her story?'

She looked him in the eye. 'That, Sergeant, never crossed my mind and I think you're very cynical to suggest it. Are you judging me by your own standards?'

She thought she saw a faint blush, which pleased her.

'You can go in the ambulance, but you'll have to make yourself available later to give a statement.'

'Of course. Thank you,' she said politely.

Half an hour later at Hammersmith Hospital's Casualty Department, Kat had been taken into a small side ward. This was partly because of the seriousness of her condition but also because of who she was. A policeman had been posted on the door, and Amelia was waiting to be allowed to see her. An initial cursory examination when she first came in proved her wound was badly infected and had spread internally. It was clear from the doctors' and nurses' faces she hadn't long to live.

Amelia had rung the office and told them where she was. Jack was still out, on his usual Friday-afternoon binge.

A nurse went in to see Kat and came out a few minutes later. 'You can sit with her now. We've given her pain relief and cleaned her up. She's drifting in and out of consciousness, so I doubt she'll talk, but she'll know you're with her.'

She looked better, with her face washed and hair brushed, but nothing could improve the shocking skeletal look. Amelia pulled up a chair and took her hand. 'I hope you feel better now you're here, warm and comfy,' she said. 'I'm playing truant from work, but I expect they'll be fine about it. I didn't tell you I've left Godolphin Road. I'm staying with a friend from work now in Barnes.'

She couldn't think of anything further to say. She certainly didn't want to mention Max, or that she really liked a policeman. What did people say to those who were dying?

'I'm glad you're here,' Kat said, just as Amelia thought she couldn't talk. Her voice was just a whisper, but she turned her head towards Amelia and smiled. 'Write that book, won't you? You could put me in it.'

'Maybe I will,' Amelia said, and stroked Kat's hand. 'Do you want me to talk to your parents, or anyone else?'

Kat's head moved from side to side, like she was saying no.

She was silent for at least ten minutes, her eyes shut, but then she opened them again. 'Don't be sad,' she whispered, her voice as soft as wind blowing through grass. 'I love it that you are, but I'm happy to go. I made a real mess of this life, didn't I?'

'I just wish I'd met you when I first moved into Godolphin Road. Maybe I could've changed how you felt,' Amelia said.

'You're a collector of lame dogs,' Kat whispered. 'No more now. Live your life for yourself.'

Amelia felt a small movement in Kat's hand and suddenly realized she'd slipped away. Tears ran down her cheeks. She laid her head on the bed and cried.

23

Amelia called the nurse in as she dried her eyes. It was all over. She was sad but, like Kat, also glad it was the end. She felt stronger for having been with her.

As she walked along the corridor to go back to the office, then home, she saw Sam coming towards her. His face broke into the widest of smiles. 'I heard you found her and called the ambulance,' he said, putting his hands on her shoulders. 'I feel I ought to say, "What were you thinking of, going to meet her?" but I won't because I understand.'

'Do you?'

'Yes.' He sighed. 'You're one of those people who need to see things through, and that's a good thing. But now I must see things through too and take you back to the station as they want a statement. Afterwards I'll drive you back to Barnes.'

That night, when Amelia went to bed, she felt not wildly happy but optimistic and complete. At the police station she was treated as a bit of a heroine because the case could be wound up now. The knot of anxiety she'd had inside her ever since Kat had disappeared was gone now. So was Max. Instead she had lovely Sam.

After she'd made her statement he'd driven her to the

river between Hammersmith and Chiswick and they'd just sat in the car, looking at the sun going down, and talked.

He said he thought she should write a book about the triple murder; nobody else knew all the strands of it as well as she did. 'The public love true crime,' he said. 'I think from what you've told me about Kat, she'd want to be immortalized in print too.'

He kept kissing her and, as much as Amelia liked living with Mavis and Peanut, she wished she had a flat of her own so she could sleep with him. She even admitted that, blushing as she did so.

Sam chuckled. 'I think of little else,' he said. 'You'd be shocked if you could look inside my head.'

'Well, maybe it's time to pull out all the stops and find a new flat,' she said. 'I need to get myself a typewriter too. I didn't realize straight away, but Max must've made off with the one he got me.'

'Good. You don't want any reminders of him,' Sam said. 'You and I, Amelia, are going places.'

'What places?'

'Well, I plan to be at least a DI in ten years. And you'll be a best-selling novelist. Maybe we can live in one of these lovely houses near the river. I did hear that Vanessa Redgrave lives somewhere around here. If it's good enough for her, it's good enough for us.'

'So you think we're going to be together for ever?'

He cupped her face in his hands, his blue eyes shining. 'Amelia, I think I fell in love with you the first time

I saw you – your ability to work out what people are about, that innate kindness you don't even know you have. You're brave and forthright, and as I've watched you dealing with all this stuff, my respect and admiration for you has grown. You're special, and you've no idea. But maybe I can show you.'

24

August 1971

'It's so hot, Sam.' Amelia fanned herself with a magazine. 'I was going to put those asters I bought into that bare patch where you dug out that horrible prickly bush. But all I can do is sit here and roast myself.'

'Well, you're looking great on it.' He laughed, looking admiringly at her svelte figure in a pink spotted bikini. She turned golden brown effortlessly after what seemed like only minutes in the sun, while he burned equally easily. He had no idea why Amelia always claimed she was fat: she had a perfect body. Not a stick insect like Twiggy, but womanly and curvy. He thought perhaps her false view of herself was her mother's doing.

Amelia had found the little flat in Barnes, the ground floor of a Victorian house, soon after Kat had died. It had one bedroom, a lounge, kitchen and bathroom, but to Amelia the real appeal was that it had cute little wrought-iron steps down to a garden.

She had attacked it, turning the somewhat seedy neglected rooms into a stylish home with the same energy and passion she had clearly used in Godolphin Road.

In the first few weeks she had lived there, whenever he had called round with the intention of helping with stripping wallpaper or painting doors, they had ended up ripping each other's clothes off, sometimes even having sex on the floor. They would roll around laughing afterwards and despaired of ever getting the flat finished. But fortunately, for the flat at least, Sam had become involved in a murder investigation of a wealthy man in Holland Park who had been tortured and strangled. This meant all leave was cancelled and he was working fourteen-hour days.

Yet each time he came to see Amelia he was always stunned by the amount of work she'd done on her own. She had kept it very white and light, but with splashes of bright colours here and there. She told him she could never wait to get home from work to start, and she'd still be at it at midnight. He thought she was amazing.

Peanut and Mavis often came over to help too. Peanut was great at carpentry and he'd put up bookshelves in the lounge and built a big wardrobe with mirrored doors in the bedroom. Most of the furniture was second-hand, bought from junk shops in Shepherd's Bush and painted. Peanut and Mavis had given her a couple of armchairs, and a lovely old carved bedstead. All Amelia had had to do was buy a new mattress.

Sam didn't intend to move in with Amelia. He remembered a Leonard Cohen track, 'The Stranger

Song', something about the man being another Joseph looking for a manger. He didn't want to be that man. He intended to marry her and do it all properly.

But then at the start of June, when he was swotting for his sergeant's exam, she pleaded with him to move in. She said the bed was too big without him, and if spiders came in, who was going to get them out for her?

The thought of being chief spider-remover and bed-filler had clinched it. In any case, he was fed up with living in the section house, the constant noise and the other guys always trying to drag him out drinking when he was studying.

Amelia had won that battle easily but he had insisted they would get married the following spring.

'About you going to see your family,' Sam said later. 'You said you would once you were settled here. Well, you are now. And look how good the whole Chiswick Creeper thing turned out for you.'

Amelia grinned. Sam was right. The Chiswick Creeper had changed her life in almost every way, even if she hadn't appreciated it at the time. Her news story about Kat and the forces that had made her kill had brought her great acclaim, and she was approached by the *Daily Telegraph* to join its staff. With the flat to do up and her new and exciting romance with Sam, she had declined the offer, but Jack had given her a substantial rise, and made her features editor.

The most exciting thing of all was that a major publisher had contacted her about writing a book on the murders. Taking Jack's advice, she was talking to a literary agent with a view to appointing him to negotiate with the publisher.

Sam had managed to persuade his DI to let him photocopy Kat's handwritten confession so that Amelia could use it as a reference tool. As he'd pointed out, without Amelia the chances were that such a confession wouldn't exist. In her spare time Amelia was making notes on the case with the intention of starting work seriously on the book at the end of the summer.

Max, whom Amelia never liked to think about, had got a two-year prison sentence. She had dropped the charges of assault as she wanted never to see him again, not even across a court room. But the police had discovered a network of fraud in which he had been involved so he got his just deserts.

'So, when are you going to see them?' Sam was always persistent when he thought something was important. 'Don't say you'll write to make an arrangement to call round. They'll ignore that. Just go.'

Amelia didn't reply. She just looked at him. In her eyes he was perfect: handsome, blond, blue-eyed, with a muscular physique. But it was his kindness, warmth and joyousness she loved most of all. He was a real man in the way her father never had been, strong, brave but also gentle. He could laugh at himself, he listened, and was so loving. She also trusted his judgement. If he said she should visit her parents, he was almost certainly right.

'All right, I'll go. How about tomorrow? Sunday is usually a good day to catch people at home.'

'Are you sure?'

Amelia laughed. 'Don't give me any opportunities to chicken out! It'll probably be every bit as bad as I fear, but I'll have done it. I suppose I ought to go bearing gifts. A bottle of something is possibly the only thing they'll appreciate.'

'Take some flowers, too. I think the best plan is always to treat people how you'd like to be treated.'

'Says the voice of reason,' she replied, impressed as ever by his common sense and innate kindness. 'Okay, tomorrow.'

Sam had to be on duty at six the next morning, and just before he left, he brought her a cup of tea. 'Another lovely morning. The sun's shining and there's not a cloud in the sky,' he said cheerfully. 'What could go wrong on such a day?'

Amelia sat up in bed to drink the tea. She loved their bedroom: it was at the front of the house and didn't get sun, so she'd papered the wall behind the bed with a pink paisley Laura Ashley design to warm it up. The biggest wall held the mirrored wardrobes, and the remaining two were covered with a barely pink paper. She'd made curtains for the huge bay window from two heavy white-cotton bedspreads, and standing in the bay was a Victorian dressing-table with little drawers and triple mirrors, which she'd painted a pale glossy grey.

Amelia often compared this present room with the horrible one she'd shared as a child with her sister. Cream gloss walls, painted by the council prior to them moving in, a blanket thrown over a length of string to serve as curtains, and their clothes, those that were hung up, behind the door on hooks. The bunk beds shook when you so much as looked at them, the mattresses were so thin they could feel the wire mesh below, and during the winter mould grew on the walls.

'You haven't changed your mind about going?' Sam asked. He looked anxious, and that was enough to make sure she didn't let him down.

'You can stop worrying, I'm going. I keep telling myself if it's too awful I can always run out.'

He leaned over to kiss her. He smelt of shaving cream and toothpaste and it was tempting to pull him back into bed.

'I'll see you around six tonight,' he said. 'But I'll try ringing this afternoon to see if you're home and how it went.'

He left then. She heard the front garden gate click, and a few seconds later he started his car. Amelia drank the rest of her tea and lay down, intending to go back to sleep, but her mind was whirling with thoughts of visiting her family later – so she got up, deciding to work in the garden while it was still cool.

It wasn't big, but it had been loved once as there were many pretty shrubs and small trees in it. Amelia had known nothing about gardening until she came here, but Mavis had shown her which were weeds, which shrubs needed pruning and those that should be dug up and replaced with something more suitable. She had learned more from books since then, but she was still at the trial-and-error stage, just enjoying watching things grow.

By nine it was getting hot again, so she went in, made herself some breakfast and had a bath. She picked a simple pink sleeveless shift dress to wear and white sandals. Then she gathered up the things she had hastily bought before the shops closed the previous day: a bottle of brandy, as she knew it was her mother's drink of choice, a large box of chocolates and a bouquet of lilies and pink roses.

It was almost eleven o'clock when she approached the house. It was marginally tidier than she remembered, no broken toys and overflowing dustbins in the front garden, and the fence and gate had been mended. But the grass desperately needed to be cut. The house was much the same. No broken windows, but they could have done with cleaning and the whole house was badly in need of painting.

She took a deep breath before she opened the gate. It was eight years since she had left, and she hadn't been in contact since. She just hoped her father was less volatile now.

The front doorbell was broken and hanging off, so she banged on the letterbox.

'Who is it?' she heard a woman ask.

'It's Amelia,' she called back.

There was silence. Amelia felt her mother and the other woman were having a confab about whether to open the door or not. Perhaps her mother was too far gone now to remember her name.

But then the door opened, and there was her mother. She looked old, even wearing a blue and white summer dress more suited to a twenty-year-old. Her face was heavily lined, with bags under her brown eyes and her hair iron grey. She was skinny too, so thin she looked like a gust of wind would blow her over. 'Our Amelia?' she asked.

'Yes, Mum, it's me. I thought it was time I came to see you.'

The house smelt as it always did, of fried food and cigarettes, but as Amelia went in, she saw it was much cleaner, and there was even a stair carpet to cover the bare splintery wood she remembered.

'How are you, Mum?' she asked. 'Who was the other woman I heard?'

'I'm not too bad, got some arthritis but that's to be expected. That was Christine, your sister, you heard. She's been living here with me since your dad died. She's nipped up to get dressed.'

'Dad died?'

'Three years ago. He had a massive stroke.'

They walked into the living room. 'I'm so sorry, Mum,' Amelia said. She couldn't have cared less about her father's death, though she thought she should. It was just the standard condolence you'd say to anyone.

'Why?' Her mother looked at Amelia with questioning eyes. 'Why would you be sorry? He was no good as a husband or a father. He made our lives miserable. You were wise to leave. I just wish I'd had the sense to leave during the war when I could've done.'

Amelia didn't know what to say. Her mother was speaking the truth, and Amelia was relieved that she didn't have to see him. But it seemed harsh not to manage a few kind words. None came to her so she handed over the flowers, chocolates and brandy.

Her mother buried her nose in the flowers. 'First time anyone's bought me flowers,' she said, with a smile. 'The boys down at the Legion sent them for his funeral, but they thought he could do no wrong. Stupid boneheads!'

The living room looked better than Amelia remembered it. A brown Rexine three-piece suite with velour cushions, a glass-topped coffee-table, and even new curtains. Still the council-painted cream walls, though, gloss paint so they could be scrubbed when marked. It made it look like an institution. Amelia noticed a vase of plastic red roses. They came free with Daz washing powder, and she'd always wondered who would want them.

'I saw you in the paper,' her mother said, beckoning her to sit down. 'I said to Christine, "Look, there's our Amelia. Fancy her writing things about murderers. But she always was good at writing stories at school."'

That appeared to be a good start, but she wanted more. She had hoped to see delight on her mother's face, some explanation as to why she'd never got in touch.

'Did you miss me when I went away?' she asked.

At that question her mother's face went blank.

Christine came into the room. She looked Amelia up and down. 'Remembered where we lived, did you?' she said.

The sarcasm was a sharp reminder that none of her family was capable of praise, of endearments, just as they didn't hug or kiss anyone. Were they born that way, or made like that by copying their parents or older siblings?

Christine looked older than thirty-five. Her long hair was bleached platinum blonde, her complexion was muddy and the tight red dress she wore showed every lump and bump on her body. She looked like she ought to be in a doorway in Soho.

'I came because I'm getting married next year, and I thought I should know more about my family. How are James and Peter?'

'Jim's in the nick. He's always in there – got a season ticket, I reckon. Pete says he's going straight, but I can't see that happening. He's got a job on a farm

364

out in Essex. Makes me laugh. Farming – what sort of job is that?'

'A nice one if you want to get away from White City and start again,' Amelia said. 'Maybe you should encourage him, rather than take the mickey.'

'You always were a weird kid.' Christine tossed her blonde hair. 'Writing your little stories or sticking your nose in a book.'

'Speaking of kids, where are yours?' Amelia asked.

'Gone into care. Best place for 'em. I couldn't control 'em,' Christine said, turning to flounce out of the room.

'She let her kids go into care?' Amelia looked at her mother in horror. 'How could she do that?'

'She's like me, couldn't cope,' her mother said, sinking down onto the settee and reaching for a packet of cigarettes on the coffee-table. 'You lot brought yourselves up, but kids these days can't do that. Their teachers question them, and social workers come poking around.'

'That's just as well.' Amelia shook her head sadly at her mother's skewed ideas of what made a decent childhood. 'And where was her husband when this happened? Didn't he have a say in it?'

'Don't be daft, girl. She married a man as bad as your dad. He couldn't give a toss about them and, anyway, he went off with another woman.'

'You know, Mum, I came back today hoping you could give me some reason why my childhood in this house was so awful. You see, in the back of my head I thought the beatings from Dad, the lack of interest from you, the squalor was somehow because of me. But it wasn't, was it? You told me I was fat and stupid so many times that I believed it.'

'Well, no bugger could say you was fat or stupid now,' she retorted, sucking at her cigarette. 'So what's your problem?'

Amelia realized she was getting dangerously close to crying, because she was feeling far too much like she'd felt throughout almost all of her childhood. 'You're the problem, Mum. Why tell a child that? Why let Dad beat me, or send me to school in filthy clothes and holes in my shoes so I got bullied? Didn't you know a mother is supposed to love and protect her children?'

'That's a lot of old poppycock,' she snapped at Amelia. 'A bit of hardship never hurt anyone. We was poor, I couldn't help that.'

'No, you couldn't help being poor, Mum,' Amelia said, getting to her feet. 'But so was everyone else round here, and most went to school clean and tidy, and their homes were spotless. But you liked drink and fags more than your kids. You were a slob, Mother dear. Christine is much the same. There's probably no hope for James either. But maybe Peter will turn out okay as Michael has. You couldn't even bring yourself to say you were pleased to see me today, or that I looked nice. So I won't come again.'

'Please yerself,' her mother mumbled.

'Drink the brandy, Mum. You always did like it better than your children.'

She left then, without saying goodbye to Christine, glad to be out of that poisonous atmosphere. She'd done what Sam had suggested and seen them, but her mother and sister's attitude to her confirmed she was right to have stayed away all this time.

She hadn't imagined how life had been in that house. But she could feel proud now that she hadn't become like them, and know that, if and when she had children of her own, they would be loved and nurtured. She would make sure they never felt second class as she always had.

Now it was time to close the door on that part of her life and open another, with her heart, to Sam's family.

They were like him, open-hearted, warm and uncomplicated. She knew they were ready to accept her as part of their family, and she wanted that.

There was one thing she could thank her own family for, and that was the insight into how influences and events in childhood mould that child for good or bad. It would stand her in good stead for writing the book about Kat and making it authentic.

Amelia felt she'd got out of her toxic home before she'd begun to slide into the way of life she'd been brought up to. Poor Kat had begun lying at an early age to convince herself she was someone special, not the reject that others saw her as. Sadly she had only alienated herself still further from other people, and in her loneliness and despair, the need for revenge had grown.

It seemed to Amelia that life was like a game of roulette. You had no control over whether you would land on a winning number or become a loser.

Of the five children in her family, she and Michael had become winners, James and Christine losers, but Peter's wheel was still spinning and, she hoped, getting away from White City and the bad influences there would enable him to land on a winning number.

Amelia was sitting in the garden with a cup of tea when Sam arrived home early.

'How was it?' he asked, and she could see from his expression he'd thought of little else all day.

'Unpleasant but therapeutic,' she said. 'Dad's been dead for three years, Mum is still the same hopeless case, and my sister Christine at least had the sense to get her kids taken into care before she messed them up.'

'Oh, sweetheart, that's awful,' he said, coming over to her and sweeping her into his arms.

'No, it's not – well, not for me. I can move on now as I know I don't have a Cinderella complex. They really were as messed up as I remembered. I've got a wonderful life ahead of me with you, Sam, and I refuse to waste another minute of it when I can be happy. Now, you sit down in the shade and I'll open a bottle to celebrate.'

'Celebrate what?' He looked puzzled.

Amelia smiled. 'That I know where I'm going now, and who I'm going there with.'

You'll Never See Me Again

When Betty escapes her marriage, she goes on the run, armed with a new identity. But she never imagined starting again would end in murder . . .

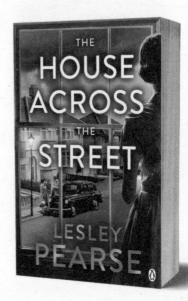

The House Across the Street

Katy must set out to uncover the truth about the mysterious house across the street. Even if that means risking her own life . . .

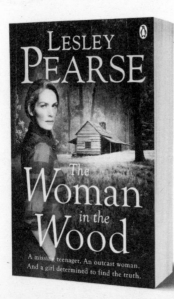

The Woman in the Wood

Fifteen-year-old twins Maisy and Duncan Mitcham have always had each other. Until one fateful day in the wood . . .

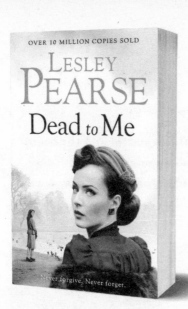

Dead to Me

Ruby and Verity become firm friends, despite coming from different worlds. However, fortunes are not set in stone and soon the girls find their situations reversed.

Without a Trace

On Coronation Day, 1953, Molly discovers that her friend is dead and her six-year-old daughter Petal has vanished. Molly is prepared to give up everything in finding Petal. But is she also risking her life?

Forgive Me

Eva's mother never told her the truth about her childhood. Now it is too late and she must retrace her mother's footsteps to look for answers. Will she ever discover the story of her birth?

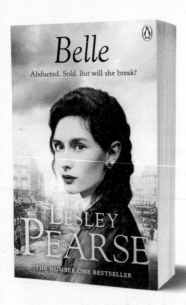

Belle

Belle book 1

London, 1910, and the beautiful and innocent Belle Reilly is cruelly snatched from her home and sold to a brothel in New Orleans where she begins her life as a courtesan. Can Belle ever find her way home?

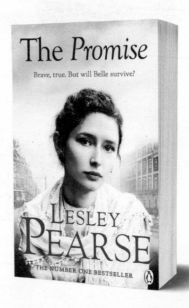

The Promise

Belle book 2

When Belle's husband heads for the trenches of northern France, she volunteers as a Red Cross ambulance driver. There she is brought face to face with a man from her past who she'd never quite forgotten.

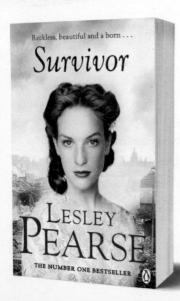

Survivor

Belle book 3

Eighteen-year-old Mari is defiant, selfish and has given up everything in favour of glamorous parties in the West End. But, without warning, the Blitz blows her new life apart. Can Mari learn from her mistakes before it's too late?

Stolen

A beautiful young woman is discovered half-drowned on a Sussex beach. Where has she come from? Why can't she remember who she is — or what happened?

Gypsy

Liverpool, 1893, and after tragedy strikes the Bolton family, Beth and her brother Sam embark on a dangerous journey to find their fortune in America.

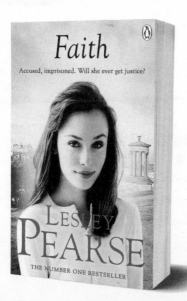

Faith

Scotland, 1995, and Laura Brannigan is in prison for a murder she claims she didn't commit.

Hope

Somerset, 1836, and baby Hope
is cast out from a world of privilege
as proof of her mother's adultery.

A Lesser Evil

Bristol, the 1960s, and young Fifi Brown
defies her parents to marry a man they
think is beneath her.

Secrets

Adele Talbot escapes a children's home to find
her grandmother — but soon her unhappy
mother is on her trail . . .

Remember Me

Mary Broad is transported to Australia as a convict and encounters both cruelty and passion. Can she make a life for herself so far from home?

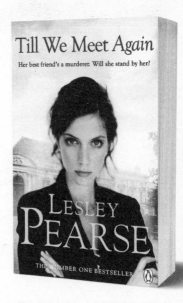

Till We Meet Again

Susan and Beth were childhood friends. Now Susan is accused of murder, and Beth finds she must defend her.

Father Unknown

Daisy Buchan is left a scrapbook with details about her real mother. But should she go and find her?

Trust Me

Dulcie Taylor and her sister are sent to an orphanage and then to Australia. Is their love strong enough to keep them together?

Never Look Back

An act of charity sends flower girl Matilda on a trip to the New World and a new life . . .

Charlie

Charlie helplessly watches her mother being senselessly attacked. What secrets have her parents kept from her?

Rosie

Rosie is a girl without a mother, with a past full of trouble. But could the man who ruined her family also save Rosie?

Camellia

Orphaned Camellia discovers that the past she has always been so sure of has been built on lies. Can she bear to uncover the truth about herself?

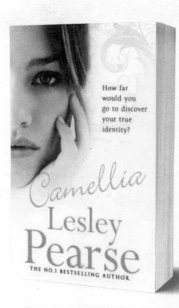

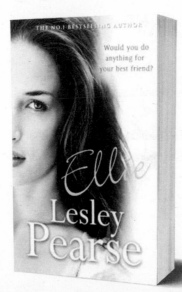

Ellie

Eastender Ellie and spoilt Bonny set off to make a living on the stage. Can their friendship survive sacrifice and ambition?

Charity

Charity Stratton's bleak life is changed for ever when her parents die in a fire. Alone and pregnant, she runs away to London . . .

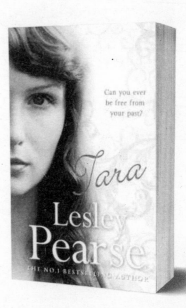

Tara

Anne changes her name to Tara to forget her shocking past — but can she really become someone else?

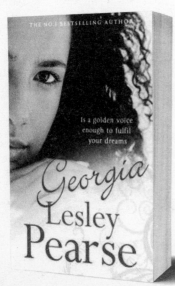

Georgia

Raped by her foster-father, fifteen-year-old Georgia runs away from home to the seedy back streets of Soho . . .